Green Fields #1

INCUBATION

Adrienne Lecter

Incubation

Green Fields #1

ISBN: 9781515279020

Cover art by S.Marko
Editing by Marti Lynch
Interior design by Adrienne Lecter

www.adriennelecter.com

Give feedback on the book at:
adrienne@adriennelecter.com

Twitter: @AdrienneLecter

First Edition August 2015
Second Print Edition November 2021
Produced and published by Barbara Klein, Vienna, Austria

To M - cat wrangler extraordinaire
Always carry a knife and duct tape.

Intro

"Do you see my panties anywhere?"

Nate gave me a suffering look. "Bree, we're standing in the lingerie section. I think I'd have to be blind not to see any underwear."

Narrowing my eyes at him, I chose to otherwise ignore his jibe. Shining my flashlight over the racks and racks of, well, underwear, I kept searching. He remained standing close to the register where he'd stopped after his circuit, ready to cover my ass should we have to make a quick exit.

"Do we have anything else on our shopping list?" I asked.

Nate took long enough to reply that I paused my hunt to shine my light in his general direction—enough to see the look on his face, but not to blind him.

"Twinkies," he deadpanned.

I couldn't help but stare at him.

"You're so damn funny, you know that?"

He flashed me a quick grin.

"Oh, I know."

"Anything else that won't make you want to eat my face off?"

He shrugged. "Don't need to juice up to find you delectable."

That didn't deserve a reply, so I instead focused on my mission.

At the back of the store, I stopped, switching the flashlight for my shotgun. A light tap on the door to the storage area yielded no answering sound, so I eased it open slowly, the creaking of the hinges ominous. Someone had busted the lock before, and the relative chaos of torn-apart stacks in the small room spoke of ransacking, but no other surprise lurked anywhere. I still took the time to do a thorough sweep before I let the shotgun slide to my hip on its strap and grabbed the flashlight from between my teeth.

It only took kicking my way through three stacks to hit gold.

"Bingo," I murmured to myself as I picked up the still-sealed cardboard box. Black, hip-hugging, one hundred percent cotton boyshorts. Chafe and stain resistant, and if I had to, I could just clean them in a tub of bleach. I'd made the mistake of going with white ones last time, and I still got the odd bright grin from Burns for running around in my "tighty whities" in camp. I so didn't need a repeat performance of that.

Pulling a black trash bag out of my cargo pants, I quickly tore open as many boxes as I found in my size and dumped the panties into the bag. When I was done, I hesitated when my eyes fell on a black pair of butt-floss undies, but, really, just the thought of maybe being stuck wearing those for four days while either running for my life or hunkering down in the car was giving me hives. But I did pick up the neon pink ones on my way back in the largest size they had—Burns so had it coming.

At my return, Nate looked up from the neat stacks he was busy packing away in another trash bag. Pulling up to him, I eyed his loot critically.

"Underwear catalogues? Seriously? What are you, twelve?"

I got a brilliant grin for that.

"The internet's been out for almost thirteen months now, and last time I counted, less than twenty percent of the people still on the road were girls. It can get very lonely in between settlements. What worked thirty years ago might very well be a veritable gold mine nowadays."

"And there you keep giving Martinez a hard time," I teased.

"And why shouldn't we? The fucker has like eighty percent of the world population to lust after," Nate replied.

"While you have, what, just me?" I asked with a wide smile.

"Definitely the better deal," he agreed, stopping for a moment to sweep his arm across the small of my back so he could pull me close. Grinning, I kissed him, wondering if we'd still have time for a repeat performance from the dressing rooms in the women's section—

Until the com went off, spewing static into my ear. I jumped, one hand on my Beretta in my thigh holster before I even reached down to the receiver unit to switch my mic back on.

"Uh, guys?" Andrej's voice came out of the speaker, the tone alone enough to make me gnash my teeth. The sound of running boots was impossible to ignore.

"Status," I barked, casting a quick look around as I tried to visually confirm what I was hearing all around me—nothing moved, and nothing made a sound. Nate quickly stuffed the remainder of the leaflets into his sack before he grabbed the trash bag holding my prized panties and added it to his stash.

"We might have a small problem here," Andrej replied. His labored breathing—a clear indicator that he was still running—told me that was an understatement.

"Define small," I replied, following Nate out of the store and hoisting the bags already sitting outside onto my shoulder as we hightailed it toward the other wing and the main staircase.

"We found a few shamblers here," he offered, only to cut off abruptly. A second later I heard gunshots go off, a good two hundred yards from our current position.

"Do you need support?" I asked, trying to gauge how best to hone in on his position.

"Negative," Andrej replied after the shots stopped. "But retreating sounds like a helluva good idea."

Nate and I traded glances as we both sped up.

"Why, you afraid of a few walking corpses?" Burns taunted over the com channel, sounding just as if he were taking a slow stroll on the beach.

"A few don't bother me," Andrej replied, followed by a chagrined, "but a good hundred do."

"What?" I hissed, just as Nate followed up with a succinct, "The fuck?"

"It's complicated," Andrej pointed out—followed by more shots, coming from much closer. The source was easier to pinpoint now as it came from the same wing we were in, from somewhere a couple of floors down around the bend. By then we'd hit the first bank of escalators. While I hastily ran down one, Nate slid down the other right next to mine, overtaking me. He did a quick sweep, then nodded to me that the coast was clear.

Pia and Martinez joined us on the next landing, dragging their trash bags along with them. As they were already overladen, I handed my bags to Martinez so I could get a good grip on my shotgun. Someone had to keep their backs free—might as well be me.

"Care to explain where you found a hundred of the fuckers hiding after we did a full sweep of the entire area?" There were always a few stragglers locked in somewhere—heck, every time I busted into a restroom I got a faceful of corpse—but that sounded like enough to put the mall as it was on the red list. No sense in wasting that many bullets for the cleanup alone.

"Well, there was this door," Andrej started.

On the way down the next escalator, I finally got a glimpse at the ground floor. In between the heaps of refuse and overturned shopping carts I could see several of our people retreating, lugging trash bags and containers along with them. The echo of boots on marble was loud, but interrupted by that dragging kind of sound that followed me into my nightmares these days. I was sure that, had I stopped to listen, I would have heard them growl and moan, too, but there was no sense in dawdling now before we got our goods stored away. Besides, even Nate couldn't have hit anything with a shotgun from three floors up.

"What door?"

"A huge-ass, locked door with a chain on it and a red X painted all over it!" Cho shouted over the com. "And this motherfucking asshole had nothing better to do than open it!"

With my hands free of bags, I took point on the next landing, while Nate lagged behind to secure our retreat. At Cho's revelation, Pia let out a curse that was half English, half Serbian, and all vile, quite eloquently answering for me.

"Seriously?" I chuffed, stopping for a moment to clear the ground floor around the elevators before I gave the others the go-ahead. Martinez and Pia ran by me toward the sunshine streaming in through the wide-open mall doors where the cars were parked outside in a haphazard cluster. I waited for Nate to join me, but when I looked up, I saw him taking up position at the glass barrier of the first floor corridor, looking out over the main mall floor, his M4 at the ready. Not a second later, he started to shoot, providing cover fire for the remaining five members of our team that came sprinting toward us.

Followed by a mass of bodies, well over a hundred strong.

Burns was the first to reach me, dumping his bags in favor of getting his AK-47 ready. My adrenaline levels spiked as every single cell in my body screamed for me to run, but instead I assumed a good defensive stance. With Nate and Burns providing cover fire, Andrej and Cho were running full out now. Seeing us standing by the escalator, they veered to the left, giving us a clear field.

Bracing myself, I pulled the trigger, not even aiming at a single screaming, half-decayed zombie coming at us. At a distance of less than thirty yards, it was almost impossible to miss. The earplugs dampened some of the sonic assault but the recoil slammed into my shoulder hard, making my second shot hit just a little higher than the first as I let loose a moment too early. It nevertheless made a head explode and the zombie right next to that one stagger, but there was still a wall of them coming at us, making my effort almost useless.

Where was a flamethrower when you needed one?

"I'm falling back," I shouted, already starting to walk toward the cars, still aiming and shooting at everything that didn't have a pulse. By the time the last shell dropped, my shoulder felt like so much raw meat, and I didn't hesitate any longer. Let the guys do their thing—I had my own job. Whipping around, I ran the remaining yards to the car, grabbing the bags someone had left right in front of the bumper. With the doors already open on the driver's side for a quick retreat, I threw the bags into the back seat and quickly reloaded as I took a stance behind the car, waiting to get a clear shot.

The staccato of the rifles thinned out as Santos and Clark came running out, almost staggering under their load of loot. Cho was walking backward right behind them, providing cover until they'd reached their car. And then it was just Andrej and Nate, and I felt like chewing my cheek raw as I waited. The howls and screams got louder as they emptied a good five magazines between them before—finally—the last two members of our team beat it.

The moment the first zombie made it out between the cracked glass doors, I pumped a round into it, hitting it squarely in the chest. Two more followed, but instead of staggering out into the light, they fell on their downed fellow shambler. Then the rest of them came pouring out around the grisly display on the ground, quickly hiding it from view. From the corner of my eye I saw Nate make it to the car, where he spent all of five seconds throwing the bags inside before the front door slammed shut.

"All clear," he shouted to me, then repeated the same over the radio. I still had three slugs in the tube so I emptied it at the raging horde before I slid behind the wheel, the shotgun jammed between my seat and the center console. I wasted precious ten seconds with strapping myself in, the belt harness tight over my full gear. Nate kept shooting at the rabid corpses through the side window until the first made it onto the hood.

Slamming my hand down on the ignition button, I kicked the car into reverse as soon as the engine howled to life, momentarily drowning out the screams from outside. Unable to hold onto anything, the shambler slid off the hood and quickly disappeared under the tires as I sent the car forward, ramming a couple of the really fast ones. Now that they lacked the funnel of the mall layout, they seemed disoriented by the dispersing targets; or maybe after being locked in all their undead life, they hadn't quite figured out how cars worked. I downed three more before I wrenched the wheel hard right, forcing the car into a turn that made my body slam into the harness. The mall disappeared from view, and as soon as I felt the tires gain traction, I floored the gas pedal. The car shot forward after hitting another bump, and then we were on the road, speeding away from the screaming mob behind us.

"Alpha clear," I barked into the radio as soon as the last zombie was well out of running distance to catch up to us. One after the other, the different cars signed in, making me relax once Cho was the last. Turning my head just enough not to lose sight of the road, I glanced over at Nate. He just finished reloading my shotgun and put it away in the rack between the front row seats before he dug into the bag at his feet—and got out one of the damn underwear catalogues.

Shaking my head in silence, I focused back on the road. The cows I had seen grazing on the way in were over the hill now, the racket we—and now our horde of followers—had made signaling them that it was wise to stay far away from anything that moved on two legs, whether it carried a rifle or preferred to use teeth and claws.

"Seriously?" I asked when my silence didn't speak loud enough.

"It's just the responsible thing to test the merchandise before we barter anything for it," he claimed, but then dropped the magazine into his lap—only to pull the blasted pink thong out. Dangling it from the end of his finger as if it were contagious, Nate inspected the offensive piece of underwear for a moment. "And there you complain about my habits."

Instead of getting defensive, I flashed him a bright grin.

"As far as I remember, you've never actually seen me in lingerie. Proper lingerie, with lace, bows, ruffles, and shit."

The look on his face was as close to shocked as I'd seen it in… probably ever, and that was saying something.

"I'd rather see you in full riot gear," he replied, pointedly looking at the lightweight kevlar jacket I was wearing. "Something sturdier than this, at least."

"I can't move in that shit," I complained. "If you had a say in my gear, I'd be bouncing around in a bomb squad blast suit or something."

Nate considered that for a moment. "Not the worst idea you've had this week."

I rolled my eyes at him, already angling for the car radio.

"Which reminds me," I started, pushing the button to open the team frequency. "Andrej, if you pull some shit like that again, I will have your ass, understand?"

"But it looked like such a promising cache!" came his amused reply. Fucker.

"It was locked with a chain and had a fucking huge red X painted all over it!" Cho interjected, still a little breathless from all the running he had to do to get away.

"Could have been a raider cache," Andrej replied.

"Because any of us would be stupid enough to leave that in a still-infested, not-cleared building?" I asked, hard-pressed not to gnash my teeth too loudly.

"Could have been stupid raiders," Andrej offered.

A million replies came to mind, but with the euphoric rush of our successful retreat slowly dwindling, I felt a little more mollified.

"Latrine duty for the rest of the week for you, Romanoff," I ordered.

"That's not fair!" Andrej complained.

"And you, too, Cho."

"What the fuck did I do?" Cho grumbled back.

"You let him fucking open a fucking door with a red fucking X on it!" I replied heatedly, but couldn't help adding a chuckle.

More grumbling ensued, but about half a mile later both acknowledged with a grumpy, "Yes, boss."

I looked over to Nate to see if he had anything to add, but he was leafing through his stupid catalogue now, making me shake my head again.

Boys will be boys.

Things used to be different. Heck, I used to be different.

I used to worry about so many things. What my nosy neighbor would say if she caught Sam and me necking in the elevator again. What color shirt to wear to work, and if it clashed with my hair. Was I eating too many carbs, or should I cut animal fats from my diet? There was always a deadline at work approaching, another weekend spent locked away in the lab—counting cells, working biochemical miracles. Had I been overlooked for a promotion? Was my involvement with my girlfriend holding back my career?

I'm not even sure what day it is, except the third day that I've been wearing the same pair of underwear, which will change the second I can pull up on the side of the road and change into the new panties I've picked up at the mall. Risking your life for a new set of clean, fresh clothes? Definitely worth it if you've been on the road as long as we have.

Sometimes it's hard to believe that it's only been a year. One year without internet, without smartphones, without a place to crash that doesn't require heavy fortifications and a watch detail round the clock to be classified as "safe." One year since we all learned that we—humans—are not the top of the food chain.

Until a year ago, I never held a gun, let alone knew how to use it. I never ran five miles, or hiked over thirty each day, for weeks. I was never hungry enough that a can of dog food tasted like a gourmet meal.

I never dreamed that I would be in charge of anyone or anything.

Why, you may ask yourself now, am I still alive?

I made a lot of stupid decisions in my life, and a single right one. Turns out, it was the only one that counts.

Welcome to our brave, new world.

One year ago…

Chapter 1

The hum of the laminar flow hood was as familiar as it was soothing. Why I noticed it now, I couldn't say. I'd spent the better part of the day in the cell culture lab, and normally I was good at tuning out the ambient noise. There was always static in the labs—the hum of electricity, the hiss of the tightly regulated air conditioning units, sometimes the clank of glass and plastic on metal as people went about their work.

Adding the last two milliliters of medium to the sixth well of the cell culture dish, I put the pipette away and closed the dish before I allowed myself to crane my neck and look at the clock behind me.

Ugh. Already after four, and I still hadn't managed to grab lunch. Normally, I wasn't that bad about keeping somewhat of a humane rhythm, but this week had been tough, and the weekend was bound to get tougher still.

Sam wouldn't be happy with me if I worked through another weekend of fifteen-hour shifts, but the paper was due end of the month, and I was so sure that with one more round of verification, I would be able to add the new conditions to the settings, enhancing the established ones. Not the greatest breakthrough in the history of science, but cell viability had been good so far.

Being careful not to touch anything outside the sterile hood, I got to my feet, then reached inside and grabbed the dishes I'd just finished with. In two hours the cells would be ready for splitting—just enough time for another viability count on the control group, and maybe a leftover salad from the cafeteria.

Warm air greeted me as I opened the incubator and placed the dishes inside, then reached for the stack right next to them. Just as I took them out, the door to the lab opened, admitting Kat. She wasn't wearing her usual white lab coat, making me guess that she was likely already leaving for the weekend. Normal people did that, I reminded myself.

"Hey, about tonight—" she started, then paused when she caught my blank look. "You remember? We wanted to head out and grab some drinks?"

Ah, right. Forgetting made me feel even more like a dork than usual. I vaguely remembered telling Sam about this, but couldn't for the life of me recall her reply. Likely ecstatic; she was the kind of girl who loved to hang out with people—any people, really.

"Yeah, sure," I offered, trying to sound like it had been fresh on my mind the entire time. "But I don't know if it's such a good idea. Sam hasn't been feeling well for the last couple of days, and I think I should stay in with her. You know, make some chicken soup, binge watch TV. Girlfriend stuff."

Kat didn't look surprised nor angry, which made me wonder if she'd already checked in with my significant other in question.

"That sounds like a great idea. Besides, Peter and Al called earlier. They can't come along, either. Both caught that bug, too."

I wanted to bristle at the sheer fact that a fellow scientist would call the latest, yet-to-be-diagnosed strain of influenza "that bug," but let it slide. It wasn't like I hadn't been guilty of the same before. Like yesterday morning when I'd tried to shoo Sam out of her studio and back into bed.

"It's probably for the best," I supplied helpfully. "I'm not sure I want to spend the evening out when everyone around me is coughing up phlegm."

"Sounds too much like work?" Kat joked, but it was a lame attempt at humor at best. Normally she could do much better.

"Something wrong?" I asked, suddenly aware that Kat herself didn't look too good. Part of me wanted to slowly inch away from her, but it was a stupid reaction, borne from too many epidemiology classes in college. If Sam hadn't managed to be my Typhoid Mary, just being in the same room with Kat wouldn't change a thing. Plus, the entire cell culture lab had stellar ventilation, even outside of the workspaces.

"I'm not feeling too awesome myself," she admitted, then barked a short laugh. It turned into a coughing fit, and now I did back away, but only so I could grab a few paper towels from the sink and hand them to her. "Thanks. I don't think it's really that virus they keep talking about on the news. Likely just a normal head cold."

"You should still get that checked out."

It was Friday, after all. Spending the weekend sick if it could be avoided by popping some pills would be a shame. I'd bumped into her way too many Sundays to ignore that her schedule was as insane as my own.

"And running a ninety-nine percent risk of certain exposure at the doctor's office? No, thank you!" she retorted, then cleared her throat. "How long have you been shut in here? They were running a new bulletin just now in the news. They're advising people to stay home now, if possible. There's even some talk about imposing a curfew. This is more serious than the average flu epidemic."

And more with the name calling. I shook my head, trying to appear at ease, even if that warning disturbed me more than I wanted to let on.

"Have they finally found out what it is? The return of the big H1N1 scare? Bird flu out to kill us all? The mega pandemic?"

"You really shouldn't joke about this," Kat reprimanded me, but couldn't help herself as she cracked a smile. "Just because the media sensationalizes everything doesn't mean it's not killing us off."

"Have there been any confirmed deaths yet?"

Not that it would be very telling. Influenza was still a leading cause of death in many demographics. It certainly killed more people each year than boating accidents. Or sharks.

"I haven't seen any believable numbers yet," Kat admitted. "But it's likely just a head cold."

I wondered if she was more self-aware than she let on, but I refused to let that send me into panic mode. I still remembered my third year of college all too well. Every lump I'd found in my body—and there had been a lot of poking and prodding involved—had had me convinced that I was a day away from dying of cancer. And look at me now—I was still around, still kicking.

"Why don't you head home and for once do what the doctors prescribe? Just vegging out in front of the TV for a couple of days doesn't sound like the end of the world to me."

"You're probably right," she conceded. "Have a nice weekend! And don't stay too long. If they really do impose that curfew, you don't want to remain locked in here, right?"

"Not if I can avoid it," I muttered, all too aware that this sounded exactly like my weekend plans. "You, too!" I called after her.

She smiled and left me to get back to doing some actual work.

Light pain whispered up my spine as I sat down at the microscope and got everything ready for counting the viability of my cells. Two years ago, working ten hours in one go had felt less of a Herculean effort than it did now, but I was determined to wrap this up before I let myself have a treat. Losing five minutes to gossip just now was bad enough. Maybe some coffee later. Coffee sounded good. To my rumbling stomach, anything sounded good right now.

Ten seconds in, I decided that I should cut myself some slack and get the coffee before I fell right off my stool, not afterward. Either my eyes were too tired to focus properly, or the ocular was seriously screwed up, and considering my pay grade, I hoped it was not the latter. After making sure that exhaustion-caused sloppiness hadn't turned me into a director of cellular genocide, I put the cell culture dish back where it belonged and pulled off my latex gloves. I washed and dried my hands thoroughly, redid my ponytail as several red strands had come loose, and shrugged into my lab coat before I left the lab. Our techs had likely left the building already, and no one would think that I'd accidentally forgotten to shut off the hood. Then again, I couldn't remember a Friday when I had left before everyone else in the entire city went out for drinks, so the chance of that happening was slim in the first place.

My phone chirped just as I reached for the door handle, making me pause. Fumbling to get it out of my pocket, I checked the screen, making sure I was still alone before I swiped the text message open.

You still at work? What a silly question, of course you are.

I bit my lip, trying hard to hide a smile as I typed my response.

You know me. No rest for the wicked.

It only took a moment for the reply to appear.

Are you up for some distraction later?

I waited for the customary twinge of guilt to appear, but it was more muted than the last time. On some level I still hated myself for this, but it got harder to care every single time. What that said about me I really didn't want to think about.

Always.

But just thinking of how he looked at me—his smile, the mischievous twinkle in his eyes—made me abandon all reservation. And the fact that he fucked like a Trojan didn't hurt, either.

Yup, I was going straight to hell, that was for sure. While my girlfriend was home sick, I was ready to drop everything so I could sneak out to hook up with some guy I'd met in a park a couple of weeks ago.

Bree, thy name is classy.

Shrugging, I deleted the message thread as I stepped out of the cell culture lab. With my mind sinking into a perpetual haze of horniness, I might as well grab that coffee now. And maybe a donut.

The corridors were almost deserted, but with my mind hell-bent on getting caffeinated as soon as possible, I doubted that I would have noticed a stampede coming my way, as long as it didn't block my route. Avoiding the main staircase, I walked three doors down and took the smaller one that would lead me to the front right corner of the atrium where the coffee and soda vending machines resided. Sure, the coffee bar in the cafeteria served something that might once have seen an actual coffee bean compared to the brown sludge that these machines spewed out, but I had just enough change in my pocket for that, and it would save me what felt like a mile of walking to the other side of the complex.

After all, I had to conserve my energy for other activities.

Convenience dictated that most days I entered and left the complex through one of the side doors, but I loved swinging by the glass cathedral that was the atrium of the Green Fields Biotech complex. Designed to be both awe-inspiring and the representative opposite of the rabbit warrens of the actual labs, it still held that sleek kind of functionality inherent to many buildings designed in the late nineties of the last century. Like a central hub, corridors led everywhere from the atrium, and more often than not it was the shortest connection to swing by the open-sided glass galleries lining the floor on three sides. Opposite the bank of elevators—also made of as many translucent materials as possible—was the grand entrance, right now letting the warm afternoon sunlight in.

Any other day I might have paused to marvel at the architectural masterpiece, but my mind was on autopilot and led me straight to my fountain of ambrosia—the coffee vending machine. A little fiddling with the controls later, I held the scalding hot plastic cup in my hands, feeling as triumphant as marathon runners had to be after finishing their race. Not that I had the first clue about running. Since high school I hadn't even owned a pair of shoes suited for it. Clogs were much better suited for lab work.

Once I'd downed the better half of the cup, I became more open to let the impressions of my environment work on me, so I turned around and looked out over the open floor of the atrium. Although it was late for a Friday and most people had already left, there was a small group by the elevators, probably waiting for the second, larger group momentarily held up at the security checkpoint.

The tall, thin man in the somewhat unfortunately fitting suit I only knew by reputation, but his nickname preceded him well into the corridors of the labs where he, as part of the administrative staff, seldom ventured. I'd never call Brandon Stone "Scarecrow" to his face, but I couldn't deny that it was a rather fitting moniker.

The primly dressed woman beside him was notorious, though, both because she was the highest earning female employee—of course also working for the administration, none of the lab rats got paid that much—and for her infamous sexual harassment training courses. As the head of human resources, Elena Glover was a legend, if one most people tried to avoid. Personally, I'd much rather spend another hour with her than the second man currently wearing a smile that was as fake as his suit was perfectly tailored.

Unlike his father, co-founder of Green Fields Biotech and renowned scientist Walter Greene, Gabriel Greene hadn't accomplished anything in his life, except maybe to impregnate half of the female administrative staff, as rumor had it. He looked as perfectly put together as the atrium around him, only that the building served a purpose, and he did not. Why the board still kept him on I didn't know, besides providing Elena with a never-ending supply of women to subject to her lectures. The last time I'd spent an elevator ride with him I'd felt in dire need of a shower afterward, stronger than any urge even when I'd been working down in the hot labs. Thankfully, his attention was focused on the arriving guests now, and he didn't even glance at where I was trying to enjoy my coffee.

Done with scrutinizing our team yet loath to quit people watching—my favorite excuse for my lack of social interaction at work—I turned to the visitors next.

The group was comprised of seven people, including two women who stood out, although both for very different reasons. The first could have been a ten-year-younger version of Elena, if Elena had ever jumped on the fitness crazy train. She was tall, reed thin, and dressed in a light beige power suit, but the way she moved spoke of strength and energy where most women with her stature were willowy husks. Her stiletto heels made the toned muscles of her calves even more noticeable, but it was easy to tear my eyes away from them when she glanced my way and I got a good look at her features. Her face was all hard angles, with piercing blue eyes and a perfectly coiffed, platinum-blonde pixie cut. I couldn't help but instantly dub her the Ice Queen, because if that woman was lacking anything, it was warmth.

The other female was the polar opposite of her. Short and kind of compact, "cute" was likely the best she could hope for, but her inquisitive eyes and slight smile transformed her face into something worth noticing. Long, dark hair and olive complexion only added to her approachability, even more so when she came to a halt next to the Ice Queen. Like me, she was wearing jeans, a tee peeked out from under her hoodie, and the way she clutched the bulging laptop bag slung across her chest made me think "geek." Considering that the T-shirt I was wearing fell firmly in the "science nerd humor" category, I guessed that said a lot about who of the two I'd rather talk to, if that was even an option.

The men of the group were altogether less noticeable. Most of them were of medium height and build, if more on the fit side of the spectrum, but when you hung out all day with scientists, it was easy to forget that there were people out there who actually thought that working out had any priority in life. All of them were dressed in the typical corporate gimp suits, and not a single hair was allowed to grow too long, or, God forbid, have its own way and stand up in the wrong direction. I'd never really been one to judge people by their hairdo, but even I had a limit where blandness turned into boring.

Finishing my coffee, I turned back to the machine, and without much further hesitation went for a refill.

Or tried to, as the machine graciously accepted the quarters I fed into it, but refused to gush its pseudo-caffeinated goods into my provided cup. It apparently took more than a multi-million dollar yearly budget to be able to afford regular machine maintenance.

More to vent my frustration than expect positive results, I smashed the flat of my hand above the control panel, only to be rewarded with dull pain radiating up my arm. Considering how many times I'd been driven to the same maneuver before, it could at least have left a small dent. Either that, or like any sentient animal I could have learned from the experience and instead hunted down a different vending machine.

"I don't think that in the history of vending machines that has ever yielded results," a deep voice remarked to my right, startling me.

"But it can be very therapeutic," I ground out, then paused. Heck, I knew that voice, and it so did not belong here.

A quick glance to my side revealed that, yes, I wasn't that overworked that I had already progressed to auditory hallucinations, but Nate was, indeed, standing next to me, his usual, easy smile on his face.

"What are you doing here?" And dressed like that, I wanted to add, but swallowed the remark as the fact that he clearly belonged to the group of visitors gave me my answer.

But it did not explain the message he'd sent me all of five minutes ago.

"Work," he offered, then his smile dipped into a register that did unholy things to the lower half of my body. "Maybe pleasure, later."

Not for the first time, I wondered why someone like him wanted to hang out with someone like me—and by "hang out," I of course didn't just mean have coffee.

That we were different kinds of people was obvious from the way he dressed. And moved, I mentally added, as he stepped around me smoothly, fed coins into the money-hungry machine, and effortlessly made it work its magic. He even got my usual choice of coffee right— black, no sugar, no anything that someone insane thought could be a substitute for cream. To top it all off, he reached for the cup and held it out to me.

"Ha, ha, very funny," I replied, but washed my momentary ire away with a gulp of coffee.

Maybe I was feeling guiltier than I thought, because just standing here with him gave me all kinds of mixed feelings. He just didn't belong here, and while I doubted that anyone seeing us together would make the connection—me in my lab coat, him with the clearly visible visitor's pass attached to his suit jacket—it still rubbed me the wrong way.

"I didn't know you were working in the pharmaceutical industry."

I had to admit, I'd never asked about his job, but between how he wore his black hair short and the tattoo on his right bicep, I'd figured he was ex military, maybe working for a civilian contractor now.

"I don't," he replied, his gaze dropping down to my chest, presumably to the ID badge that was affixed to the pocket of my lab coat—spelling out my name, Brianna Lewis, PhD—because I couldn't think of any other reason why he would ogle the goods that

I kept neatly stored away. Unlike in cheap porn flicks, working in a lab didn't really do a lot in terms of sexy outfits. Most days I even wore a sports bra because of the added comfort and lack of wires that could poke distractingly into parts of me that, same as my nose, I couldn't scratch or readjust while my hands had to stay as clean as possible.

"Is that a periodic table of elements?" he inquired. Looking down, I was reminded of which ill-conceived notion of science humor I'd picked as today's outfit.

Smirking, I pulled the lapels of my coat apart to let him get a look at the print on the shirt.

"Yeah, go ahead, make me feel like an exhibitionist," I joked, just a little bit self-conscious. That my libido didn't mind about that notion, I ignored. It was exactly what he'd guessed, only spiced up by the loving words of, "Chemists do it on the table—periodically." If Elena Glover ever got a look at it, she'd have a field day with me. Then again, she seldom ventured into the labs, and for evaluation and training days I usually toned it down a bit.

"Very clever," he remarked, still looking genuinely amused.

"Strike! Now my undoubtedly sharper-than-average intellect has been validated! You really know how to charm a girl!"

His eyes told me quite candidly that he, in fact, did, but I wasn't fazed by it. Or not enough for me to let it show. I hoped. After all, I had first-hand experience of his… talents. No further charming required.

"Speaking of work… I'd better get back to my cells. They can get oddly demanding at times. And I shouldn't keep you from your Corporate Barbie and Ken meeting, as you clearly don't intend to answer my question."

That got me a different kind of smile, both feral and alluring. As much as his sudden appearance here rubbed me the wrong way, I wouldn't have minded dragging him off to some empty seminar room this very second.

"Sound advice. Some things shouldn't be kept waiting." He turned away then, not quite dismissing me, but halted before his back was to me completely. "A word of advice in return?"

"Oh, yes, please!" I gushed, blinking my eyes coquettishly at him while offering a truly insipid smile.

"Drink that coffee quickly."

That was not what I'd expected, but considering what that brew turned into once it got cold, it made a lot of sense.

"Guess I will!" I called after him, shaking my head at the same time. I got a vaguely pornographic grin in return before he pulled on his professional calm mask from before. Nate—a very strange man, but then he had to be if he chose to bump uglies with me. Across the atrium I caught Elena Glover glowering at me, which made grinning brightly and saluting her with my cup even more rewarding.

Taking a tentative sip, I turned to the stairwell I'd come down before and made my way back upstairs. In passing I smiled at one of the janitors who was taking advantage of the almost abandoned hallways, pushing a cart for collecting waste before him. He nodded in return.

The first explosion hit the complex just as I ducked into a supply room for a shortcut, pitching me forward and sending the remainder of the coffee scalding over my hand.

Guess I should have heeded Nate's advice.

Chapter 2

S hock can be a wonderful thing. It distorts reality and makes you realize just how easily your perception is manipulated.

I could tell with certainty that it was a series of seven explosions that rocked the building down to its foundations and consequently sent glass beakers and bottles flying and breaking everywhere, but I didn't know how I ended up in the middle of the room, huddled under my coat in a sea of glass shards, my right hand aching from the residual coffee burn. Pain in my knee gave me a hint, and when I looked at my stinging palm, I saw light scrapes there, as if it had been dragged fast along some uneven surface.

Disoriented, I tried to get up, but a half-hearted stagger was all I was capable of. Then my mind cleared a little, and the sense that my head was swathed in a cocoon of cotton dissolved into a distinct ringing in my ears. Aftershocks from an intense sonic assault—something like that might happen when half a building detonated, I figured.

The air around me was full of dust motes that started to settle slowly, and when I tried again, I managed to climb to my feet as my inner ear reclaimed its sense of balance. Confusion was still at the front of my mind, but the rising sense of dread crawling up my spine made my stomach flip.

What the fuck had just happened?

I didn't even consider natural causes. I'd never been in an earthquake, but those had definitely been man-made explosions.

Were we under attack?

The notion was so ridiculous that I laughed, although it came out more like a strangled cough. We were smack in the middle of the U.S. of fucking A. There was no way anyone in the world could just send a bomb down on us—besides, I doubted that the explosions had come from above or outside. I might be wrong, but they'd felt like they'd originated from somewhere below me. That left terrorism as the obvious second option, but why would terrorists attack a biotech company? Sure, genetic engineering and vaccine production were multi-billion-dollar markets, but from what I remembered, the company had only recently broken even, considering the investments that had been required to fund it and get everything running smoothly. Research was a costly business, and contrary to other fields of industry, the work force didn't come that cheap, either. There couldn't be more than a hundred people left inside the building, so it wasn't even a good soft target, compared to any mall in the country.

So what was going on?

And what Nate had to do with that I didn't even want to consider.

More ludicrous ideas were amassing to swamp my mind, but I shoved them away. I needed to think now, not lose time playing guessing games. The dust stung my eyes and made them water, but a quick rub took care of that problem.

Looking around, I tried to reorient myself. One of the shelves behind me was blocking the door I'd entered through, so I tried the other direction first, only to find the second door locked. Cursing under my breath, I reached into the pocket of my coat for my keys, but then remembered that I'd left them on my workspace. In the lab. Fantastic.

Turning back around, I waded through the trash now littering every available lower surface, moving gingerly to minimize the risk of cutting myself further. When I reached the shelf, I gave it a halfhearted push, but it didn't budge. I wondered for a moment if I should cry for help, but doubted that anyone would check this room when security protocols stated that people should use their designated exit routes in case of emergency. Getting myself out on my own was likely the safest bet.

Studying the shelf, I realized that the problem was two-fold. One of the other shelves was partially leaning on it, making it impossible for me to shove it back where it belonged. The other problem was that only half of its contents had spilled out—the rest was still weighing down the steel frame.

It took a lot more time than it should have to empty both shelves one more or less destroyed object at a time. I started with the ruined glassware, using a pack of hand towels to get the shards out of the way. Then came books and boxes filled with back issues of magazines, followed by other lab supplies like plastic tubes. And yet more plastic tubes. After the fourth box of them I started to wonder if I'd stumbled over a hidden cache of sorts.

And then, oh wonder, I managed to drag the last two tanks of 96% alcohol solution off the shelf, the muscles in my arms and lower back screaming. I straightened and took a deep breath, and after a last glance at the added chaos my efforts had created behind me, went for the frames of the shelves.

Five pain- and frustration-filled minutes later, I managed to pull the door open just enough for me to push myself through.

Outside, chaos reigned.

Compared to the destruction inside the supply room, the hallway looked almost undisturbed at a first glance. Down the corridor, a ceiling panel had been dislodged and was now hanging haphazardly suspended from a single hinge, but besides that there was only the omnipresent settling dust. Four doors down I saw Bruce, one of our division's techs, leaning against the wall, but he looked okay, a frown of confusion on his face. I tried calling to him, but my voice didn't even sound like anything human in my ringing ears—I doubted that he had fared better. His utter lack of reaction underscored that guess. Instead of trying to resort to interpretive dancing for communication, I went the other way. We had a first-aid kit in our lab, and as it was closer than the atrium, I decided to patch myself up now before being ignored when people with actual medical emergencies should get treated first.

While I was aware that I had dust and residual shards of glass in my hair that only came out reluctantly, the cuts on my palm had already stopped bleeding, and the light burn on the back of my hand was likely only visible to me anyway. Belatedly I realized that I should just have stuck it under cold water, but I had other priorities right now than a small ouchie like that. And if the damage to the building hadn't ruined the faucets, there would be running water in the lab, too.

I vowed to myself that once I found out what was going on here, I'd check on my cells next, but the way they were packed into the incubator, I doubted that more than a little medium spillage had happened. Of course I would have to destroy the entire batch, seeing as ground shaking detonations kind of screwed up standard protocol conditions, but with luck I wouldn't have to wipe down the inside of the incubators.

Reaching the corridor just outside my lab, I felt like my hearing was starting to actually work again, judging from the sound of raised voices and the hammering of feet hitting the floor that I thought came from the general direction of the atrium. I briefly wondered if I'd sustained any permanent damage, but chose not to dwell on it until I had a chance to talk to someone more qualified about that. And not to mention find out what was going on.

With over three hundred separate labs, double that in storage rooms, and cell culture labs on top of it, the complex was a true labyrinth that took most people months to learn to navigate properly. I'd been working for Green Fields Biotech for over two years now, and I still got lost sometimes when I was forced to stray from my usual corner of the building. Pretty much the only parts of the complex that had a clear-cut layout were the atrium and the biosafety level three and four labs—underground in the adjacent building—but when you were dealing with visitors or highly infectious—not just potentially lethal—material alike, it was common sense not to addle anyone's minds any further with architecture.

Thinking about the hot labs made me grow cold instantly. There was a reason why they were housed underground and in a separate building where everything was reinforced to the highest standards of building security. When I'd gotten my initial training for BSL-3 and BSL-4 labs, I'd marveled at the sheer number of fail-safes that were calculated to withstand earth quakes, tsunamis, and meteorite impacts without anyone inside getting harmed, or, likely not even noticing that the world outside was quickly going to hell.

Had anyone been working down there today, and now found themselves locked in with a caved-in connective tunnel?

The idea alone made me want to hurl, and my hands started to shake before I could still them. There was a reason why I was working on the analytic end of the experiments now, where the worst that could happen on a daily basis was dry skin on my hands from all the alcohol and antiseptic used for disinfection.

I told myself forcefully that it wasn't me down there, and right now I had bigger concerns. Like finding a first-aid kit and a bathroom, and getting to the atrium. In that order.

A few deep breaths and I felt remotely like myself again, ready to tackle the problem at hand. My knees were still a little weak but fully functional as I speed-walked over to my lab. When I looked over my shoulder, Bruce was no longer standing in the corridor, but that didn't come as a surprise. Most people who worked here—at least on the lab floors—were very capable, and it didn't take a lot to find the next exit. Unless, of course, you were me and preferred gallivanting through the building on semi-useless quests like unnecessary coffee runs.

The lab was just as I'd left it hours ago before heading into cell culture, only now there was glass and overturned furniture everywhere. Except for me, it was empty.

By then the back of my hand had gone numb, and I decided that I was done feeling sorry for myself. I rummaged around for the first-aid kit, but when I found only a huge roll of gauze inside and no antiseptics, I decided that plain water would do just as well. The tap was still working, and I gritted my teeth as I cleaned up the shallow cuts. I doubted that there would be scars.

I left the useless first-aid kit on the corner of my workstation that wasn't littered with glass and soaked with spilled liquids. The lab techs would have a field day preparing all the buffers anew once the cleaning crew had taken away what couldn't be salvaged. I just hoped that the company would pay both groups overtime aplenty. Policy likely dictated that by Monday morning everything would resume as if nothing had ever happened.

The only thing left for me to do was make my way to the atrium now, which I should have done fifteen minutes ago.

I couldn't say why, but once back out in the corridor I peered into the labs I passed. Maybe I was simply curious or maybe it was just starting to dawn on me that this was a really scary situation, and the need for human interaction and reassurance grew with every step I took. That was probably the reason why I felt instantly elated when I saw a security guard step out of the small kitchen down the hallway instead of wondering what he was doing up here.

I found myself beaming a breathless smile at him as I hastened my step, and after an initial moment of critically checking me out, he returned it with a nod.

"You okay?" he asked, his voice holding a familiar light accent, something Slavic. It was then that I finally recognized him—Joey? Johnny? Luke? I simply couldn't remember, but he was one of the regular guys at the security checkpoint downstairs. When I was close enough to read his name tag, which read "Andrej," I remembered that he was the guard I frequently shared my coffee breaks with at the ill-fated vending machines. He'd once told me that he came from Chechnya initially, and his wife was part of the cleaning or cafeteria staff. Very hard-working people, happy to be exploited by corporations like Green Fields Biotech.

"Yes, just confused," I offered. "Do you know what happened?"

He shook his head but seemed distracted. Likely he was no better off than me. Or maybe he simply didn't understand me yet; if he'd been downstairs, which I guessed might have been closer to the origin of the detonations, his hearing might still be compromised, while I could already discern single words, if vaguely. I doubted that he had any real emergency situation training, and signing on as a lowly security guard couldn't have let him expect to find himself in a warzone.

Thinking along those lines made me come up with another explanation for the frown on his face.

"Is your wife working today? Are you looking for her?"

His frown deepened, and almost as an afterthought he pointed at his ears and shook his head.

"Marta, your wife?" I shouted, feeling just a little stupid.

"Oh, no, at home today, sick day," he supplied, then looked around me down the corridor. "We should go back to the atrium. People will know more there."

For a moment I got the weird feeling that he was laying on his accent more heavily than usual, but that was likely another sign of stress. I could barely hold my thoughts together in my own language; communicating in another when you were still more deaf than not must have been hard.

"Sure. Did you find anyone else still on this floor?"

He shook his head and motioned for me to follow, either because he hadn't seen anyone, or he was tired of playing guessing games of what I might have said. Sighing inside, I fell into step behind him, telling myself that he'd probably checked all the other labs already and I was just postponing the reasonable course of action. He didn't seem to be in a hurry, so I figured that whatever had happened hadn't threatened the general stability of the building.

We were just crossing a smaller corridor that ran parallel to the open-sided glass gallery around the atrium when the small voice at the back of my mind, usually reserved for sitting in the driver's seat of my paranoia bouts, came alive.

Why wasn't the alarm going off?

Explosions of whatever kind should trigger sirens all through the complex, in most cases coupled with the sprinkler system activating itself. I still remembered vividly when a couple of months ago the alarm had been triggered late on a Sunday night when one of the acid tanks in the basement had sprung a leak. I'd been soaked through and through by the time I had made it outside, and the wailing of the sirens had given me quite the headache.

Whatever the reason for the explosions, the alarm system should have been working full force. So why wasn't it?

Once I started wondering about that, other small details sprung to the foreground. The emergency lighting that should have illuminated the quickest escape routes was still turned off. Every third door in the corridors was a security door that should have shut itself at the initial triggering of the alarm system to prevent fire and aerosols from spreading. The ventilation system was still running although it should have been shut off for the very same reason. And why was it so damn quiet only twenty minutes after someone attempted to bomb us into the stone age?

I was just about to try to ask Andrej about the alarm system when we passed a crossing corridor, and I caught the barest glimpse through the far glass wall into the atrium. It only lasted the two seconds it took us to reach the other side of the hallway, but that was more than enough.

Men, dressed in black and camouflage, some wearing balaclavas, others grim expressions and an abundance of assault rifles. At least I thought those were assault rifles—outside of movies and video games, I'd never seen an AK-47 or the likes. They all had a hard, inherently hostile air around them.

Those were definitely not security guards, and I doubted that the resident SWAT team had suddenly changed their entire gear.

My heart started racing at the same time as a fist-sized knot took residence in my stomach. Those guys down there had looked exactly like your run-of-the-mill terrorist gang, straight out of a bad action movie. Never having had anything to do with terrorists, either, I couldn't say if they'd looked any more realistic than the guns they were toting.

Either it was a stroke of luck or just bad timing, but just then Andrej's radio went off, making me give a little shriek. He shot me a quick look as he responded, shutting it off almost before whoever was on the other end had a chance to talk. Of what he ground out, I only got a single word—"roundup"—but that was enough to send my heart beating at a speed likely to bruise my chest from the inside.

Maybe the smart thing to do would have been to ask Andrej what that was about, but my hyperactive mind now latched on to things about him. He was supposedly as half deaf as me, but had looked up at the sound I'd just made. While he wasn't carrying a gun openly, I could see a bulge at the back of his pants that looked like more than a haphazardly tucked-in shirt, and I'd never noticed before that he wore combat boots rather than cheap knock-off dress shoes. And wasn't Chechnya right on top of the list of countries giving rise to militant crime syndicates?

I was fully aware that I was likely rocking a strong bout of paranoia paired with some unfortunate prejudice, but after the way the last hour had gone down, I was more likely to follow my instincts and maybe end up making a fool of myself than ignore them and end up dead.

Casting around frantically, I searched for a way of escape and found it on the sign on the door right across from where I was standing. It even gave me the perfect excuse for my behavior.

"I have to, uhm, use the bathroom. Is that okay? I really have to pee," I offered, hoping that my rising panic simply sounded like appropriate urgency.

The hint of suspicion that I thought I'd seen creep onto Andrej's face promptly vanished, and he even got the door for me. Gallant terrorists, then.

"Of course. I will check the other rooms, then wait here for you. Is good?"

"Okay." I nodded, and hastily dashed into the restroom.

The first thing I did was actually use the toilet, because seeing the stalls instantly reminded my body of its physical needs. Besides, if something hinky was going on here, I had no idea when I'd get the next chance of an undisturbed bathroom break. Once I was done, I didn't flush, though, hoping that this way I could delay Andrej checking in on me until I could come up with a good plan.

I couldn't use the main door and try to sneak out that way, that was a given. The wide corridor outside provided no hiding places at all, and he'd be able to see me from anywhere down the hallway. I also didn't know if he was really going to check the labs or had hunkered down outside the door, ready to drag me off to who knew where the moment I stepped outside.

The nasty voice at the back of my mind was very happy to supply the name of a possible suspect, but like before, I quickly stomped down on that impulse. That was one more thing to worry about that I didn't need in my life right now.

The bathroom was in the middle of the wing, so there were no windows I could crawl through—not counting the fact that we were on the third floor and I had terrible acrophobia. That left my options very limited, or so I thought, until I looked up. There was another panel dislodged there, right above the stall next to the one I was standing in. And not only was it not a normal ceiling panel, no, it looked like a vent.

Before my mind could supply hundreds of reasons why I shouldn't do this, I stepped onto the closed toilet seat directly underneath the vent and examined it more closely. Behind it I could just make out the gleaming interior of the air duct.

Seeing as this was the only option I could come up with, it was better than no option at all. And what was the worst thing that could happen if I was wrong, and I was about to embark on a hilarious journey of freak-out driven insanity? I was already the girl who was bound to lose it. My fame could hardly increase if they found me wedged in an air duct tomorrow.

The real problem wasn't contemplating whether people actually crawled around in air ducts outside of bad spy flicks, but how I could get myself up there in the first place. Even stretching, I could just reach up to wrap my hand around the frame of the vent; there was no way I was going to pull myself up and into the duct like that.

Looking around for something that might give me a higher vantage point for additional leverage, I ended up trying the flush tank next. That helped, but barely. Only when I swung one leg up onto the stall partition did I manage to heave myself up far enough so I could pull my head and torso into the duct. That I made enough noise scrambling to alert the entire building was secondary. Right then I felt like a regal queen of physical accomplishments. With a last push I managed to get my legs up, too, then shimmied back so I could reach down and grab the grille, closing it shut underneath me.

It was only then that I realized just how little space there was left around my body inside the duct. Did I mention that I not only rock acrophobia, but claustrophobia, too?

For the next three minutes, all I could do was try to get my breathing under control and not start screaming at the top of my lungs. The already tight space seemed to close in on me by the second. Air was blowing in my face, stinging my eyes and making it even harder to breathe. Any moment now the floor of the duct would give way underneath me and I would break my neck on the toilet seat, and...

Even with the sound of my pulse racing in my ears, I clearly heard Andrej call out for me, which had a starkly sobering effect. Holding my breath, I counted to ten, then inched backward until I was completely off the vent and could just barely see down into the stall if I craned my neck.

Another shout, then I heard the bathroom door open, followed by heavy steps. He checked all individual stalls, then let out a hostile sounding curse in what I presumed was Russian. At least it sounded Russian. Did they speak Russian in Chechnya? I vowed to myself that I would find out once I was out of the air ducts again, and maybe safely ensconced in a warm blanket with a cup of hot tea. Come to think of it, right now I really didn't give a damn.

I couldn't see Andrej, but he must have gotten his radio out, because there was a burst of static before he spoke again, this time in English.

"Boss, I lost her."

There was a pause, just long enough for me to notice just how absent that accent could be if he tried. Maybe he didn't even have an accent? He likely wasn't even from Chechnya in the first place. Right now, that was the least of my concerns. Part of me still hoped that this was all a huge misunderstanding.

"Lost who?" came the static-laden reply. I didn't recognize the voice, but then the radio likely contorted it beyond recognition. I also didn't know who was head of security, so I couldn't even try to match it from memory.

"The girl I found when I went to double-check the third floor. Can't remember her name. She's medium height, average physique, long hair in a ponytail—"

"You can stop right there. You know that I haven't had time to memorize the ID pictures of all 2,583 employees. Do you have a name?"

"No."

A pause, and the voice got slightly strained, as if he'd long gotten bored of the conversation.

"Do you know which division she's working for?"

"Third floor's all minimum security, can't have been anything vital. I think she's a research assistant or a lab tech. Way too young for group leader."

Even with fear clogging my throat, indignation reared its ugly head. I'd worked damn hard to earn my PhD, and I was a long way from a mere "research assistant," damn it! Wisely, I kept my mouth shut, even if it made me taste bile.

"Any idea how she got away?"

"I checked the other doors in the corridor, but always kept an eye on the bathroom. She couldn't have gotten out."

"Apparently your incompetence is as well defined as your arrogance. Unless you want to tell me that instant combustion or sublimation is possible?"

"What?"

"Never mind," the voice replied, sounding smug that he'd delivered a blow convoluted enough to confound his target while making it obvious that he'd been outsmarted. "I doubt that a single girl can wreak much havoc, even if she was Bruce Willis's daughter. Get back to the checkpoint. We need you for baseline security. Stage two commences in thirty-five seconds."

"Understood," Andrej harrumphed into the radio, and must have turned it off as no response followed. I heard him take another tour up and down the aisle of stalls, then the door swung shut behind him.

I was just about to wonder what the aforementioned "stage two" might be when the lights went out, leaving me in utter darkness.

Chapter 3

If there was a single advantage to being wedged in an air duct, I certainly couldn't think of it. Being wedged in an air duct with the lights out was even less of a fun walk in the park. Add a healthy dose of bone-deep fright caused by ominous conversations after a series of explosions, and I think I deserved a medal for not simply losing my shit right then and there.

One thing was obvious—all the breathing exercises in the world wouldn't get me out of there.

As I saw it, I had two options. Option one, I could stay where I was for an extended period of time, then drop back down into the bathroom and try my luck from there. Option two, I could stop being a passive crybaby and take matters into my own hands, right fucking now.

I started crawling and pushing myself forward before common sense could convince me otherwise. Waiting might have made more sense, but I couldn't be sure how much of a dupe the conversation I'd overheard had been.

The only upside I could find to crawling through air ducts inside a biotech complex was that they seemed to be clean. At least everything I touched felt clean, although my mind was happy to supply armies of rodents and insects lying in wait for me. As much as I tried to move at a constant, steady pace, it was more of a stop and go deal, and with every push I felt the aluminum around me groan. I had no doubts that if I happened to move above someone standing guard, they'd only take a couple of seconds to figure out what was going on.

It felt like I'd spent hours inside this sweaty, narrow hell when the random colors dancing before my eyes started to take on shape and eventually morphed into actual light spilling through another vent. Energy reserves I didn't know I still had mobilized themselves, and I managed the last few yards in record time. I could only guess at how far I crawled, but realistically I figured I'd made it about four to five rooms farther down the complex.

My heart sank when I finally reached the vent and realized that I was now above the small kitchen where I'd met Andrej the guard. That was not the reason for my rising dread, though. Through the slits in the grille I could make out two people, both dressed in black fatigues, entering. How they'd missed the bumping noises I'd been making was beyond me—if they'd even missed them.

They were both men of average height with buzz cuts that made them even less distinguishable. The rifles in their hands looked menacing, and from my vantage point I saw that they both had knives and guns strapped to their belts and thighs. Realistically speaking, they wouldn't even need any weapon to take me down as I wasn't exactly a kung-fu master in disguise. From up close it was obvious that they weren't part of a police unit, and I doubted that the military would send rescue personnel in armed to the teeth.

The walls closed in around me even more, ready to suffocate now, but I did my best to keep my breaths as even and silent as possible. With my heart hammering in my throat, that was quite the feat. If I made it out of here alive, I'd definitely treat myself to some chocolate cake.

Why chocolate cake was what came to my mind right then was beyond me, but the insane irony of it made me grin for just a moment.

Less than an hour had passed since the explosions, and already my mind was cracking. I was so not the survivalist type.

Endless minutes crept by as I watched the armed men stand around, doing nothing except talk between them in a harsh language that once again sounded Russian to me. Sweat was slowly trickling down my neck and temples, and it was only a matter of time until the steady flow of air that hit my face would make me sneeze. Then it was just a question of whether they shot me right where I was inside the vent, or dragged me down beforehand.

I really didn't want to end my existence in an air duct.

A sudden burst of static from a radio startled me. How I managed to jerk but not hit my head or anything else on a duct wall to alert them to my presence was beyond me, but they still seemed oblivious as they both got out their radios, and after a few more words stepped out of my field of vision.

I allowed myself a slow exhale as elation gripped me hard, but the fun part wasn't over yet.

Forcing myself to remain immobile until I'd counted down from one hundred was pure torture.

It also gave me time aplenty to look around the room and discover that I'd have to make the drop down onto the table completely unaided. This was so not going to work.

I considered continuing my journey inside the vent, but, quite frankly, if I didn't get out of this space right now I would go insane, and then all the supporting furniture I might find in another room wouldn't help me one bit. Just to be sure, I waited another endless minute before I shimmied back, then reached for the vent and tried to pry it loose.

It only took me a little bit of fiddling to unlatch whatever mechanism held the grille shut, and it swung down almost without a sound. Like the vent in the bathroom, it remained secure on its two hinges, but my mind was all too happy to conjure up images of the metal clattering cheerfully down onto the floor, sending the terrorists right back to me.

Moving forward until I could look down into the room, I lowered myself onto my stomach until I could take more than a glance around. The kitchen, and what I could see of the hallway beyond the door, looked abandoned, but that didn't make me feel any better. The table I planned on dropping onto seemed miles away, and I didn't doubt that the distance was just enough to break my neck or ankle if I botched it.

As going face first was not an option, and there was no way that I could wedge my knees underneath my body inside the vent, I had to crawl forward, then start easing myself out of the hole in the ceiling, feet first.

I was sure that the guards would be back in time to see my slow and painful descent.

I was sure that I would have a stroke if anyone touched my legs while I was trying to make it down.

At first, things seemed to be going surprisingly well. The hinges of the vent were on the forward side, making the grille press against the front of my thighs as I lowered myself, giving me ample room to kick my legs once they were out of the duct. With the main part of my weight still safely distributed to my torso, I even got the hilarious feeling that I might just make it.

But when I inched further backward until my butt was through the hole, gravity hit me with a vengeance.

As tedious as it had been to heave myself up into the duct, the descent worked a lot faster. I only had a moment to realize that there was nothing my frantic hands could grasp in their scrambling for purchase, then I was suspended in mid-air.

I hit the table feet-first, the impact jarring my entire body. Pain shot up to my hips, and then I toppled forward, narrowly missing a chair as the floor rushed up to greet me.

The shock of the second impact, mostly buffered by my hands and chest, was immediate. For a moment, I was too stunned to even try to breathe, and when I found my lungs empty, panic set in. Agony raced down my back from where my chin hit the floor, and that "seeing stars" kind of vertigo gripped me hard. It wasn't exactly a testament to my stealth skills that I only let out a low groan, but nothing more would get through my clenched teeth.

Rolling onto my side, I hugged my legs to my chest and simply wallowed in pain for a few seconds. But man, that hurt!

I had no idea how long I'd spent curled up on the floor, but once the pain levels went down into mere discomfort territory, I forced myself up onto my knees, then stood completely. I ached all over, but surprisingly, nothing felt broken. I also didn't hear shouts or the sound of rapidly approaching boots, so my fall seemed to have gone unobserved.

Looking around, I instantly felt like a deer caught in the headlights, out in the open as I was, but I still forced myself to scramble up onto the table and close the vent. This time my descent was a lot slower, if no less awkward with the way my legs were still shaking.

Holding my breath, I inched toward the door and peeked outside.

The corridor was as deserted as the last time I'd seen it. I tried to strain my ears, but the only thing I heard was my own pulse.

Suddenly, a cart came rolling out of a lab to my far left, toppling over as it hit the opposite wall, sending beakers smashing to the ground. I hastily clamped a hand over my mouth before I could shriek, ducking back into the kitchen. The men must have been in the lab adjacent to my own, wreaking even more havoc, it seemed. Why was beyond me, but of all the things I was dying to know, that one was pretty low on my ever-growing list of concerns.

Another crash followed, and when I peered outside again, I saw that they were going through my lab next. The way they were progressing, they'd be back in the kitchen in about a minute, with three more rooms in between.

The obvious conclusion was that my best escape route was down the other way, but just as I had that epiphany, I heard a similar crash come from over there. Either they had split up, or another team was joining them.

That only left the rooms on the other side of the corridor, seeing as the next connective hallway was well behind the quickly narrowing window of movement that still remained to me.

Thinking hard, I tried to decide which room might be best to hide in. Right across from my lab was the cell culture lab where all my experiments were conducted, but considering the speed they were working at, I would run straight into their arms if I went for that. Next was the large room where our floor's freezers and nitrogen tanks were stored, together with the huge centrifuges. I could probably hide behind one of those, but there was ample open space in between where I would get caught faster than I could duck away.

Right across from the kitchen was the warm room for bacterial overnight cultures, packed with the suspension culture racks, two supply cabinets, and a workspace that was always so crowded on top and underneath that no one would notice if I pushed something away to create a small hidey-hole. Besides, it was set to a moderate sauna temperature of 37°C, and much preferable to the next door on the right that led into the -20°C cold room.

With my mind made up, I only had to get there before anyone saw me. Easy peasy, eh?

Not.

The destruction crews were approaching fast. The one on the right was still two doors down, but the one on the left had now reached the lab next to the kitchen, with only a small supply room in between. Any moment now they would be done with it.

Another cart came crashing out into the corridor to my right, and I didn't hesitate anymore. Pushing myself off the door frame, I ran the three steps it took to traverse the hallway, grabbed the heavy door handle of the warm room, and pulled it open.

Never before had a slow moving door been that much of an annoyance to me.

Noise and heat came at me in a moist wave, but I didn't care. Pushing on the inside now, I begged for the stupid door to open a little faster. The moment the gap was large enough for me to duck inside, I did, then pulled hard to make the door shut again.

Normally, the mechanical hums and whines of the shaking culture bottles were soothing to me, but right then they turned into a searing hot knife at the back of my mind. It was impossible to judge how much noise the door had made as it shut, or if the sounds from inside the room had been audible beyond the corridor. Then again, they must have heard me crashing down out of the duct in the kitchen, too, and simply attributed it to the work of the other crew. Maybe that worked again?

I didn't plan on pushing my luck, so instead of remaining just inside the door, I hastily stepped up to the workspace and started shoving the chemical waste containers aside to create some space at the end of the bench, right up to the wall. The best I could do with the table legs was a small crevice that made the ducts look roomy, barely wide enough for my shoulders to fit into, but it was better than being caught and dragged off to who knew where. Time was definitely working against me, so before I could have another freak-out because of the limited space I had to cram myself into, I crawled inside, backward, dragging one of the containers as close to me as possible.

And then, I waited.

Here at least it wasn't pitch black, even if my hiding space was pretty much the darkest corner of the room. I could still see a sliver over the containers surrounding me, except for the one I'd halfway pulled in behind me. Sitting there with my knees to my chest and my arms somehow wrapped around them, I could at least look at my watch, what little good that did me.

The display read 5:07, an endless thirty-two minutes after I'd left the cell culture lab. To me it seemed like a small eternity already, and the constant level of adrenaline pumping through my veins was starting to take its toll. Try as I might, I couldn't keep my fingers from shaking as I waited and hoped, sitting in my corner, sweating like a pig as the drone of moving flasks surrounded me.

Then the lights went out and I was suddenly sitting in the dark, while the flasks came to a whining halt as the machines stopped. In the sudden, eerie darkness the sound of the door swinging open was ominously loud, and I held my breath as I watched three people step into the room.

Chapter 4

Crammed into the small space at the end of the workbench, I couldn't see much besides some artificial light spilling into the room from outside, glinting on drawn weapons.

I hadn't thought it possible, but my pulse started racing even more, to the point where I was certain that they had to hear my frantic heartbeat even though I didn't move a muscle. Wedged in as I was, I wasn't even sure if I could have moved had I wanted to. My muscles already started to burn, and the pain from my glorious exit from the ducts flared up anew. I did my best to ignore both.

It got immediately easier when I heard a harsh, cold female voice talk in perfect English, with only a hint of an accent that I couldn't place. It was a different one than Andrej's.

"Are you sure that you saw someone come in here?"

My heart thudded harder while a fearful whimper tried to wrench itself from my throat. They'd seen me! They had fucking seen me!

"Well, not exactly," a male voice replied, a lot less sure than the woman's.

"We heard some noise," a second male voice supplied.

"Crashes," the woman responded snidely. "As in teams combing through rooms all over the building?"

If I had to take a guess, she was annoyed with having to delegate tasks that were beneath her.

"Maybe?" the first man replied, somewhat chagrined.

"Could you two be any more incompetent!" the woman bit back, having none of it.

"We think there was someone in the kitchen." The second man stood up to her, if with less confidence than before.

"In the kitchen," she echoed. "And then ran into this room, without either of you actually seeing anything."

"Yes," guy number one backed up his partner. "We were busy getting the protocol books, as we were told to."

Protocol books? Did they mean the lab protocols all personnel were required to keep? What use could that be to anyone? From experience I knew that it was hard enough to make sense of my own notes from a few months back. Having to rely on those of anyone else in my work group was a real bother, and to anyone not familiar with the experiments at all, it must have looked like so much gibberish. Why were they looking for that of all things? That was definitely something to think about once my mind wasn't about to turn into full flight mode.

"Then where is that ghost you were chasing?"

A bright beam from an industrial strength flashlight zoomed across the room, not even close to my hiding space.

"But we saw—" guy number two started, but was swiftly cut off.

"Fucking idiots," the woman grumbled. Maybe she said more, but it got lost in the deafening sound of a rifle going off as bullets ripped through glass, plastic, and walls alike.

The first seconds I was too startled to scream, although I doubted anyone would have heard it. Pain ripped through my ears, sharp and all-consuming. I felt still more shots going off and hitting all around me, but didn't hear them anymore. Then I managed to shove my left, uninjured hand into my mouth to mute the scream that I could no longer hold back. The muzzle flashes continued for about five seconds, then cut off, and moments later complete darkness surrounded me again.

The sonic assault after the explosions had been bad, but it was nothing compared to the pain and disorientation that I felt now. All I could do was bite down on my hand and weep silently—presumably, as I still couldn't hear anything—and wait.

The utter absence of sound went away as the unnerving drone of tinnitus set in, but I welcomed it. I'd never heard gunshots in real life, let alone unprotected and from up close, and it was not an experience that bore repeating.

I knew when my hearing returned as I could make out the animalistic sounds coming in haphazard intervals out of my throat and chest. I didn't make them consciously, but I couldn't do anything to stop them. It cost me enough to remove my hand from between my teeth, and my whining cut off in a sharp bark of laughter when I realized that I should disinfect the possible bite marks soon so they wouldn't get infected. Because human oral bacteria were the likeliest cause of danger to my life right now.

I didn't check my watch for a small eternity while I listened to the sound of my heartbeat slowly calming down. Getting out of my crawl space seemed like the last thing on Earth that I should be doing. Just sitting there sounded like a damn fine idea.

One thing was certain: these people didn't belong to any military force trying to help with the rescue effort. Combing through the labs I could have somehow reasoned away, but who in their right mind opened fire with an assault rifle inside a small room just because they were annoyed and possibly trying to scare up someone hiding in it? I had no idea if they'd been wearing ear protection, but even with noise-canceling headphones, that must have been a hell of a racket. Whatever was going on was not a humanitarian mission.

I knew that my panic attack had passed when I felt curiosity seep into my thoughts.

Checking my watch, I realized that I'd been very content to just be alive and hide from the world for almost an hour.

Staying put was likely the smart thing to do. I didn't have food, but there was a sink at the other end of the room by the door, and as I didn't hear the faucet dripping, I assumed that it wasn't ruined. I was still sweating, but not as much as before, so I assumed that the environmental controls had been completely turned off as the lights went out, letting the room cool to normal temperature slowly. The scent of bacterial growth medium lay heavy in the air, making me guess that the culture bottles had taken the brunt of the rifle shots. The idea of leaving my cozy space to crawl across a floor full of glass, growth medium, and genetically modified enterobacteria wasn't exactly the definition of having a good day.

The dark, sarcastic part of my mind supplied that at least the E. coli would have company if I had to defecate sooner or later. Would some unlucky undergrad student have to analyze the contents of that, too?

My amusement was rather short-lived, and I tried to relax as much as possible in my current situation. Stupid notions aside, I had to decide what to do now, and only considering unrealistic options didn't make my day any brighter.

If they were terrorists—and all signs pointed straight at that— there was no guarantee that I was safe just because I was hiding here. From what I could tell, they'd made a first round through the building to stir up all remaining personnel, which I'd evaded through means of air duct crawling. After that, they'd started tearing the labs apart to snatch up information. It still made no sense to grab the lab protocols if they could just as easily have checked the recent publications of each work group to see who was doing what, but maybe I was missing the point altogether. That part I was still very hesitant to make my mind up about.

The utter destruction of the bacterial cultures could either have been step three, or just a declaration of madness in general. Both seemed to fit the bill so far.

Extrapolating from that, it was hard to take a guess at what would come next, but I didn't think it beneath them for using the air conditioning system to gas out whoever had so far eluded them. Maybe I was just being understandably paranoid, but suddenly it sounded like a damn good idea to get to one of the safety checkpoints and outfit myself with a first-aid kit and a gas mask. If the coast was clear, I might either make it outside from there, or sneak down into the biosafety level three labs to don a light hazmat suit and respirator unit. I'd never been in the L3 labs housed in this part of the complex, but I knew that not all of them were with the hot lab I'd been working in that was set up in its separate bunker.

Then it occurred to me that what they might be after was likely in one of those labs, and a cold shiver that had nothing to do with the drying sweat all over my body ran down my spine.

Green Fields Biotech was mostly working in pharmacological and medical basic research with a few patents in vaccine development to spice things up, but as far as I knew, the most hazardous materials in the complex were your run-of-the-mill chemicals, not viral banks full of Ebola. We were a leading research lab for tuberculosis treatment and coronavirus vaccines, thus the L3 and L4 labs, but I couldn't fathom what a bunch of terrorists wanted with bacteria and viruses that vaccines and treatment methods were readily available for.

It was then that I wondered once more if anyone had been in the L4 lab when the explosions had gone off. Suddenly the fact that the ventilation system and climate control was shut off took on an entirely new meaning.

Chapter 5

Until then, hiding had sounded like a perfectly acceptable option, but the moment I realized that the entire building could be compromised by a rapidly spreading disease that was unpleasant at the least and very likely lethal, every breath that I took turned into an inevitable time bomb. I'd landed my current job because of my thesis work on SARS. I was only too aware what might spread throughout the complex if the chain of security was compromised.

Technically, the L3 and L4 labs were working completely autonomous, and the most likely security breach might happen by someone taking contaminated material outside with them. The gauntlet of decontamination showers and airlocks should prevent that if only trained personnel got anywhere near the hot labs, but the would-be Rambos who were combing through the labs up here and shot bacterial culture flasks for fun didn't sound remotely qualified for that.

Thinking about all this, I realized that my priorities had just rearranged themselves.

First, I needed to know exactly what was going on, right now.

Second, I needed to get out of here, whatever the cost.

It occurred to me that my reaction dipped not just a little into the melodramatic range, but I really didn't care.

So bolstered was my survival instinct that I made it out of my tight, not-so-comfy space and across the wet, glass-strewn floor before dread's icy grip fastened around the back of my neck again. Yet, my mind was set, and not knowing got more and more unnerving by the second.

Easing the door open, I looked outside.

Once again the corridor lay abandoned, but in a much worse state than before. Carts were overturned, papers strewn everywhere, and substantial parts of the floor were covered in undefined liquids. I was doubly glad about my sturdy lab clogs, hoping that thick plastic would protect me from all the spillage.

The kitchen across the corridor was dark now, but soft evening light streamed through the open lab doors. This time I wasn't fooled by the absence of patrolling guards and waited a full ten minutes before I opened the door completely and stepped into the hallway.

I was met with silence, my uneven breaths the only sound in the world.

First things first, I told myself, and slowly made my way to the nearest lab door. I would have preferred my own workspace, but for what I had in mind, any would do.

There wasn't a flask still full or a beaker left whole, but I'd expected as much. Ignoring the general state of chaos, I stepped around the worst of it and worked my way through to the desks by the windows. Where I expected the neat array of black lab journals to rest was only a glaring hole in the otherwise overflowing bookcase.

Next, I looked for the computers. Even with most people bringing their own laptops, each lab had a mostly outdated but still functional desktop unit. It didn't come as much of a surprise that the monitor lay smashed on the floor, and the case of the tower was a bullet-riddled ruin.

The landline telephone hadn't fared much better, and the emergency line at the other end of the lab was dead.

After this lab, I checked the next two and found still more of the same.

The fourth lab was where my workplace had been since my very first day on the job, and seeing it in shambles now made me grow cold on an entirely different level. Trying hard to ignore that, I quickly traversed the room and reached for the top shelf near the window, almost howling with triumph when my fingers closed around the plastic casing of my cell phone.

My surge of hope died when I looked at the display and saw that I had no service, neither for calls or mobile internet. There was always stellar reception here, even when I took the phone with me into the lower floors to search for old publications in the archives, or used part of my lunch break to call Sam from the bathroom. Even in the thick of winter I'd never had connection problems. This was not the norm.

Even if it was useless, I still held on to my phone but turned off the sound and vibration alerts. At worst, I could play a round of sudoku if I found myself wedged into another dark, cramped space, or throw it at someone's head to distract them.

Armed like that, I stepped back out into the corridor, and after a moment's hesitation made my way into the cell culture lab. Maybe it was stupid to go check on my research when I had more pressing matters to attend to—like possibly staying alive—but as I was already here, I might as well look inside.

Like everywhere else, the lights were shut off and the ever-present hum of the air conditioning units was glaringly absent, but that wasn't what made me halt in my tracks right inside the door. The already muted daylight spilling in around me wasn't enough to let me see more than a quarter of the room, but it was enough. The devastation I'd seen around the normal workspaces was nothing compared to what I glimpsed here. All the incubators were open, two even yanked off the bench they'd been sitting on and were now lying on the floor, cell culture dishes and red, spilled medium everywhere. All the hoods were trashed, and in front of them were heaps of shattered glass where the pipettes had all been smashed. A glance at the ceiling showed that they'd even yanked out the UV light tubes used for basic decontamination overnight when no one was working in the lab. Feeling a little brave, I hit the light switch, but nothing happened. The power was cut for good.

With a sinking feeling in my stomach I went next door, only to be greeted with yet more of the same.

A general power outage meant that within hours, most of the samples in the freezers would thaw and be lost forever. After how the labs had been destroyed, I'd kind of expected the freezers to be open, if not their contents ripped out and strewn across the floor. They'd even toppled over the liquid nitrogen tanks and ripped out the cell bank racks stored inside.

Whatever they were after, they did a damn good job destroying everything in their wake.

As I slowly backed out of the room, I realized that part of the terror I'd been feeling since my slow flight from the warm room was dwindling. Their methods might be barbaric, but it looked as if they knew exactly what they were after. Maybe I was being too optimistic, but I hoped that meant they knew what to leave alone.

This still didn't really explain what was going on or why, but I was determined to find that out next.

Swinging by my lab one last time, I grabbed the first-aid kit that still rested weirdly undisturbed on the counter and set out to finally get some answers.

Chapter 6

The closer I got to the atrium, the more my courage waned, but I forced myself to keep slinking from door to door, ducking into rooms whenever I found one unlocked. Traversing the main corridor quickly was almost impossible as several trashed cabinets blocked the direct path, and someone had ripped off an entire section of wall paneling in one place.

It was then that I saw the first heavily armed patrol making rounds, and almost turned back. I definitely felt like the cat whose curiosity was about to be the end of her. But something kept me going, and with every dash I got closer to where I hoped I would find at least some answers.

A last terrifyingly slow walk through a seminar room that was barely less than pitch black because someone had torn a door off its hinges, letting in some natural light from the direction of the atrium, and finally I reached my goal.

One look down the three floors of glass facade, and I wished I'd never gotten up this morning.

At first glance, it wasn't even that bad. No one was lining people in lab coats up and executing them, at least as far as I could see. But there were plenty of people milling around who were obviously the worse for wear, some even wounded, with black-fatigued, armed men and women holding them at gun and rifle point. Two of them were slowly walking from one casually clothed, mostly lab-coat-wearing person to the next, and kept pushing people toward one of two groups. The smaller of the two wasn't all scientists, as I recognized Gabriel Greene, Brandon Stone, and Elena Glover among them.

Besides that, the atrium had undergone a terrible transformation.

The sprawling glass foyer, next to the security checkpoint and the niche with the vending machines, was partly caved in, likely from one of the explosions that had set off what had since turned into the worst day of my life. What panes of glass were still intact were quickly disappearing behind barricades made of desks, cabinets, and sand sacks. From my vantage point I could just get a glimpse at the side entrance, which was reduced to a giant heap of rubble.

In the corner between the two entrances, taking up more space than most small family homes, was a bank of computers and suspended monitors smack in the middle under the huge flat screen that usually displayed the company logo and short informational clips. It was turned off now, but someone was fiddling with cables that they'd yanked out of the wall, connecting it to the rest of the setup. The entire area was ringed by what

I thought were generators, explaining why the computers were working and where the electricity for the bank of ultra-bright floodlights came from.

Studying the monitors, my stomach sank further. I knew that the complex had a patchy net of security cameras, mostly for the classified areas, but I didn't put it beyond the corporation to have hidden cameras operating elsewhere, too. If the terrorists managed to hijack that feed, creeping around would get a lot harder. In hindsight, the likely cause of why I was still up here and not down there was that I'd been in the right place at the right time. The roundup crews must have been sloppy because they'd known that soon the cams would do their job for them—if you wanted to call shooting randomly at bottles and computers "sloppy."

Movement near the foyer caught my attention, and I leaned forward a little to catch a better look without giving my position away. There, almost at the exact same spot where I'd walked by him many, many times, lounged Andrej. He'd ditched his guard uniform for darkly patterned camouflage fatigues and a matching cap. Next to him, John—another security guard—was industriously chatting with a petite woman who I knew worked in the cafeteria. As I scanned the combat-gear-wearing crowd, I recognized several, if not all of them. Realizing that this operation must have taken months to plan and execute if they'd successfully infiltrated all the supply positions made me grow more than just a little uneasy.

Was there anyone around I could still trust? In a way, that new level of paranoia made me feel even worse.

Then two people marched into the middle of the room, and when I say "marched," I mean it. I recognized the tall, blonde woman as the Ice Queen who'd been with the group of visitors, and when I heard her bark orders at some of the troops, I realized that it was the same voice from the warm room I'd been hiding in. Putting a face to the madwoman who'd randomly shot around and probably damaged my hearing forever didn't really make me feel any better.

The man beside her, who held himself with so much confidence that he couldn't be anyone but the man in charge, was Nate.

Huh. Guess that explained why he'd told me to finish that coffee quickly.

For several seconds straight, my mind was simply frozen.

It was one thing to put two and two together and suspect that the "visitors" who had so coincidentally chosen the Friday afternoon when there was a terrorist attack to take a tour might be involved. Realizing that I'd been having an affair with the man who'd likely pushed the button that triggered the downward spiral of violence and destruction was quite another.

As I stared at him, my mind kept filing away details, because taking the next leap of thought was simply too painful. Running into me in that park all those weeks ago? My ass.

Like most of his men he'd donned combat boots, but that seemed to have been the only concession to the changed circumstances he was willing to make. He was still wearing his suit, although he'd loosened the tie, and when he gestured toward the elevator banks, I saw that he carried a gun in a chest holster underneath the jacket. Considering the omnipresent layer of dust here—likely due to the destruction of the entrances—he still looked almost impeccable. Maybe his dark hair was a little more mussed, but it still seemed on the more respectable end of the "straight out of bed" style range.

Right then I felt utter revulsion that I'd ever considered him attractive, among other things. Suddenly, the light discomfort from the burns at the back of my hand felt a lot more like a stigma than an accident.

I must have overstayed my welcome as far as my luck was concerned, staring down at him, as the next moment his head suddenly jerked around and up, and our eyes met across the distance. What I saw in them sent my heartbeat into overdrive, but not with longing. His stare was cold, calculating, and full of recognition. Just as I knew who he was, he knew me.

It took me just one second to shrink back and push myself against the wall, well out of sight, but it was too late.

"Romanoff?" I heard him call below, his voice as hard as the look he'd given me.

"Boss?" Andrej replied. I guess that explained who he'd been talking to on the radio when I'd been hiding in the air ducts above the bathroom.

"Didn't you accidentally lose someone up on the third floor?"

A brief pause followed.

"Uh, yes."

"And didn't you repeatedly reassure me that you'd searched every nook and cranny up there to find her again?"

"Yes."

"Then can you explain what Miss Brianna Lewis, PhD, is doing up on the third level gallery, watching our industrious little operation unfold?" He added a dramatic pause there. "Why don't you go get her right fucking now? The positive outcome of our mission likely depends on her cooperation, willing or not."

I missed Andrej's reply altogether, which wasn't that much of a surprise, considering the worst revelation yet.

They knew who I was, and for some reason that I really didn't understand, they needed me.

With adrenaline yet again poisoning my veins, I turned tail and ran.

Chapter 7

S tealth had so far worked best for me, but with panic gripping me hard, I found myself hurtling through corridors and up flights of stairs before my mind caught on again and forced me to reconsider my new tactic.

From what I could tell, I'd chosen my path at random, ducking through destroyed labs, seminar rooms, and stairwells almost as fast as they loomed up ahead. I'd made surprisingly good progress, I realized, when I recognized the hallway I was currently running along. I'd made it out of the wing my lab was in and into the main building, down one and up two floors, which left me a short distance from the smaller, upscale cafeteria the administrative staff flocked to mostly.

So far I hadn't seen or heard anyone give chase, but I didn't know if that was a good sign, or just one of how much of a headless chicken I'd turned into. Fact was, I didn't really know the layout of the building outside of the main connective routes, leaving me at a dire disadvantage compared to the force partly comprised of the people who cleaned the entire complex on a day-to-day basis.

Looking around wildly, I chose one of the smaller corridors turning away from the main hallway and started half running, half walking toward the end of the complex I thought was farthest away from the atrium. Maybe I'd find another exit there? I dimly recalled that there was a small parking deck around the back that might be my best chance.

Taking another corner fast, I was momentarily blinded by the bright rays of the setting sun. Another day it would have made me smile, maybe even pause a moment to revel in it or take a picture with my phone.

Now it was simply a nuisance, and I turned away after one slow blink.

Only to come face to face with my new worst nightmare.

How he had gotten there or known which direction I would take was beyond me, but he hadn't just arrived. No—Nate was leaning against the wall with all the casual posture of a man who'd been waiting for someone who was inevitably going to arrive right where he expected them to. The same lopsided smile that I was intimately familiar with was fixed on his face, but his eyes still held that cold, calculating quality that made my blood turn to ice.

"Hi, Bree," was all he said, but it was enough.

I whipped around as fast as I could, taking off in the direction I'd come from. Probably not the smartest move, but that way I might stand a chance of not getting lost in the next thirty seconds.

I didn't hear him come after me, but before I was out of range the ominous sound of radio static followed me, making it clear that he was sending his bloodhounds out. For a moment I considered going for another duck-and-cover round, but the faster I moved, the less likely they'd be able to predict my route, or so I hoped.

Running down a couple more corridors I found myself back in more familiar territory, but that was almost as much a curse as it was a blessing. The pounding of feet drawing closer let me know that they were on my trail, and I had to vanish quickly.

More by accident than plan, I grabbed the next door handle available and shut myself in the adjacent room.

Cool air welcomed me, and I realized I'd stumbled into a cold room. I instantly started to shiver, but then decided that I could have hit a worse lot. Getting my phone out, I fired up the flashlight app, holding it up to study the ceiling.

While the cold room wasn't connected to the central air ducts, I was sure that there must be some kind of sealed vent up there. The room also came with a thick, insulated door that would likely muffle sound, and workbenches lining the wall that cut the distance to the vent down to what I might manage somehow.

Frantic casting around was rewarded when I found a differently colored panel in the ceiling right above a bench. Taking my phone between my teeth, I quickly waded through the overturned stacks of petri dishes and plastic containers and used a chair to climb up onto the worktable.

My fingers were already going numb from the cold, but running them around the frame of the vent didn't yield any results whatsoever. Sheer frustration made me resort to violence, and I was surprised when the vent cover came off completely as I smashed the stool I'd used to climb the table right into the ceiling.

I didn't hesitate to wonder whether the crash was loud enough to be audible outside, but put the stool on the bench and used it to push myself up into the air duct. There was nothing I could do about the vent, seeing as the plastic cover had come loose from the hinge, but I kicked the stool away for good measure.

Then I was doing what I was painfully familiar with already and dragged myself deeper into the hellish enclosure of the duct.

I wasn't sure about the layout of this floor, but I passed what felt like two vents on the way forward before I reached one I could actually see, suspended over a connective hallway as it was. In my panic to get into the ducts I'd dropped my phone, but then it was next to useless, anyway.

Peering down through the grille, the only thing I saw was the monotone non-color of off-white and gray tiles of the floor. If possible, this duct was even narrower than the last, and I had trouble drawing deep breaths. Straining my ears, I listened for movement and almost yelped when a black-clad figure walked by right underneath me, rifle at the ready. Then Nate followed, and it took all my resolve and inner strength to force myself to remain immobile right where I was.

I didn't doubt that if either of them had stopped and looked up, they would have seen me through the vent. That none of them were checking the ceiling sounded like the best news I'd gotten all day.

Another endless minute passed without anyone following them before I allowed myself to move on. The moment my torso passed the vent everything around me was dark again, but I almost welcomed that.

On and on I crawled until I felt another vent under my fingers. I didn't even know in which direction I was crawling, so I gave up wondering what might be the purpose of the room underneath me. It was dark and quiet, so it would serve me just fine.

Then a volley of bullets hit the ceiling underneath the duct and ripped right through it so close to my feet that I felt them whiz by, sending me scrambling forward with mindless terror.

Bumps and groans of metal followed my progress, but I didn't care.

They knew I was in the ducts!

And they were shooting at me!

Suddenly, cold aluminum hit my fingers, and because I was too stupid to stop, I smacked face-first into the side of the duct. Stifling a mewl of pain, I felt around with my fingers, realizing that I must have hit a corner. Inching my body around it was a slow, painful affair, but when I started moving in the other direction, I realized that it could be my salvation. If they'd followed my progress so far, they were likely waiting in one of the next rooms. Now if the duct took a turn, I might end up somewhere they weren't looking yet.

But for that plan to work, I had to slow down and avoid making any noise, and that was a lot harder than it should have been.

Seconds seemed like hours as I inched forward, flinching whenever metal groaned around me or parts of my clothing scraped along the duct. With no way of judging time or distance, it was impossible to estimate anything, so eventually, I simply stopped and listened.

The sound of my thundering heart was deafening. My entire body was shaking with every panting inhale. How anyone in the entire building could still be oblivious to me hiding in the air ducts was beyond me, yet five minutes—or hours—had passed since I'd heard voices anywhere.

Adrenaline was still coursing through my veins at what felt like a lethal dose, but the rising panic that was clogging my throat told me that my mind was regaining enough capacity of clear thought that, very soon, I would freak out. I'd never been good in dark, tight spaces, and what had happened today already was enough fodder for nightmares for the rest of my life.

A door banged open somewhere in front and below me, making my body jerk in what might have been a jump in a less restrictive space. Wedged in as I was, I couldn't have moved a lot, but it was just enough to give away my position.

"I think we have a winner," a lightly accented voice taunted. I recognized it—the Ice Queen. Seconds ago I'd thought I was already as afraid as I was going to get, but a new sense of dread started creeping up my spine. With her, anything was possible.

In my head, I started counting down from ten, hoping against hope that I'd heard wrong or that she'd just said that in case I was hiding somewhere out of sight and she hoped to startle me.

The unmistakable sound of a gun being fired, the bullet zooming inches by my face, convinced me otherwise.

If I'd still been capable of rational thinking, I might have tried to remain immobile and hope that I could continue playing possum, but the primitive part of my brain had long since exhausted that option. Without the need for further encouragement, my body propelled itself forward, arms and legs scrambling to help. Light filtered through the single hole the bullet had left, then I was beyond that panel, trying to reach the security of the wall.

The only warning I got was a deep groan of metal, then gravity took hold of me and wrenched me down toward the floor several feet below me. I had just enough time to open my mouth to scream, then the impact jarred me hard enough to stun me for several seconds. Pain exploded in my left knee and entire right side, but adrenaline was still kicking me hard and I was on my feet before anything else registered.

Movement to my left made me duck right instinctively. I more fell than ran through the door, staggering out onto the open corridor that looked the same in both directions. My momentum carried me to the right, so I kept going in that direction, my lab clogs scrambling for purchase. Rubber gripped linoleum, and strength that should have left me hours ago propelled me down the hall.

Gunshots rang out behind me, bullets spraying chinks out of the wall to my left. I wanted nothing more than to stop and cower, but I kept on moving.

Another voice, this one male, shouted across the din.

"Don't kill her yet, we might still need her."

Nate, again. The "yet" sounded more than ominous. Right then I was happy not to dwell on it, though, as I ran for my life.

The door to a staircase loomed up before me, and as it was on the side of the corridor not currently getting riddled with bullets,

I gabbed onto the handle and pushed hard. The door gave way too easily, making me stumble into the dark, but somehow I managed to stay on my feet. The exit let just enough light in for me to grab onto the rail, and up I went.

The pounding of my pulse in my ears was almost loud enough to drown out my pants and the squeaking noises my shoes made, but I forced myself to still listen for signs of pursuit. After three turns I figured I must be up one floor, and still no shouting or shooting behind me. In a way, that was even worse. I wasn't stupid enough to hope that they didn't know exactly where I was.

The fact that they were giving me a head start, as if to turn this into a "sporting" hunt, made my blood run cold.

Another turn, and I realized that I could actually make out the silhouettes of the steps I was running up. Craning my neck upward over the railing, I realized that I'd hit the staircase at the very end of the building that led up to the flat top roof through a greenhouse floor.

The nasty voice at the back of my mind helpfully supplied that this was a one-way street I was going up, seeing as there was no other way down off that roof once I got to the greenhouse.

With more and more light spilling into the stairwell, I made out the door to the next floor.

It was locked. Same as the doors to the next two floors above me. And by the time I considered running downstairs again, the cacophony of shouts and pounding boots on stone that I'd been dreading all along started up below.

With burning lungs and protesting muscles making every step a torment, it was tempting to just give up and wait for them to catch me, but something deep inside of me simply wouldn't let me do that. Using a last spurt of energy, I ran up the remaining flight of stairs, right past the shadowy outlines of plants behind glass all around me, and burst through the door onto the roof.

Outside, only the sound of the wind blowing in my face met me. What hair had come loose from my ponytail was blasted into my face. Raising a hand to shield my face, I turned around as I took a last few staggering steps toward the end of the roof.

The sun had almost completely set now, painting the sky in deep orange and red, with dark blue and purple advancing around it.

Hours had passed since the explosions. I had no idea how long it would take for police to set up a perimeter around the complex, but when I looked down, expecting to see the flashing red and blue lights of a sea of police cars and ambulances that were gathered on the ground amidst a crawling, black mass of people, I only found the grounds deserted. Not quite undisturbed, though. Squinting, I could see something dark cutting through the grass before the fence, interspersed with uneven, circular patches. It took me a moment to realize that those were craters. Had the terrorists surrounded their headquarters with mines? At this point, nothing was beyond them, I figured.

Whipping around, I saw that the door to the stairwell was still closed, but it was only a matter of time until it would open. Looking up at the sky, I saw a single helicopter circling over the city, but it must have been miles away. Raising my arms, I waved them frantically, but already knew that it was in vain. It was then that I noticed several plumes of smoke rising from different parts of the city, and as I turned around, the wind brought the distant wail of sirens up to me. The sun was setting rapidly and there should have been street lights on aplenty, but even most of the buildings I saw around were dark.

Had they hit several targets at once, to keep the police busy? But even to my panic-stupid brain, that idea seemed ridiculous.

What the fuck was going on?

Panic made me whip around again, and my gaze fell onto the opposite roof. There were two dark-clad figures moving around, and with some squinting I identified them as police snipers, the white letters blazing across the dark blue fabric of their bulletproof vests. One of them had just gotten a radio out and was talking into it, his eyes fixed on me.

Hope burst in my chest, sending tears to my eyes, but that might have been the wind, too. I kept waving and screaming, a smile spreading on my face. Any minute now they'd call in that I was up here. Any minute now...

I guess I noticed that I was missing something, like that the other sniper wasn't looking at me but instead focused on something on the ground. Or maybe my subconscious picked up noise behind me that my mind simply didn't want to process. Because when a strong hand came down on my shoulder, fingers digging in harshly as I was yanked away from the balustrade, my body didn't startle.

But in my mind, I screamed.

I tried to tear away, but it was a frail, half-hearted gesture only as strength leaked out of my overworked muscles. Defeat, leaden and heavy, crushed the flare of hope, making everything, even drawing the next breath, impossibly hard.

Across the roof, the sniper raised a hand to his temple in a sloppy salute before he turned his rifle downward. At the edge of my vision, I saw Nate mirror that salute before he grabbed my upper arm with that hand.

They had the janitorial staff, security, and now even someone inside the police force?

I'd never stood a chance of getting away.

Chapter 8

O n the way down to the atrium, I tried to wrest Nate's grip off me twice, but it was more a token gesture than real effort. If anything, that seemed to amuse him, but I figured it would. I knew that he was stronger than me; he'd proven that time and time again, if under somewhat different circumstances. Hungry, scared to death, and still in the throes of feeling utterly betrayed and defeated, I must have been like a helpless kitten to him. The only positive thing I could say was that he didn't manhandle me, but then my untimely descent from the air ducts the second time around had left me bruised and hurting all over to count for a good substitute of a pounding. With adrenaline now leeching out of my veins, I felt every pulled muscle and bumped bone three times as much as before.

He'd come up to the roof with three others, and the rest kept flocking to us until I was surrounded by a crowd of black combat gear and rifles. I didn't know whether it was shock or defeat that kept me from freaking out—maybe a little bit of both. Or survival instinct, although I didn't feel like mine was honed enough to count as such after the string of mishaps I'd made that had played right into their hands.

At least he didn't rub my nose in it. Yet.

Full darkness had fallen by the time we hit the ground floor. Even though not that much time had passed since I'd last seen the atrium, the transformation had continued at a steady pace.

Gone was the crowd of people herded together, with only the small group around the boss's son and the HR hag remaining. They'd now been brought into the glass cube that had previously housed the reception area. Among them I saw a few scientists, too, some still in their lab coats or scrubs, but I was pushed toward the computer station before I could make out anyone's face.

There, the cute girl with the messenger bag that had been with the "visitors" had made her home, her eyes trained on a trio of screens while she typed so fast that her fingers were a blur. It came as no surprise that she was one of them; by now I was ready to see anyone I had met in the past year as a terrorist. Next to her, the Ice Queen was leaning against one of the tables holding all the equipment, a somewhat satisfied smile on her face that didn't reach her eyes.

"Do I need to get out the scanner, or have you verified her identity yet?" she asked, almost bored. I really didn't like the way she kept looking at me, like the cat who'd just caught the mouse, full of gleeful promise of violence.

"I don't think that will be necessary," Nate replied suavely, then gave me a hard push as he let go, sending me stumbling toward the Ice Queen. "Just frisk her, then bring her to the others."

I did my best to hold my breath and straighten, my jaw set defiantly as she patted me down, but I likely still looked slumped over and disheveled. My hair was all over the place, my coat dirty and torn, while she still managed to look prim in her black fatigues. She didn't draw out my torment, either, simply moved her hands over my body in quick, sure motions. In short order I was divested of my lighter, notepad, pen, and a few other random items that I kept in my coat pockets. I'd already lost my phone in the cold room and had no idea where the first-aid kit had ended up, but I got the feeling that I'd somehow disappointed her.

Maybe she'd expected someone who'd eluded them to carry a small arsenal, too?

Right then, I couldn't have cared less.

Once she was satisfied that I was left with only the clothes on my back, she grabbed my arm and pushed me toward the glass cubicle. I tried my hand at some passive resistance, but she simply stabbed two fingers into my lower back where I presumed my left kidney was, and the resulting burst of pain had me doubled over and panting, but walking along just fine. I thought I heard a snicker from one of the guards standing around, but maybe that was just my imagination.

She led me to the back of the cubicle where two fatigue-clad figures stood guard—a man and a woman. When they opened the door for us, she gave me a hard push that made me stumble into the cube. The door closed just as I looked back at her over my shoulder, but she was already strolling industriously off into the darkness beyond what the floodlights illuminated. Clearly, I was dismissed.

Instead of dwelling on that—and, quite frankly, I was also kind of glad that they didn't show any more interest in me after what I'd overheard before—I took quick inventory of the people sitting unevenly distributed around the room.

Besides Greene and Elena, they'd also snatched up his assistant, Brandon Stone, the scrawny, tall guy who was likely the most competent of the trio. They were sitting huddled together all on their own. I'd already seen them on my unlucky recon trip, and of all the people who were with me inside the cube, they made the most sense to me. If there was ransom going to be paid for anybody, it would be for them.

The rest of the people were all scientists and tech staff, all of whom I'd seen and greeted in the halls one time or another, but I didn't even know their names. The only one I was familiar with was the only other woman besides the HR hag, who was sitting by herself in the corner facing the computer stations.

I hadn't seen Thecla Soudekis in some time, and then only in passing. She'd aged in the past fourteen months, and I guessed the stress of the day hadn't contributed positively to the look of worry etched into her features. Back when I'd been her right hand down in the hot labs, she'd always been brimming with energy. Now she looked as weary as I felt.

For a moment, I hesitated before I shuffled over to her. Next to her corner, toward the front of the atrium, was the only non-occupied space I could comfortably take if I wanted to lean against the glass walls like everyone else, so it only made sense that I went there.

She gazed up when I approached, and the look of resentment paired with utter terror made me pause. Then recognition dawned on her face, and she managed a small smile before it fell.

"Bree? Is that really you?"

I tried to offer a smile in return, but it felt fake, so I dropped it quickly.

"In the flesh."

"What are you doing here?" she started, then her eyes roamed up and down my body and snagged on my less than presentable exterior. "What happened to you? Did they do that to you?"

This time I didn't imagine the snicker, and it was definitely coming from Greene's direction. I glanced at him for a second, but chose to focus on Thecla instead as I sat down beside her. It was either that, or keeling over any minute now when the last of my strength left me.

As much as I would have liked to blame Nate and his troupe for my scrapes and bruises, that wouldn't have been entirely fair. Reaching up, I redid my ponytail into a loose bun, in passing noting that there were a few more scrapes on my palm that I hadn't even noticed. Right then, the irregular aching in my left knee was the most painful bruise, but I probably looked worse than I felt.

"No, at least not directly. I spent some time crawling through the air ducts, and I hid behind the trash in a warm room. Plus, all the spillage and glass, it's like a war zone out there."

Thecla nodded sympathetically, then snatched my right hand up as she noticed the cuts there. Studying it briefly, she suddenly got up and started pounding on the glass. I was so astonished that I didn't even try to stop her.

"Hey, can we get some antiseptic and bandages in here? You keep yapping on about humane conditions, but this is a joke. If you keep us locked in here for God knows how long, you should at least give us a means of administering basic level first-aid."

Andrej just looked at her through the glass, unimpressed, but when she kept shouting, he got out his radio and said something into it that I didn't get. The inside of the cube, closed off on all sides as it was, turned out to be surprisingly soundproof.

Half a minute later, Nate came strolling up to Andrej, looking like he was just passing by a shop window for all the attention he turned to us. I honestly wouldn't have cared if he'd never noticed me again, but when Thecla explained to him that she needed to bandage my hand, he gave a curt nod and sent me a brief, intense look that made my stomach sink. Somehow, being the center of his attention so soon after my capture—or ever again—wasn't a comforting thought.

Instead of bringing her the kit, he came inside and crouched down before me, fixing me with his gaze as he raised his brows.

"Your hand?"

Until he said that I hadn't realized that I'd crossed my arms over my chest and stuck my hands into my armpits, instinctively protecting them. All the work I do requires fine motor function—like dentists and surgeons, biochemists tend to be pissy about their fingers. Facing him now, I couldn't help turning it into a gesture of defiance.

"My hands are fine. Just a few scratches." And because fear must have numbed the part of my brain that housed my survival instinct, I added, "And what is it to you? Your people were shooting at me. A bullet to the head is a bigger deal than a few scrapes."

He flashed me a quick grin, and the fact that it was genuine made me want to crawl right into the wall of glass at my back.

"Either you hold out your hand to me now, or I'll have some of my men hold you down while I clean you up. You decide what it's going to be."

There wasn't even a hint of threat or bravado in his tone, just the clear confidence that whatever I chose, he'd get his way, and that was just fine with him. I was partly tempted to let him go for option two, but then the less people touched me, the better. My pulse still picked up as I forced my arms to sink onto my knees, then extended my right hand to him, palm up.

He scrutinized it for a second, getting a bottle of antiseptic and some cotton balls out of his suit pocket. His grip as he took my hand was firm, but he was surprisingly gentle as he started cleaning the cuts. It stung but I gritted my teeth, trying not to make a sound. The familiarity of his touch was way worse than the physical discomfort.

Watching him take care of me with such single-minded focus unnerved me on a deeper level than I was ready to admit. To stop my gorge from rising, I started talking, again proving that I had no sense of self-preservation.

"Why do this yourself? You must be very busy, organizing all this mayhem and stuff."

He paused and glanced at my face, and that unnerving smile resurfaced.

"Right now? Not particularly. Most of the setup is complete, and my people have been selected to be self-sufficient as well as efficient. The only holdup we've suffered so far was catching you."

I pursed my lips, ready to spew more vitriol, but at the last moment swallowed my comeback. When he realized that I was deliberately remaining silent, he gave a small shrug and went back to cleaning my hand.

"As for why I'm doing such a low task myself, I'm a strong believer in only delegating things I cannot do better."

"Why not let us have a first-aid kit and be done with it? Most of us here have good basic medical training."

My argument genuinely amused him.

"And let you have a whole arsenal of harmless-looking weapons? You can easily blind someone by splashing antiseptic into their eyes or make them choke on a roll of gauze. If you're quick, you might even kill someone by puncturing their carotid or aorta with safety scissors or a pen if you employ enough brute force." Looking up and catching my gaze, he went on. "You're quite resourceful. You've proven that. Everyone else in here took us less than twenty minutes to round up, yet you forced us to play hide and seek for almost three hours. What makes you great at your job turns you into a loose cannon to me right now. I might be many things, but I'm not stupid."

No—the stupid one? That would be me.

My palm looked a lot better once the crusts and dried blood were gone, but I didn't protest when he got a roll of gauze out next. Who knew where that might come in handy? That I pretty much underscored the truth of his accusation by thinking that gave me a strange kind of satisfaction.

"I pretty much sabotaged myself at every turn. I wouldn't call that resourceful," I admitted.

Making sure that he'd secured the gauze properly, he gathered up his supplies, even the used cotton balls. His eyes had taken on an almost predatory gleam as he looked at me as he straightened.

"Pia was rather impressed with your ability to evade her and her men not once, but twice with the very same trick. I planned for a lot of things, but not that a physically underdeveloped lab rat would make it into the air ducts and be able to hide in plain sight. She's a hard woman to impress. If she thinks that you're tough enough to go toe to toe with her, I don't take any risks."

Turning around so he could cast his gaze over the other hostages, he nodded toward a bucket I'd noticed in another corner, next to the door.

"You missed my briefing from before, so I'll repeat the essentials for you. I don't give a fuck about what you think about what we're doing here, but it is in our best interest to treat you as humanely as possible. There's bottled water to keep you hydrated, you will be fed, and my men have strict orders not to use excessive force unless warranted. If you hunker down, don't make trouble, and do as you are told, you'll get out of here relatively unharmed. Try to screw with us, and all bets are off. Capisce?"

He waited until I nodded before he went on, but I got the impression that he was talking less to me personally and more to the hostages in general.

"It is also in your best interest to try to uphold the moral laws of society as you are used to them under less strenuous conditions. This is not some badly scripted Hollywood action movie. In this scenario, there will be no heroes. In real life, heroes get executed, and they make conditions worse for everyone. I would also advise you not to act like egotistic douchebags, but that's up to you to decide. I will hold you all accountable as a group; if you force us to take actions, our response will be swift and brutal. If this makes things more bearable for you, see this as a social study. How long does it take for one or all of you to go nuts and go for each other's throats? The fact that you are working for this company means that your intellect is well above average, and you should be able to staunch any impulses that will lessen your chances of survival. Nothing speaks against all fifteen of you making it, provided you don't force our hands. The rest is up to you."

He let those words sink in, then turned to me one last time.

"You should have drank that coffee fast when I told you to." He didn't need to glance at the reddish burns at the back of my hand for them to flare up anew. "Maybe that will be a lesson to you in the future."

His previous statement had intimidated me enough to make me hunch my shoulders and pull my knees closer to my chest, but maybe it was because of that tension that my temper snapped.

"You think? Well, if I'd imagined in my wildest dreams that you would bring down half the building on us, I might have chugged it down in one go. But if I'd suspected that might happen, wouldn't it have been smarter to just walk out of the building in the first place so some deranged criminals couldn't lock me up inside a glass cube?"

Nothing I said fazed him, but then I hadn't expected it to. He left without saying another word, but not without gracing me with one more terribly amused grin. A direct threat to my life would have rattled me less.

Tension drained from my muscles as I forced myself to relax and settle into the wall at my back. Letting my head sink against the cool glass, I stared up into the dome of the cathedralesque atrium above, barely visible in the gloom. It was only then that I noticed the utter silence that had fallen inside the cube. Before, when Thecla had inspected my hand, there had been murmurs and quiet conversation, but when I looked back down, I found everyone staring at me.

"What?" I ground out, glancing at Thecla for support, but she was wearing an equal expression of bewilderment and suspicion.

"What was that about coffee? You know that guy?"

Her voice was a dry, pressed rasp, and suddenly I understood what she was getting at.

"What?" I echoed eloquently. "No, of course not!" The disgust inside of me made that lie sound somewhat convincing.

Before I could explain, Greene piped up from across the cube.

"Didn't look like that when you were cozying up to him at the vending machine. Rather convenient that no one could overhear you then, and five minutes later, half the building lies in ruins."

I glared at him, then straightened, doing my best to appear dignified, or as dignified as possible with my legs now tucked underneath me.

"Excuse me? The only reason why I was down in the atrium is that you and your company are too cheap to provide vending machines for each floor, and the coffee machine in our kitchen has been out for weeks. And why I was even still in the building is because I have a deadline to meet next week, and your CFO put so much pressure on my group leader that he pretty much forced me to work eighty-hour weeks to get enough results so we would get enough funds to keep the project running until we were ready for publication. Meanwhile, you and those other two were waiting for them, greeting them with open arms. Doesn't that sound ten times more suspicious?"

Greene looked as if I'd slapped him, but then shook my accusation off.

"That's a convenient alibi, but you were talking long enough to exchange instructions. I know that we're paying you geeks well, but apparently some people aren't above corporate espionage. My father is a fool to still trust the loyalty of his employees."

My first impulse was to get up and slap him, but I'd never physically attacked anyone in my life, and remembering Nate's speech quenched the last bit of aggression.

"It was just coincidence. Believe me, I wish I hadn't gotten that coffee."

Greene looked downright disappointed that he hadn't gotten more of a rise out of me, but then something else occurred to him, making his face light up with malicious glee. I'd never liked him, but he was quickly becoming my least favorite person, and considering who milled around outside the cube, that was saying a lot.

"So they chased you through the building for three hours? Sounds like a lot of bullshit to me. A pudgy thing like you shouldn't be able to do a single push-up, let alone get into an air duct. Do they even make them wide enough that you'd fit inside?"

I had no idea when I'd hopped onto the body shaming express, but that insult struck me hard. I hadn't been able to protest Nate's assessment of my overall physical fitness and muscle mass, but Greene's comments were way out of line and completely unfounded.

Why I had to not only swallow the bait but also add fuel to the flames was beyond me, but I was incapable of not biting right back at him.

"You'd be surprised what I can do with my body. I like to be on top. I can support my entire body weight on one arm for way longer than just a single push-up."

His triumphant smile in return told me that, yup, he'd definitely scored that point, and before I could add anything to amend the steaming heap of crap that I'd just barfed up, the HR hag came to his rescue, of course.

"Miss Lewis, I would like to remind you of the general rules of conduct that are in effect for all employees? And your shirt is definitely not approved according to regulations."

I knew when I'd lost and when it was best to tuck tail and shut up, so I did just that, although it made bile rise in my throat to look away first. Saying that he'd started it would have made things worse, so I dropped the subject altogether when everyone seemed ready to move on.

This time when silence settled it was no longer as strained, but people seemed to have run out of conversation material. I busied myself with staring at my bandaged hand for a while, then looked over my shoulder toward the monitors. Last time I'd seen them from above, they'd just started to set up feeds from security cameras, but now the system looked fully operational. More than fifty small windows showed ever-changing angles of corridors and labs. Only a single one on a separate screen remained the same, and when I realized what it was, I felt a new shudder of dread race through me.

Turning to Thecla, I didn't wait for her to acknowledge me before I gushed, my voice shaking ever so slightly.

"Do you know what happened to the L4 lab? Was someone down there working when they set off the charges?"

What I didn't ask was whether she thought that the airlocks had been breached and we were right now breathing air full of one virus or another that might kill us within the next weeks.

Her brows drew together, but the absence of fear on her face was already easing my rising panic.

"Not as far as I know. We shut everything down Wednesday night. Scheduled maintenance, you understand?"

I didn't need her to glance pointedly at a knot of fatigue-wearing people who had all belonged to the janitorial staff to get her drift. I was sure that they specifically lacked the special training to do maintenance down there—we had service contracts with external businesses for that—but what she wasn't saying came across loud and clear.

Of course, when you had the foresight to infiltrate every possible branch that would make your operation go more smoothly, including the local police, you wouldn't risk accidental exposure to agents that required the highest level of biosafety regulations. It had likely only taken undercutting the competition's offer to land the job.

"Did you manage to call Sam?" Thecla asked, drawing my attention back to her. The question surprised me, mostly because it was so personal. We'd never really discussed details of our lives outside of work, and I hadn't realized she was aware that I was in a relationship, let alone with whom.

"No, the phones weren't working. Not even the emergency services. Guess that was the first thing they did, cut us off from the outside world?"

Thecla shrugged and started sharing what little information she'd gathered by overhearing conversations over the last three hours.

As I'd suspected, the party of "visitors" made up the core command group, and the first thing they'd done was grab their three-people welcoming committee directly after detonating the charges.

As no one from the other high-level security labs was with us in the cube, we didn't know what had happened there, but Thecla assumed that they had been offline for maintenance, too. It made sense to do all that work in one go, of course.

The infiltrators had started rounding up people immediately, first under the pretense of establishing a triage station in the atrium, then to make sure that no one was buried under the rubble, but ultimately to sort through the personnel and single out this select group of hostages.

Looking around, I could understand why everyone was here except for me. Thecla was the head of the L4 lab, five of the other scientists were the group leaders with the biggest, most productive labs attached, and the others were in charge of other high profile projects. Greene likely had had the bad luck of being the only man with anything close to corporate decision competence who'd still been in on a Friday afternoon in the midst of a flu epidemic.

Me? I was a nobody who'd maneuvered herself even further out of the spotlight a year ago. It made absolutely no sense to throw me in with the rest.

Since finishing the roundup, they had established their perimeter outside, which turned out I was right about. They'd set up the monitors and built the barriers, and as far as Thecla knew, all exits had been rendered useless by the detonations except the one at the foyer of the atrium.

That only left one question unanswered.

"And I presume the bucket's for basic human needs?"

Her grim nod confirmed my suspicion.

"Yup. So far I've avoided getting anywhere near it, but it's only been three hours. Give it a little more time, and we're all going to get really uncomfortable around each other."

I had to admit, the idea of peeing into a bucket in front of fourteen other hostages and who knew how many terrorists outside wasn't the most comforting thing I could come up with, but I could imagine a lot worse. Then I caught Greene leering at me from across the cube, and quickly remedied that assessment.

That guy was trouble, and I had the sinking feeling that before long things would get a lot worse than they were right now.

Chapter 9

Time soon slowed to a crawl with nothing to occupy my mind with and Thecla not at her most talkative. There wasn't much I felt like talking about, either, so I figured I wasn't better company. And what I probably should have been mulling over—my connection to the man who was responsible for us sitting here inside our see-through prison—was the furthest thing from what I actually wanted to think about.

More out of boredom than interest, I turned around and studied the monitor array. Maybe a part of me hoped that there were more duct rats still out there, but it didn't seem likely. There hadn't been that many people in the building to start with, and I doubted that more than a couple had considered hiding rather than following the security protocols and flocking to the atrium. The only thing the cameras picked up were lots of dark-clad mercenaries making rounds. That they were mercenaries I didn't dispute any longer. I still had no clue what this was about and how they were getting paid—and what for—but I didn't expect to find out anytime soon.

What I was more concerned with was the question of whether we would make it out of here alive.

While I couldn't find it in me to disagree with the notion that they were a bunch of trigger-happy lunatics, the analytic part of my brain was asking nagging questions. Like, what did I really know? Besides being shot at myself, I hadn't seen them execute anyone. The conspicuous absence of most of the people I'd watched getting herded together in the atrium could mean a veritable blood bath, but I figured Thecla would have told me about that if she'd observed it happening—and I hadn't heard any screams or shots except for what their hunt for me had produced. That thought came with a bitter taste for me. Had my failed adventures inadvertently led to my imprisonment? But there was still that matter of that special coincidence…

I quickly cut that train of thought short. There was no sense in beating myself up over this until I could talk to him—and if I had my way, I would remain oblivious for the rest of my hopefully very long life, thank you very much.

The cute tech girl was meanwhile busy typing away on her keyboard but then stopped, and the large screen switched to a generic view of the start of a presentation, from the looks of it. Just seeing that made me frown. Once she was done, she signaled her boss, who posthaste went to grace us with his presence—way too soon, if anyone had asked me, which they, of course, did not.

I knew that this couldn't be good, and the way my stomach heaved, I wondered if I was already developing ulcers. He pretty much confirmed my fears when he stopped just inside the door and stared right over to where Thecla and I were huddled.

"Remember when I said that you would all benefit from showing your explicit cooperation? I need a volunteer."

It came as no surprise that no one spoke up, and the floor at his feet held a sudden high potential of interest for the entire group. What did astonish me was that he didn't grab me by the arm and yank me up, but instead turned his hard stare on Thecla.

"And I'm volunteering you."

Her reaction was as immediate as it was understandable. He hadn't yet fallen silent when her arms came around me, and she grabbed me hard enough that the discomfort of my fresh bruises roared alive. I couldn't help but take her hand and squeeze it just as hard as we both stared up at him in our shared horror.

I felt like the lowest invertebrate for being immensely glad that he hadn't chosen me.

Antics of any sort apparently weren't what he considered excusable behavior, because instead of repeating himself, he drew his gun from his shoulder holster and pointed it with steady disregard straight at me.

So much for my guilt trip.

"Dr. Soudekis, you already published five papers using Dr. Lewis's research here without even crediting her in the footnotes; do you really want to ruin her career further by threatening her life? You have a lot to make up for and likely not enough time to achieve that. Is adding to that list instead of subtracting from it how you want the world to view you?"

I had no idea what he was talking about, but I was definitely going to check her publishing credentials when we made it out of here alive. Not that that was a top priority for me, but the human mind likes to latch on to such wonderful details while it is working hard on ignoring others.

At first, she didn't react, but then she gave me one last hard squeeze and let go. Her jaw was set in determination as she got to her feet, and Thecla looked almost regal as she faced her captor.

"Very well. What would you have me do?"

His answering grin was nothing if not feral.

"I'd like to have a chat with you, nothing more."

"I think I can manage that," she replied low under her breath, and sent me a last, long look. "Be brave." Then she stepped up to him and didn't look back. Without putting his gun away, he signaled her to precede him out of the cubicle, and closed the door behind them.

My eyes were glued to her progress as she followed his directions and stepped in front of the huge screen. I admired how calm she looked right until he took position in front of her, crossing his arms over his chest, gun still out in the open but pointed downward. Before, the walls of the cube had seemed to hold out more sound, but with them both standing just a couple of feet away, I could more or less make out what they were saying.

"I presume you have a suspicion what this is all about?" Nate asked, his jaw set in a surprisingly grim way. How Thecla avoided his gaze spoke volumes—volumes that made me uneasy on an entirely different level. It made me wonder if she actually knew him—if not in the same way as I did, any kind of familiarity freaking me out. What kind of business did a high-ranking scientist and current leader of the BSL-4 division of a biotech company have to do with terrorists? That my thoughts weren't that different from what Greene had accused me of didn't go by me unnoticed and immediately made me second-guess myself.

"Maybe," she pressed out when he made no move to spare her answering.

"Maybe?" he echoed, his voice taking on a playful lilt that gave me the creeps for a different reason. The promise of violence in his tone was not even thinly veiled.

"Probably," Thecla amended, quickly looking up, but she returned to studying her own hands twisted around each other a second later.

"Take a good long look at me. Maybe that will probably help turn that into a 'definitively'?" he suggested.

Her eyes kept flickering up to his face, but I thought it was his gun that had started moving ever so slightly as he tapped his upper arm with his free hand as if he were counting down the seconds. I only saw them both in profile so I couldn't be sure, but she seemed ready to break out into a sweat any moment now.

Looking around, I tried to read anything off the faces of the others, but my compatriot hostages all looked incredibly relieved that they weren't out there on the hot seat, and Nate's people were more concerned with looking that bored kind of alert that made me think of robots on stand-by. One or two of them were checking their weapons; the Ice Queen was sharpening a knife, the sound of metal on whetstone just barely audible through the glass but setting me on edge nevertheless; and two of the former security guards were busy screwing around with the one infernal coffee machine that had miraculously survived the cave-in of the entrance but was still more intent on eating quarters rather than spewing out brown slush. Giving up, they instead got some chocolate bars from the vending machine next to it, the shattered glass front making their work easy pickings.

"Let's talk about your research," Nate suggested—as much as being asked at almost gunpoint could be considered a "suggestion"—leaning back against one of the tables that held the array of monitors.

"My research?" Thecla asked, sounding surprisingly guarded.

"All of it. Not just the part in the official documentation."

His words set me on edge, and I wasn't even the one on the hot seat right now. Was that the reason why they had been tearing the labs apart? Looking for something that simply wasn't there?

Thecla licked her lips, betraying nerves, but then that could have been just from the situation. "I have no idea what you're talking about."

Nate kept looking at her, unblinking.

"Now that is something I cannot believe. You killed, what was it? Fourteen people in cold blood? No, fifteen, right?" He added a brief pause there, but Thecla didn't react. At his ludicrous accusation, she seemed to have turned to stone. "I know that you stored the data somewhere, and you're going to tell me all about it now. A woman as meticulous as you wouldn't just let her findings go to waste."

I had absolutely no idea what he was talking about, but even from several feet away, I could see that a shudder ran through her body. I was still waiting for her to vehemently protest—I would have, at the very least—but all she did was look at somewhere between the floor and Nate's knees. Tearing my eyes away from her, I looked at my fellow inmates and was met with a lot more indifference than I expected. That everyone was still hunkering down was one thing; but Greene seemed to be the only one listening to the conversation, tension making the lines of his jaw stand out stronger.

Could there be anything to this accusation?

There was one possibility out there that made sense, if only just a little. Thecla had been involved in vaccine research, so maybe there had been complications in a clinical trial? But that sounded far-fetched at best; Green Fields Biotech did the preliminary research, yes, but not the actual human trials. It was someone else's responsibility—like the FDA's—to make sure that no one could come to harm. Granted, there were always nutjobs out there who'd want to blame scientists for sheer bad luck of patients, but Nate had never struck me as that irrational. Then again, what did I know? Not even in my wildest dreams had I ever figured that he'd be the kind to take hostages and detonate bombs.

"Giving no answer is an answer, too," he remarked just then, pulling me back out of my musing. He looked more relaxed than his words made him sound—a fact that was underlined when he put his gun down next to him and briefly switched his attention to the techie still seated beside him. "Have you looked through her files yet?"

He got a curt nod from her, and a moment later her fingers were flying over the keyboard again.

"Lots of spreadsheets, saved papers, everything you would expect. I've randomly checked the files, but nothing looks suspicious. She must have stored the interesting stuff somewhere else."

Was that a hint of satisfaction that I saw flitting across Thecla's face? But that couldn't be, right?

Nate seemed to have seen something, too, because he narrowed his eyes, then picked up something from a box resting on the table. It took me a moment to recognize the egg-shaped object as a hand grenade. My pulse picked up and I felt something in my chest seize, unease quickly making room for outright fear. Thecla swallowed convulsively, her gaze fixed on the grenade, but she remained silent.

"Know what this is?" he asked, holding the grenade out to her, making her tense even more. "Course you do. Makes me wonder. You handle deadly viruses in your lab on a daily basis, but you're afraid of this?"

Silence stretched again, leaving me too much opportunity to consider why they kept a box of ordnance just lying around in the open like that. It was broken not by Thecla's reply, or Nate's next question, but by a weirdly menacing moan coming from the direction of the vending machines across the atrium. My nerves already felt laid bare by what was going on right in front of me, but while it didn't actually sound like much, there was a subliminal quality to it that made something inside of me run cold—a brain-stem, instinct-driven reaction.

Through the gloom outside of the floodlights, it was hard to make out details, but one of the two guys who had been busy decimating the contents of the vending machines had gone still. I couldn't see the look in his eyes, but his features were strangely vacant. Bored, likely, as most of Nate's people seemed to be that I could see guarding us or the atrium, but there was something completely unnerving about it.

That was, until his face suddenly turned into a grimace, his eyes widening with rage, and he launched himself at his buddy who had been standing right next to him the entire time. The attack was all mindless brutality and direct violence, the rifle strapped to his body completely forgotten as he grabbed the other guy's head, and went straight for his jugular. With his bare teeth. Howling with rage and triumph.

The whole incident only took seconds and was so bizarre that my mind didn't quite catch on to it until he wrenched his head back, blood spraying everywhere. His victim let out a scream that cut off immediately when he was attacked again, his fingers going limp on the pistol he'd barely managed to draw, making the weapon clatter uselessly to the floor. All around the atrium, heads turned, but I wasn't the only one simply perplexed by what was going on.

Nate didn't seem to have the same problem.

Staring at what was going on over there, I'd missed what had happened to the grenade in his hand, but he was halfway across the floor, his gun out, by the time I noticed him. Every line of his body sang with tension, but the look on his face was closed off, concentration taking over.

"Jones?" he called, loud enough that it even drowned out the sickeningly wet sounds coming from where the guy—Jones presumably—was now savaging his victim on the floor, tearing chunks off his neck and face like there was no tomorrow. He didn't react, and that seemed to be all that Nate needed. In quick succession, he pulled the trigger twice, first hitting Jones in the shoulder—which didn't even make him jerk around—and then in the head, spraying blood, bone, and brain matter everywhere. That finally did the trick and made the now lifeless body topple onto the other, but as he drew close enough, Nate sent another bullet into what was left of his head, and two more into the victim's.

After the deafening blast of gunfire, silence fell, but only for a second. My eyes were still glued to the gruesome bloodbath over there when a high, keening sound made me look back to where Thecla stood—a grenade clutched to her chest. Her eyes were impossibly wide, her entire body shaking with dread, but it wasn't Nate or his gun that she was staring at, but what had started leaking blood all over the floor at his feet.

"I'm… I'm so sorry but I can't do this anymore! It's out there! That's not a world I can live in anymore!" she screamed, her words barely intelligible.

Nate whipped around, his eyes briefly latching on to the grenade, but he ignored it over focusing on the frightened woman's face instead. My breath caught, fear so visceral that it was clogging my throat gripping me.

"Easy there—" he started, but cut off when she pulled the safety pin, her fingers grabbing the now armed detonation device even harder. For one insane moment I almost expected her to lob it at Nate and the others, but instead she sagged down onto her knees, folding her body around the grenade.

"You know what's out there, I know you do!" she shouted at Nate, her eyes impossibly wide. "And I know it, too." Then her gaze zoomed to me, and for a second, she looked almost calm. "I'm sorry—" she repeated.

The grenade went off.

Chapter 10

Every breath I took hurt in my chest. Not in the way your lungs start to burn from exertion or the first stages of suffocation. No, it was a stronger, more deep-set kind of pain.

Tears had been burning in my eyes for over an hour now, but I refused to let them fall. Not because I was afraid that it would make me look vulnerable—right then it was hard to care about anything else than what my mind had latched on to. That sound, more felt than heard and somehow… wet. That spray of blood where a familiar face, hands, and torso had been. The mangled remains, barely human above where the grenade had carved a cavity into her chest to expose the spine and what little was left of the rib cage.

Those tears were born of frustration rather than sadness. My mind felt like it was stuffed with cotton, repeating the same sequence over and over and over—making me wonder whether I'd slipped into a state of shock.

There was only a single thing my thoughts kept revolving around—the conviction that I was going to make it out of here alive. Whatever the cost, whatever it took, whatever I would have to do—I was going to survive this.

Considering how the last couple of hours had gone down, it wouldn't be easy, and I wasn't sure if I wouldn't hate myself coming out of this. I could dwell on that later, maybe spend the rest of my life in therapy, but I wasn't going to let anyone get the better of me.

While I'd been hiding in the air ducts, I'd been convinced that there was no worse state to be in but sitting here, locked in yet on display with absolutely nothing to occupy my mind with; I realized that I actually preferred the former. Inactivity seemed to make my predicament ten times as bad. Before, I had limited control over my life.

Now, I had a bucket looming in the corner, and the acrid smell of burning flesh in my nostrils.

Of those locked in the glass cubicle, Greene and I seemed to have been the only ones observing Thecla's interrogation—brief as it had been—and how it ended. Instinct had made me throw myself away from the wall closest to her just as the grenade had gone off, making me end up half sprawled across Greene at the other end of our prison. The look he had given me was just as frantic and confused as I'd felt, and the fact that he hadn't even groped me, just shoved me off him, spoke of how shaken up Thecla's suicide had left him. His shock had worn off much quicker than mine, but back in my corner—all on my own now—it was easy to ignore the occasional smirk he aimed at me.

The explosion had torn the terrorists out of their momentary stupor; the Ice Queen had stepped in quickly and organized that someone sloshed some kind of flammable liquid over the three bodies and set fire to them before they had even fully bled out. The resulting stench made me want to retch even an hour after they had doused the remains with fire extinguishers. All that was left were two uniform, gray sludge heaps that drew my eye whenever I looked out into the atrium, but I tried very hard not to. Which was impossible, of course, as such things go.

About half an hour after Thecla had ended her life, I'd succumbed and grabbed some bottled water in an attempt to wash the taste of blood and bile out of my mouth. I kept telling myself that dehydration was my worst enemy right now—if I ignored the gun-toting psychopaths, that was. Sam always reprimanded me that I wasn't drinking enough on a good day, and today was definitely not one of those.

I hadn't yet finished drinking when I felt that all-too-familiar twinge start that told me that, very soon, I'd have to throw any staples of normalcy overboard and use that bucket. Honestly, the idea of public urination had lost a lot of its horror after seeing my former colleague reduce herself to so much bloody gore.

Trying to postpone the inevitable seemed like a stupid thing considering that I didn't expect anything to change until morning, and there would be more than one trip to the bucket in store for me by then, but I still remained in my corner until discomfort turned to light pain. When I got up, I felt my cheeks flame up but tried to ignore it. I hadn't been the first to succumb to that basest of urges, so it shouldn't have made that much of a difference.

Stepping up to the bucket, I fixed the dark corner in front of me with my gaze, and tried to go through the motions as mechanically as possible. The guards outside where a short distance away but none of them even glanced in my direction. Any normal human being should have had the urge to lend someone in my position some privacy, and, just to be sure, I'd waited until Nate had left the atrium. Not that I thought that watching me pee would be of any interest to him, but anything I considered decent or intimate was definitely something I'd exclude him from.

Sadly, I'd overestimated the group-building strength of the exercise of being locked in with thirteen other people. I was just about to crouch down, strangely happy about still wearing my lab coat to glean even a shred more privacy, when I heard Greene's voice sneer off to my right.

"Finally some entertainment! Too bad that you're not more of a looker, or this could have become actually interesting."

Screwing my eyes shut, I did my best not to react. The quicker I was done, the quicker he'd be out of material to taunt me with. Why anyone in a situation like ours would act like he did was beyond me.

"Does that work for you, cowering there like a baby getting potty-trained?" he went on.

Embarrassment turned to anger, but I forced myself to take it out on myself by sinking my fingers into my thighs, rather than letting him see that he got under my skin. I vaguely remembered reading somewhere that people dealt differently with grief and loss—in his case, it seemed to one-up his usual asshattery.

I knew that I should have stood above this. Why did I let him have so much power over me? Why—

"Something I've always wondered about. Is it sexually gratifying for women to urinate? When you fuck a woman just right she's going to piss herself, too, so is pissing reminding you of getting fucked?"

My back went ramrod straight, and before I could put a muzzle on my temper, I'd already fixed him with a glare, and words were coming out of my mouth. "Want to know what I've been wondering about? Are you one of the guys who needs to watch porn where girls puke into each others' mouths to get off?"

His eyes narrowed, but he was still sporting a lazy smile where he kept lounging against the glass wall as if it was the sofa in his living room. "Why, is that something you engage in on a regular basis? I think I'd want to watch that, yeah."

Pressing my lips together tightly, I turned as much of a cold shoulder on him as I could, looking around for something to clean myself with.

"No toilet paper provided, but if you ask me nicely, I'll consider licking you clean. Just like home, eh?" came his next jibe.

I hated how a twinge of defensiveness crept in with the intertwined anger and mortification, but it helped me to take a mental step back. This exchange was bordering on surreal, and it was about time I learned my lesson and shut my mouth.

Thankfully, they hadn't taken away the pack of tissues I carried around in my lab coat, so I put one of those to good use. I briefly wondered if I should have held on to them longer; a more charitable person than me might have offered some to the others, but then none of them was even looking up, let alone coming to my defense, so they didn't deserve unsoiled underpants. Dropping the used tissue into the bucket, I returned to my bottle, using that water to rinse my unbandaged hand. With what was going on, caring about germs seemed like a silly thing to do, but years of practice were hard to overcome.

As I settled back into my corner, I caught Greene still leering at me and did my best to ignore him. Not that I'd done such a stellar job so far, but the night was still young.

Then my gaze was drawn back to where Thecla's charred remains still lay where she'd sunk to the floor, and I realized that it really was about time for me to get my priorities straight.

Chapter 11

Time continued to crawl by at a snail's pace.

I'd been awake for more than eighteen hours, had a hellish three hours of both physically and mentally exhausting game of cat and mouse behind me—I should have been ready to keel over any second now.

It wasn't like I wasn't weary to the bone. I simply couldn't relax enough for my mind to shut down. And time to think was the last thing I needed right now.

A short while ago, Nate had returned to the atrium. He had been gone for over an hour, although from the productivity level of his men, that wasn't easy to tell. Everyone seemed to know what they were doing, and besides short intervals of downtime where they stood around and chatted in low tones, all of them were busy. The only static people were the guards at the cube door and the foyer barricade, and even they switched in a team rotation schedule of forty-five minutes. I'd never considered myself a hyperactive person, but not being able to do anything while everyone else was occupied was slowly driving me nuts. I could see several of them looking over to the larger sludge pile that had been two of their fellow mercenaries. What had that been about, anyway?

Then again, the moment Nate walked into the cube and fixed me with that intent stare of his, I wished I'd never whined that I was dying of boredom here.

"I need another volunteer," he addressed his hostages in general, but there must have been a reason why he looked at no one else but me.

I stared back, trying to pack all the contempt and revulsion I felt for him into my gaze, but he looked unconcerned. No, actually he started to smile, which was ten times more creepy. That man had the worst sense of humor, and I had the sinking feeling that I'd soon get to see a whole lot more of it—of the real him, because that wasn't a side I recognized from before today.

"Anyone?" He cast a token look around, but as no one else would meet his gaze, he was all too soon back to focusing on me.

"Why, getting bored? Wasn't watching a woman kill herself because she thought that was her only way to avoid getting tortured entertainment enough for you?" I ground out. This time I even sounded pissed off and less like a scared little girl.

The wry twist coming to his lips made that smile almost genuine, and thus so much worse.

"It gets old after a while," he replied. I didn't move as he turned around and walked back out of the cube. Only then did it occur to him that he was on his own, and a hint of annoyance flitted across his face as he glanced back to me. "Make no mistake, you are coming with me. If I have to drag you out kicking and screaming, that's all the same to me."

"So you'll do it yourself, not let two of your flunkies handle me again? Are you no longer afraid I might crease your suit jacket or something?"

The look he gave me was absolutely unreadable, but as his pose remained laid back and relaxed, my jibe must have failed to hit the target. Not much of a surprise, really. Whatever had happened between his flunkies didn't seem to have rattled him much, and he'd barely had more than a whispered curse under his breath for Thecla.

"Do you want me to force you everywhere at gunpoint? I have no moral objections to that, besides looking utterly ridiculous. If you couldn't tell, let me state this in explicit terms. I am trying to be civil. If you have no intention of repaying the favor, there's no need for me to continue behaving this way. Do you really want a glimpse at what lurks underneath once the kid gloves come off?"

I almost sputtered at the implication that so far he'd tried to make things easy for me, but my mind proved that, deep down, it was capable of procuring some sense of self-preservation, making me shut up before I could do more than inhale deeply.

There was no use in provoking him. If he was going to kill me next, I could do nothing to stop him, but cooperating might go a long way toward not spending my last minutes in terrible agony.

Getting to my feet slowly, I did my best to walk out of the cube with my head held high.

I was going to survive this, I was going to survive—

I was almost out the door when Greene reached for my lab coat and brought me to a momentary halt. When I glanced down instinctively, he bared his teeth at me in a perverse imitation of a smile.

"Have fun getting gang-raped, girlie."

That was the last thing I'd expected him to say, although I should have known better by now. Consequently, I had to abandon my no-talking-back policy.

"What the fuck is wrong with you?" I hissed, only to get laughed at in the face.

I tried hard to feel morally superior as I stalked out of the cube, but the best I could hope for was probably looking like a bristling cat.

When I stepped up to him, Nate gestured toward the corridor leading deeper into the middle part of the building, and I fell into step beside him. Four of his men followed but at a distance; apparently my stunts warranted some kind of extended supervision, or he just liked to bring yet more muscle with him to intimidate me. That Greene could be right, I didn't even consider for a moment. Glancing sideways at Nate, I couldn't help but think of the notion as ridiculous. He seemed like many things, but not like a rapist. And it wasn't like he hadn't already gotten that from me with my full consent.

At the door to the corridor he got out a flashlight and turned it on, forcing me to keep abreast with him if I wanted to see what possible pitfalls were lurking on the floor. Here, things didn't look any less chaotic than in the wing where I'd been spending most of the day before my untimely capture. The strobes of light the guards were directing barely touched my heels.

We walked in silence until we reached a staircase, then went up two floors. He still seemed relaxed, but I couldn't help getting jittery as adrenaline pushed my heart rate up steadily. I caught him looking at me out of the corner of his eye a couple of times, but he did nothing to initiate conversation. For what it was worth, he seemed to be taking a late night stroll through the building, never mind the chaos his troops had left.

I'd thought boredom was bad before, but I'd clearly been wrong. If this went on for much longer, I was going to have a meltdown!

As if he had read my thoughts—which probably wasn't that much of a feat, jumpy as I was—Nate stopped in the middle of the hallway and turned to face me, the beam of his flashlight hitting my knees. There was just enough illumination to see his face, but not read the look on it clearly.

"What I don't understand is why you take every single bite of bait that he leaves for you. You must be aware that your intellect is substantially superior to his, and any woman should have enough pride to see what a weak scumbag Gabriel Greene is. What is your excuse for letting him lead you along as if he'd put a leash around your neck?"

The accusation stung, although I wasn't even sure if he meant it as such. Maybe his observation felt like that because I silently agreed with him. That didn't mean that I was ready to give him the answer he was looking for.

"Why, annoyed that he gets more rises out of me than you do?"

Even in the gloom I saw that his smile was a real one.

"I admit, that rankles somewhat, although I consider myself far enough above him that anything concerning him is nothing I see as a serious insult. Will you answer my question now?"

"Why should I?" I questioned.

Now that smile turned cocky.

"Maybe because you've long ago realized just how much I enjoy our banter, and common sense tells you that it's in your best interest to remain in my good graces?"

That came as a real surprise, and not exactly a pleasant one.

"Don't you think that if that was my main concern, I'd just tear off my clothes and jump you?"

One of the guards snickered, and the sound was so familiar that I recognized it as Andrej's. Why having him along was kind of soothing to me, I really couldn't say, but it helped me lose some of the tension that made my shoulders ache. It did nothing for the fierce burn in my cheeks, though.

Nate shrugged, smiling faintly now, and nodded for us to resume our walk who knew where to. This time I didn't resist. Even I knew what battles were worth fighting, and which weren't.

"There's always that," he replied, and that lopsided grin was so achingly familiar that it made something inside of me break, followed by a deluge of self-loathing. Mostly to change tracks, I chose to give him that answer if he really wanted it.

"Stress, I guess. Might be the by-product of getting chased through air ducts, shot at, and incarcerated."

"So your natural reaction to getting pushed is to push back? You do realize that if he snaps, you're going to bear the brunt of every single offense you offer him?"

That had occurred to me, but I'd avoided thinking about it in more detail. As much as Greene was barking up my tree, there was a huge difference between stupid bravado and setting action to his words. I'd known guys like him all of my life—they were all talk, and nothing much behind it.

"I don't think it will come to that," I offered.

"Because you're such an amicable person who can talk herself out of a tight corner?"

"No, because he's a coward. It's easy to verbally abuse the weakest link in a chain, but taking action would mean he sets himself up for possible failure. I don't think he's that stupid."

"As things are right now? I agree with you. But if you keep pushing, he's bound to push back, and he will reach his breaking point well before you."

That statement made me pause. Just because he was a violent lunatic didn't mean that Nate might not be a good observer. I'd never really been good at judging people's character—case in point.

"And you are telling me this why? Wait, let me guess. Next you'll offer to play my knight in shining armor and rescue me from the big bad wolf?"

His snort held a bit of condescension.

"You shouldn't mix your idioms. It subtracts from the intelligent assessment your statement is based on."

"Which means?"

He looked at me sideways as he stepped around an overturned cart.

"Sometimes it is better to say outright what you mean."

"Would you do me that very same courtesy? After lying to me for weeks?"

He paused, wincing, then shrugged as if it was all the same to him.

"Let's talk shop then, shall we? Yes, I can offer you protection. I would even offer you money if I believed you'd be susceptible to bribes. Sadly for me, I know that it wouldn't work. You're that stubborn kind of idealistic person who does what is right rather than what is best for her. You help me, I make sure that Greene doesn't get anywhere near you. Deal?"

My mind screamed at me to not even consider it, particularly as it was a rather vague suggestion, but I didn't want to prove what sounded a lot like an accusation true again.

"And by 'help' I guess you mean more than the cooperation you've demanded from all of your hostages?"

He inclined his head.

"A lot more than that, yes. Think about it for a while. For now, we've reached our destination."

I looked stupidly at him, then over to where he directed his flashlight. We'd stopped in front of a bank of vending machines, all shut off because of the lack of electricity. Just seeing them made me shrink back a step, alarm going off in the back of my mind. Ignoring my reaction, Andrej stepped around us and got out a key, opening the doors of the four machines. I bet it wasn't even a copy, but a bona fide maintenance key used for restocking the machines every day.

Nate got out a huge, black plastic trash bag and handed it to me.

"Your glorious task is to forage food for your fellow compatriots to eat. Not exactly a beacon of healthy nutrition, but I expect that most of you have been living off this kind of diet for extended periods of time. A couple of hours more won't kill you."

I stared at him for a few rushed heartbeats, then took the bag and went to work filling it without a word of protest, but my mind was screaming at me to stop. The urge to grab a candy bar and stuff my face should have been so strong that my stomach convulsed in anticipation, but the imaginary stench of burning flesh was back in my nose, making me want to retch instead. It was easy to tell myself that my fear was irrational, that my observation must have been pure coincidence. Also, Nate was right—tens, if not hundreds of people must have eaten from these machines, and last time I looked, no one had turned into an insta-cannibal yet.

The sack was two thirds full by the time I got the last two previously refrigerated, pre-packaged sandwiches out of the machines, my eyes lingering embarrassingly long on them as I dumped them inside. When I looked up at Nate again, I saw him smirk right back at me.

"Just how long has it been since you last ate something?"

At first, I didn't want to reply, but there really was no sense in holding that information back.

"Five-thirty in the morning. That's when I got up and grabbed a banana and some leftovers from dinner."

"The breakfast of champions," he scoffed, then nodded at the bag. "C'mon, eat something. You must be starving."

I held his gaze for a second, my fingers tightening around the heavy plastic of the bag.

"Thanks, but I'm not hungry."

His eyes narrowed a fraction, and I caught him sending a look to Andrej over my shoulder.

"If it's because of your friend—"

The condescension in his voice made my hackles rise, but I forced myself not to betray my ire.

"Wouldn't you know it, most people don't get hungry when they watch someone blow themselves up. Besides, I can't stand this sorry excuse for chocolate."

Nate seemed to weigh my words for a longer time than was warranted before he gave a curt nod and signaled for me to start walking back the way we had come. Three hallways over, we took another turn, this one deviating from the way we'd used before. When he saw me look down the other corridor, he explained.

"We're swinging by the cafeteria. There should be some fruit and salad left."

It was then that I could finally pinpoint our exact location.

"Should it worry me that you know your way around here better than I do?"

"That was rather obvious from your flight this afternoon. Are you aware that you could have made it a lot harder for us to find you if you'd taken any other way than the one you did?"

I fixed him with a glare but chose to think about my reply before I offered it.

"Considering that my mind is mostly occupied with science while you infiltrate buildings and detonate their entrances, I think that's one of the obvious consequences."

I didn't know whether I deserved the laugh I got, and I certainly didn't like how I wanted to preen that I'd gotten it out of him. I was obviously losing my mind.

We walked on in silence until we hit the next intersection, where two of the four guards left us. I looked after them questioningly, and Nate was only too happy to comment on that, too.

"You didn't really think that any of us considered so much manpower necessary to hold you in check? I alone would be more than enough to subdue you should you get any stupid ideas into your head. You know that I'm physically capable of it."

"You think?" I asked, sarcasm heavy in my voice. He studied me as if he thought I was serious, then narrowed his eyes at me.

"That is exactly what I was referring to before we got to the machines."

I tried to remember what that had been about, but the promise of food had short-circuited my memory.

"You mean that my smart mouth will get me in trouble if I don't take your gracious offer and betray everything I believe in?"

I really didn't like his smile now, feral as it got.

"What you think of as irony sounds more like the yapping of a Chihuahua next to the bark of a proper dog. As I've already told you, you don't know all there is to know. You should wait before you get all high and mighty on my ass."

"Why not enlighten me now if I'm so ignorant? I know that you've infiltrated this organization on all levels. The thing with the snipers on the roof proved that you have the police in your pocket, too." Pausing, I wondered if I should let that point slide, but then chose to surge forward. Maybe if he finally behaved like a real ass to me, I could just cut out that piece of me that still had issues trying to get over him. "I'm not sure how much Hollywood productions deviate from real life contingency plans, but the building should have been surrounded by police right now. Or the national guard, considering that you caved in all the entrances. Sure, you hit the jackpot with that flu epidemic, but it simply makes no sense that no one should have noticed that we've been off the grid for hours now."

His answering smile told me that he was mostly humoring me and not taking me very seriously.

"It took me almost two years to plan this operation. Trust me, even if we'd take the entire weekend, no one would come looking for us."

"But why? Why do this? Why—" Why force a woman to commit suicide? But that part I didn't add.

He considered for a moment, but then shook his head.

"Soon. With no evidence to show you, you wouldn't believe me, and I don't have that much time to waste at hand. You'll get your chance to see what I mean if you truly want to. I hope for your sake that you'll do the smart thing then."

We continued on toward the cafeteria, down another staircase that I was sure I'd never even seen, let alone used. Mulling over his words, something else he'd said picked at my brain.

"You really do think that you're a better person than Greene? He might be a douchebag, but he has yet to drive someone into ending their own life."

I was surprised that his shoulders tensed at that, but when he rounded on me, I realized that it wasn't because of my jibe of what he'd done to Thecla. Heck, for all I knew, he still thought he could wash his hands clean of that.

"Don't compare me to that miserable excuse of a man. There's a clear hierarchy of predators out there, and the lowlife who thinks he's a big guy because he can rape women is just a step above those who violate children. I'm in an entirely different sphere than he is."

Interesting assessment, but I kept that to myself. Why I couldn't keep it at that, I didn't know, but likely the same weird wiring in my brain that made me flare up at Greene made it impossible not to goad Nate on. With him, at least I felt safe to do so.

"So it has never crossed your mind to take advantage of a hapless woman?"

Vitriol was sparking from his eyes, but his voice sounded surprisingly sweet. Of course he was making fun of me, but still.

"You mean like drag you into the next suitably clean room and have my wicked way with you up against the wall? Like in that motel, down on I-79?"

Suddenly, he was standing way too close to me, and breathing got uncomfortably hard. My mind screamed at me to back down, but instead of doing the sane thing, I leaned closer until we were almost touching.

"Yeah, something like that."

He smiled, a wide, welcoming, almost charming smile that was freaking me out because it looked genuine for a second before his eyes hardened, making me feel like an insect under scrutiny. I'd seen that smile enough times before to know that it usually turned into something else. Had it all really just been pretense? And for what? Just to screw with me? Literally?

"No, that thought has never crossed my mind." He let that settle in, then stepped away, giving me room to breathe. When he resumed talking, his tone had dropped back to normal, casual even. "I've never seen the supposed power in a man forcing himself on a woman. Take yourself. Unless you have a black belt in a martial arts discipline that is vastly superior to the handful I've mastered, it's highly unlikely that you could even hope to best me in a fair fight. You're shorter, lighter, your physical fitness level is lower than mine, and your reflexes aren't trained. I'm not stating this to put you down. It is a simple fact that I've trained for this mission for the past year and a half while you've been busy saving the world one cell culture dish at a time. How would it empower me to overpower you when we are so unevenly matched?"

I shrugged, somewhat uncomfortable with having to utter those words myself.

"Rape is about power and control. The rapist has it all, and the victim has nothing. It's as simple as that."

"As far as control is concerned, that might be a correct assessment, but I don't see the merit in that. Now, power—that's a completely different point."

"It is?"

He nodded. "Let's stay with you for our example. Wouldn't you agree that, Greene maybe excluded, I'm the least likely person in the building you'd want to have sex with right now?"

I wondered for a moment if I should ask about the women in his crew, but decided that it was beside the point.

"Pretty much, yeah."

He grinned as if I'd complimented him.

"Now, wouldn't true power be if I somehow managed to get under your skin, that my personality and charm were both so strong that it would make you overcome your revulsion and that sense of betrayal that your eyes are screaming at me? That is real power, not taking something from a woman that she can't defend. Only it takes a true idiot not to realize that. Hence someone like me will always stand well above someone like Greene."

I had to give it to him, what he said made sense. It creeped me out, but yes, it made sense.

The rest of the way to the cafeteria we spent in silence. I didn't dare speak up again, lest he make me even more uncomfortable than I already was.

Once we got there, I couldn't help but deflate a little more. The cafeteria, large enough to house a good portion of the well over two thousand employees at once, was lit sparsely with more floodlights, but that wasn't what made me pause just inside the doors. In the middle of the room, tables had been put together and turned into a long, exceptionally well-stocked buffet.

"Are you actually planning to keep us here for the weekend?" I asked, my voice sounding smaller than I felt comfortable with.

"No," came his reply before he gave me a gentle nudge. "Now grab some fruit and salad. I don't have all night."

He watched me closely, then pushed me toward the door that would lead us back to the atrium. I went without protest, but also without the previous enthusiasm. I couldn't say why, but seeing that feeding station suddenly hammered down the possibility that I wouldn't just have to tough out the night before I could return home and never leave the safety of my own four walls again.

At the edge of the glass cathedral that housed the prison I was about to be sent back into, Nate reached for my shoulder and brought me to a sudden halt. I tensed, about to shake off his hand, but he let go before I could get to it. His face was completely void of emotion, but his eyes were still bright with intensity that I couldn't make sense of.

"A word of advice, if my previous warning hasn't made it through that thick skull of yours yet. My offer stands—you help us, and I will make sure that your stay here will pass with more comfort and less danger to your well-being. I can't force you to take it—I also wouldn't if I could. You can call me a liar and a cynic, but I believe in personal choice and freedom, and it is your right to choose to be a mindless, blind sheep rather than rise above that. You are of use and value to me, but only if you so choose. If you duck your head and ignore my offer, you are of no use to me, and consequently I will not be interested in you any longer. I remain with what I've promised all of you before—if you don't provoke us, we will not torture or hurt any of you, but if you're useless otherwise, we won't step in when things go wrong inside that glass cube."

Whatever it took, I told myself again. Whatever it took.

But right then, that incentive, that knowledge just wasn't enough to make me betray myself.

I held his gaze as calmly as I could and hoisted the bag higher onto my shoulder. It weighed a ton, but it was nothing compared to the grief and frustration dragging on my heart.

"Got any other grand statements to proclaim, or can I join my fellow hostages inside the nice, cozy glass cube with the sanitary bucket?"

He stepped aside and gestured toward the middle of the atrium.

"Join away."

I wondered if it would be too much to ask whether he'd let me use the restroom before he sent me back, but I'd pretty much barred that way myself, so I trudged on without another word. By the time I'd made it to the cube door, he was long gone, proving even more how insignificant I was. And I hated myself for just how much that grated.

This time I got more attention from the other hostages. Apparently the promise of food got their concern up while Greene's verbal abuse was something they were happy to ignore. I dumped the trash bag in the middle of the cubicle and retreated to my corner without touching anything.

I didn't tell them about the cafeteria, and I certainly didn't share the few candid tidbits Nate had dropped along the way that were news to me.

I did notice that, of everyone who'd remained behind, Gabriel Greene was the only one who didn't scramble for anything to eat— and when I caught his knowing gaze, I got the sense that, like with Nate before, he knew more than he let on. Suddenly, staying away from the candy bars sounded even more like the wise decision of the century.

Exactly what was it that I could do that made me interesting to Nate? And somehow I just knew that it was that exact same thing that got Greene staring at me with that uncanny level of hostility, even if he tried to hide it behind that machismo act of his. It had to have something to do with my academic career, and not just my nice smile or my other assets.

I didn't find any answers, and staring out into the atrium where the security station showed yet more guards patrolling hallways but not much else didn't yield anything, either.

Chapter 12

It didn't take long for most of the food to be gone. Even with Nate's promise to keep us fed, everyone was bound to hoard as much as possible, and while the sack had been full to the brim, twelve people could eat an astonishing amount of food in a short time. I wondered if I should feel privileged for knowing that there was a lot more available in the cafeteria, besides the undisclosed number of vending machines that hadn't been raided yet, but somehow that didn't make me feel better. I had the distinct feeling that asking for any of that would come at a price, and if our ordeal would only go on for another day as Nate had hinted, I wasn't going to compromise myself for food.

Besides, not eating anything when everything still reeked of grilled homo sapiens wasn't hard. And anything that kept me from needing to use the bucket was an advantage in my book.

I'd half expected Greene to greet me with a similar comment than the one he'd sent me off with, but it took him an entire ten minutes to stop staring at me as if I held all the answers. Once he got bored of that, though, he was back in the game.

"I wonder what took you half an hour to get the food here. The next vending machine outside of the atrium is, what, three minutes away? Five tops. Let's say five. You don't look like you can do it in three."

I gave him a baleful stare, but that was all he was going to get out of me this time. Try as I might, I couldn't quite shake off Nate's warning. Maybe I had underestimated Greene because I assumed that, his taunting aside, he wasn't thriving on making this difficult on all of us.

Like before, Greene didn't need my participation to amuse himself.

"So that's about fifteen minutes tops, five each for the way, and how long could it possibly take to fill a bag with food? That still leaves the other fifteen minutes unaccounted for. Want to entertain us with what you were doing in the meantime?"

Holding my tongue was easier when I tried not to look at him, so I stared out into the atrium instead. What was it about that guy and the candy bar?

Not replying might have helped to not feed the troll, but that didn't keep him from volunteering more of his idiocy.

"I bet you loved sucking his cock. Or did he fuck you straight up in your ass? It's always the ugly chicks who dig the perverted stuff the most. I bet you came almost instantly—"

Closing my eyes, I did my best to tune out the drone of his taunting. Not that it helped much.

"I mean, really, the way you keep slobbering after him even now is disgusting! Do you have no self-respect?"

That did catch my attention, but only for a moment. Greene's eyes narrowed when he realized that I hadn't listened to him ramble at all, but before he could launch into another tirade, the door to the cubicle swung open, admitting the supposed victim of my adoration.

Only when I didn't feel myself instinctively shy away from him did I realize that something terrible had happened in my chat with Nate—somehow, even fully aware of what he'd done and was capable of, talking to him had made me think of him as a normal human being again instead of a monster. And because my mind was capable of worse feats than what Greene could come up with, I felt myself wonder if there was something to that attraction thing Nate had mentioned in the weirdest discussion about rape that I'd ever had with anyone.

That was the point where self-preservation did kick in and the cringing happened, but only after I'd spent a good twenty seconds gazing up at him, likely not looking as disgusted as I wanted to. He wouldn't have been smirking otherwise as he held out a cup of coffee to me, of all things.

This man was so going to be the end of my sanity.

I stared at the steaming cup, at a complete loss for what to do. Why was he doing this? Just minutes ago he'd been all, "I won't do anything for you unless you do something for me," and now he was bringing me coffee?!

My bewilderment must have been obvious, as Nate started explaining as he set the cup down beside my left knee.

"Considering that you spilled your last cup of coffee because some raving lunatic set off explosives all over the building, I figured I owe you a fresh one. Besides, as I told you before, you do something for me, I do something for you."

He even had the audacity to flash one of those purely male smiles at Greene as he left the cube. That he wasn't hit by a fountain of scalding coffee for his trouble was a testament of me trying to be the better person.

That move certainly proved that he did nothing that wasn't calculated. I didn't think for a second that it was a white flag, or even a small thank you for playing along as I got the food for us hostages. What I'd thought was mostly idle banter had obviously been him casing the situation. In Greene's behavior he had found a weakness that he could exploit.

Shit.

I was still staring at the untouched cup when Greene got ready to deliver what I was sure was another prime example of his level of sophistication, but I cut him off before he could get started.

"Go ahead, give it your best. If it's something I haven't heard yet, you can have the coffee."

Sadly, he wasn't as much of a one trick pony as I liked to believe, and switched tactics immediately. Settling back on his haunches, he regarded me with a lazy smile playing around the corners of his mouth.

"Oh, you should have it. I'm sure you did something to deserve such a treat." He paused, his grin turning nasty. "As much as I like to amuse myself with the notion that it's for doing a good job licking his balls and asshole, I think the truth is much more sordid. First, you just happen to talk in the foyer minutes before the hostile takeover, which clearly was a last check-in to see if everything is ready. Then you marvelously disappear while everyone is rounded up, only to get thrown in with us once we've had enough time to stew and come up with the most horrifying scenarios in our heads. They give you two hours to gather intel, then you get plenty of time to check back with him to relay it. Oh, I know what that coffee is for. Just watching you eye fuck him all the time makes that quite obvious."

He fell silent with a look of grim satisfaction on his face, leaving me completely flabbergasted. Of all the things he'd spewed, this was the worst. The problem was, it also was the most plausible, and as the others listened on, I could see agreement in their eyes.

That was the reason why no one had stood up to defend me. They all thought I was a traitor at best, a planted mole at worst.

And just like that, things had gone from bad to much, much worse.

Chapter 13

I had barely finished the coffee when Nate was back, this time
with four of his men, two of which each grabbed Greene and me
and dragged us outside without a single word of explanation. I
didn't protest but also didn't help along, and consequently landed
on my ass in front of the computer station where they deposited us
both. The box of grenades was gone—I checked.

While I slowly got to my feet, Nate leaned against the work table
to our right, assuming a relaxed pose with his arms crossed over
his chest. He could have been chatting with old friends, or trying to

make new ones. I had no idea how much exactly he knew of what Greene had accused me of, but it couldn't be coincidence that he kept pushing like this now.

"You probably wonder why I asked my associates to bring you here," he began.

I remained mute, determined not to give him anything unless someone put a gun to my head. Greene was more cordial about the situation, almost mirroring Nate, yet sans a table to lean against.

"Oh, no, the reason is perfectly obvious. You want information from me, and she's here to play the second part in your weird 'good cop, bad cop' scenario. Don't bother, it's not working on me."

Nate seemed to consider that, then gave a brief nod of acknowledgement. I could have strangled him right then and there, but had the sinking feeling that in this situation, whatever I did, I'd just doom myself.

"Very well. I would still like to remind you both that it is in your best interest to cooperate with us and not make a nuisance of yourselves. This will all be over much quicker if we get what we want sooner."

Greene snorted.

"Okay, I'll play along, mostly because I'm bored. You got me there. What exactly do you need us…" he overstressed that word "… to cooperate with?"

Turning to the cute techie, Nate nodded at her.

"Bring up the first list, please."

I was surprised that he asked, not demanded, but she acted as if she was used to that. Maybe she was.

A few seconds later, the screen that had been tuned into the camera feeds switched to a list of project titles. I scanned them quickly. I knew a few of them, and the rest also sounded like what Green Fields Biotech was working on. Greene scrutinized the list, but his face remained blank. Nate waited, and when nothing came from either of us, he cleared his throat.

"Do those projects sound familiar to you?"

Again I chose not to react, and Greene took his time finding a reply.

"So this is about the capital of the corporation, if I may venture a guess? Undercover corporate espionage only got you so far, and now you need me to resolve the last remaining details and tell you all our dirty little secrets."

He got a somewhat amused smile in return.

"Something like that. Provided you actually know what your father's company is up to. Your reputation isn't exactly built on being a capable CFO."

I hadn't realized that Greene had gotten a promotion recently, but it explained why he was grinning with satisfaction now.

"You'd be surprised about what I know that people don't expect me to be capable of."

Nate shrugged. "Then care to tell us a little bit about all those projects?"

"And what's in it for me?"

Another shrug. "What do you want?"

I was surprised at the direction their exchange was taking, but then Greene proved again what he was really made of.

"Easy. What I want is her." He indicated me with a sideways jerk of his chin.

I blinked, not believing what I was hearing. Before it could sink in properly, my stomach turned into a tight, uncomfortable ball as Nate seemed to consider it.

"Define that."

Greene snorted.

"Gladly. I'll even be so gracious as to offer my side of the deal first. I tell you everything that I know, and once we're done, you give me an hour with her in a nice room where no one comes in and will distract us. I can get more specific if you want me to, but I'm getting a sense here that you'd rather get on with business, and while I do her, you can do whatever you came here for."

My initial shock wore off about the time Nate donned a pensive face.

"You can't be seriously considering that?!"

He raised his brows at me as if my outrage came as a surprise to him.

"Why? Don't you think that's a fair trade? We get what we want while you take one for the team?"

If there had been a weapon readily available, I would have gone for it now, but in the same careful calculation he'd shown before, Nate seemed to have ditched his gun and knife before having us fetched from the cube. His eyes held an unspoken challenge as he kept holding my gaze, and I was pretty sure that he knew what was going through my mind right then.

"So, do we have a deal?" Greene cut into our staring contest.

"I don't know, do we?" Nate asked me, still playing along.

"The hell you don't!" I shouted, not caring if every last soul in the building heard me. "You can't just give me away as a bargaining chip!"

Too late I realized that I'd inadvertently strengthened his base, sounding more like an offended lover than anything else. Greene's triumphant leer was making me sick.

Before I could put my foot even further into my mouth, Nate proved that he was still the real master manipulator of this game.

"Well, it seems like the lady doth protest, so maybe I can come up with an acceptable compromise? Whoever of the two of you tells me the most useful information gets what he or she wants. In your case..." he indicated Greene "...you get to do with her whatever you like. But if she outdoes you, you both go back into the cube to contemplate the senseless boredom of your existence."

The plan was excellently executed, and I would have admired his plotting if it hadn't left me at such a disadvantage.

"How is that fair? I don't gain anything from you sticking to exactly what you promised all of us, and I still have to give you information?"

"That's the only deal you'll get. Take it or leave it."

His hard gaze kept boring into me, and he didn't have to repeat what I already knew. I'd just have to agree to help them, and he'd instantly pluck me out of this situation.

I wanted to cry with frustration but couldn't let either of them see me that vulnerable. So I gave the barest of nods, then stared up at the list in front of me. That list that I really couldn't say anything about, even had I wanted to.

Of course Greene agreed as well—after all, he had nothing to lose and a lot to gain. With rising unease I listened to him prattle on about each project, naming the group leaders, group size, how many patents they'd already churned out, the net revenue the company gained from the different projects. That went on for three slides without me getting even a hint of a chance, and my stomach sank lower and lower. I couldn't judge how valuable that information was. I figured most of it a simple Google search might have revealed. Maybe it was published in the quarterly statements. Maybe it was exactly what the terrorists were after.

Greene looked more satisfied with each item he ticked off the list, and by the time he hit the last point of the third page, he was smirking outright.

"And what can you tell us about Project Destiny?"

It was a weird name for a project. The others sounded a lot more scientific and self-explanatory, yet Greene hit it in stride.

"Oh, that's a real cash cow. Not quite ready for milking, but I can tell you, it's big. Group leader's Dr. Thecla Soudekis. She's been working on this for the past six years. Small staff but high financial input because all the work is done down in the..." There he suddenly cut off, and when I looked at him, I saw him blanch visibly. His eyes went wide and his show of confidence wavered, but he caught himself almost instantly. "In the basement. No patents yet, but promising. What's next?"

Nate didn't react for a moment, which for him was a glaring tell. Looking closer, I realized that his posture had changed, too, but on a much more subtle level than Greene's. Suddenly there was tension in his shoulders and torso, and while he'd been tapping one foot idly on the floor before, he'd stopped now. His attention was focused razor sharp on Greene only, whereas before he'd glanced at me often, continuing his silent taunting.

Whatever Project Destiny was, it was more to him than the multi-million-dollar revenue deals Greene had summarized before.

A few seconds later, he eased up again, but some of that tension remained, even when he looked away and nodded at the techie once more. A few taps on the keyboard and the screen changed, now showing something I felt a lot more familiar with than the quarterly statement.

Out of some perverse curiosity I kept my mouth shut, although I knew that this was my moment to shine and hopefully talk myself out of the choice between becoming Greene's sex toy or an active asset of terrorists. Just peachy.

"Any of that ring a bell?" Nate asked, still focused on Greene. I wondered briefly if he was testing him.

Greene frowned, but his stumble from before was all but forgotten.

"Technical details. I recognize some of the numbers. Those are things we have patents for. Yes, definitely patents."

I had to bite the inside of my cheek to keep from laughing out loud. Nate looked over to me and offered me an almost nice, small smile.

"You know, if you do keep quiet, I might let him have a go at you simply out of spite. I told you before that I'm not dependent on your cooperation, and I certainly don't need you fully functional, either."

That cut my mirth short rather quickly, while Greene continued to smirk. It was definitely about time that I put him in his place.

"Those aren't patent numbers or even patented material, technically. Those are cell lines. Every lab all around the world uses them. Green Fields Biotech might wish they'd be holding those patents because then they wouldn't need to do anything to earn millions every day, but they're older than the company, some by decades."

The techie switched to the next slide, and I just kept on going, because it was just more of the same.

"Viral vectors, most of them from coronaviruses."

The next slide made me blink, and I stared at Nate a moment before I went on.

"That's the first page of the materials section of my PhD thesis."

He gave a noncommittal shrug as if to say that he could also play into my hands, not just against me.

It went on like that for several minutes. The information honed in on the research I had been doing, or had cooperated in—first the more recent projects, then some of what I'd been working on down in the hot labs. That made me uncomfortable but for different reasons than giving him what he wanted. I was sure that not a single word I said was news to him. He could have easily gotten all of that off the web or the company servers. I had no delusions that, by now, they'd hacked into those successfully. I hadn't forgotten the techie's comment about Thecla's data.

All the while Greene wore a grim face. At first I thought it was simply because I was catching up, but when I realized that he had started to sweat, I wondered what that was all about. He couldn't have been that desperate for sexual gratification.

Then the screen changed again, and I stared at the diagrams for a full ten heartbeats before I turned to frown at Nate.

"Very funny. That's a fake. Something either of you copy pasted together in Photoshop and did a bad job labeling."

He cocked his head to the side, his eyes never leaving my face.

"What would make you say that?"

"Because it's bullshit."

Now I got a variation of the look Greene had received when he'd been talking about Project Destiny, and I felt a cold shiver ghost up my spine.

"Please explain anyway. Indulge me."

I was getting a really bad feeling about this, but went on simply because this was ridiculous.

"This looks like some bad mashup of three different virions. It's even labeled there—from Coronavirus, Influenza A, and Ebola virus. Those do not even belong to the same order or class of viruses, so they could never be combined like that. Nidovirales have a positive sense RNA genome, the other two are negative sense—even if you completely ignore anything else, this cannot exist. I know that we crazy virologists like to draw diagrams where virions look like colored Lego pieces all randomly arranged to make up these pretty geometric forms, but there's a lot of biochemistry behind that. I repeat, this is bullshit. Did I pass that test? Can we move on?"

I was sure that I was the only one present who'd understood a word of what I'd said, and I had to admit, I'd likely simplified it way too much, but I couldn't fathom that it was important. As hoaxes went, this one wasn't even a good one.

And yet Nate kept staring at my face as if he was reading and judging my every reaction. This was making me increasingly nervous on its own, and I hoped he wouldn't read that as something it really wasn't.

"Next slide, please."

The screen changed to an equally fake electron microscopy image, likely approximating what the hoax virion sequence from before might look like structurally.

"Very funny. Next, please."

Nate pushed off from the table and I had to steel my spine not to instinctively back away as he walked over to me and stopped so close that he just had to lean in and whisper into my ear.

"Just indulge me. Explain what you're seeing. I swear, it's not a Rorschach test, and the right answer isn't 'penis.'"

If there'd even been a hint of laughter in his voice, I might have relaxed, but he sounded so damn serious that it was suddenly hard to swallow.

"Well, if we went out on a really long limb—and I'm talking pure hypothesis here—the mashed-up virus from the previous slide might look like this under an electron microscope. No idea if it's a good approximation—I haven't done Influenza since undergrad, and Coronaviridae look nothing like that. They're like spheres with halos. That's what they were named after when they were first discovered. Like they had a corona surrounding them."

His face remained impassive but there was something lurking behind his eyes, and I decided right then and there that I never wanted to find out what that was, let alone be on the receiving end of it.

"And you insist that this is fake. You've never seen anything like this, never heard anyone even joke about this?"

I immediately shook my head.

"I'm a hundred percent positive that I haven't. The only thing making less sense would be using a DNA virus or a reverse transcribing virus, but, yeah, I told you, it's bullshit."

He pursed his lips, looking almost pensive, but the intensity of his gaze never lessened.

"And what would you say if I told you that this is real, and I have proof of that?"

My heart skipped a beat before it went into overdrive, fear closing my throat until all I could get out was a raspy, "That's not possible."

Realistically, it wasn't, but then prior to 1981 the world hadn't known about HIV, either, and there were still conspiracy nuts out there who believed that it was an engineered virus rather than a clusterfuck resulting from hygienic misconduct. Yesterday I would have laughed such an idea off, but then it had seemed equally fantastic that a handful of terrorists would just walk in through the main entrance, blow up half the building, and let their perfectly planned mission ruin my entire life.

Then again, I still didn't know why they were doing this, and suddenly the knowledge that none of them were running around wearing hazmat suits and gas masks was incredibly reassuring.

"Where did you even find those pictures?" I asked, my voice shaking although I tried to keep it steady. I had the distinct feeling that I really didn't want to know the answer to that question.

Nate was only too happy to destroy my bubble of denial.

"Those, and a little video clip that I'm about to show you, were found in Mr. Greene's personal inbox. Apparently he didn't get the memo that if you are dealing with something that is highly confidential, you don't just leave it in your trash."

The moment he stopped talking, the screen switched to a new view. Half of it was black, while the other was taken over by a video app that started playing a moment later. That was about when I held my breath, and I just knew that by the time I would let it out, my world wouldn't be the same any longer

On screen a woman appeared, most of her body obscured by the green suit she was wearing, complete with a respirator and face shield. It was the gear everyone was outfitted with down in the L3 labs—not quite as safe as the L4 positive pressure suits, but not that far removed. I recognized Thecla even before she started speaking.

"This is Dr. Thecla Soudekis, time course study number five. Both subjects were infected twenty-three hours and thirty minutes ago, progression is happening at an increased rate of approximately one point two, symptoms are consistent with previous studies."

She used that same droning voice I was familiar with from hundreds of lab logs she'd recorded with me in the room, but something was different. Focusing on her surroundings, I couldn't help but wonder where she was standing. It looked like an observation lounge and must have been part of one of the L3 labs or else she wouldn't have been wearing full gear, but nowhere I'd ever been fit the surroundings. Something else I noticed was that she seemed stressed, downright harassed, and that was not something I'd ever associated with her. Even in moments of severe danger she had always been calm and collected, the perfect leader who knew at any second that it was that very collected calm that would get her and her people out of there safe and unharmed.

In an uncharacteristic, unnerved gesture she reached up as if to touch her face, almost knocking the face shield askew in the same motion. She glared at her own hand then, before she looked straight into the camera again. Now her gaze held challenge.

"Maybe if that Glover hag would get us subjects that were representative of any decent health standard we could go about this in a scientific, analytic manner. Half of the symptoms could be from withdrawal; last week we got one that was just coming down from a high. How do you expect me to do my work when I can't even get a decent blood panel?"

Nobody answered her, but then who would, in her personal log?

Another moment passed before she sighed, then droned on as if the outburst had never happened.

"Progression is slightly accelerated, likely due to the physical condition of the subjects, not a deviation in the viral vectors. I recommend another series of six tests to exclude the possibility of outliers before progressing to the next stage. Variation five shows absolutely no positive impact; if anything, it accelerates the deterioration."

The screen went dark and air whooshed out of me, loud and shaky enough that I had no doubt that Nate was aware of it, close as he was still standing to me. As far as I could tell, he hadn't paid any attention to the video, his eyes remaining zeroed in on me.

I had no idea what Thecla had been talking about, but this didn't sound good. Not good at all. We had an animal BSL-4 lab down there where we worked on rodents sometimes, but even though I told myself that she must have meant that, it made no sense. Mice didn't have withdrawal, nor did they come down from a high. They were also not selected by the head of our human resources department.

But maybe there was an explanation for that. There had to be. Likely, Thecla had just been vexed and used things in conjuncture that had nothing whatsoever to do with each other.

I might have managed to talk myself into believing that if the video hadn't resumed a moment later.

Now it showed a graph—what I assumed was an image of the progression rate she had been talking about. Thecla's narration continued as a voice-over.

"Time course study number five-point-five has been terminated at the sixty-hour mark. Subject iota has expired at fifty-six hours and twenty-two minutes, subject kappa at fifty-nine hours and forty-five minutes. I have performed autopsies and the samples are waiting for analysis."

She paused, and it sounded like she had to swallow convulsively before she forced herself to go on.

"This is a time lapse of the progression rate, taken in ten minute intervals. I recommend heavy sedation for time course study round six."

The graph disappeared and was replaced by the full body images of two men, completely naked, who were secured to hospital beds by a number of thick leather straps. One of them looked about thirty, thin enough that individual ribs were clearly visible. The other was likely about sixty, but it was hard to tell from his matted hair and beard. He wasn't in much better physical condition than the younger man.

A display at the top of the images showed the time progression, starting at zero, increasing by ten every second as the images changed.

At first, they both seemed to be sleeping, but soon the unsecured parts of their bodies started whizzing around between images as they'd moved in the ten-minute time frames between the shots. They started to look feverish around the nine-hour mark, and dark bruises started appearing at thirteen-twenty. At fifteen they were both clearly writhing in pain, which even translated into the stills. At twenty, they both started bleeding out of several orifices and open wounds.

I was violently sick all over the floor in front of me long before the time lapse images reached the high fifties and the screen turned black.

Chapter 14

For what felt like the millionth time, I checked my watch. I couldn't believe that only one hour had passed since I'd seen that video. It felt like a lifetime to me.

What had happened directly after I'd purged the meager contents of my stomach was still more a haze than anything else. I knew that Nate had asked me something, but I hadn't been in any state to offer a coherent reply, so he had me escorted back into the cube. Now I wondered if I'd suffered some short-term psychotic break, but the nasty voice at the back of my mind kept chanting that it was all just denial—making me both a coward and a drama queen.

The longer the night dragged on, the more I tended to agree.

I wanted to somehow rationalize away what I'd seen, but the events of the day had sapped enough of my strength to prevent me from putting any unnecessary effort into a lost battle.

Was the biotech company I had pretty much devoted my life to capable of conducting illegal experiments on unwitting patients? Absolutely. As much as I would have loved to let my idealism flag fly, if there was money to be made, they'd find a way.

More shocking was Thecla's obvious involvement, but had I ever really known her? She'd been my supervisor, she'd let me handle the stuff that was beneath her, and like all good girls in the field I'd taken the bad with the good and hoped that one day in the future I would be in her position and able to shine while others got to shovel shit instead. I wanted to believe that she was a better person than the video made her out to be, but I hadn't really known her, and she hadn't been a close friend. People had a lot of reasons for what they did, and there was still a glimmer of hope out there that I just didn't know enough, but the sobering fact was that most scientists I knew were fatalists. Someone was going to do it, so it might as well be them if the money was right. The worst of them even justified their actions by saying that they'd be faster, more careful, humane.

And really, weren't we all animals in the end? It worked well for mice and chimpanzees. Why not humans, too?

I certainly felt like an animal right now. A betrayed, beaten animal with nothing left to do but curl up in a corner and wait for the inevitable. What that might be, I didn't want to imagine, but I had a pretty good idea from what direction danger would come. Ever since he'd had me thrown back into the cube, some of Nate's polished veneer had come off. Over the last hour I'd watched him pace up and down in front of the cube, and he didn't try to hide the way he kept staring at me.

I had something that he wanted—experience of working in a hot lab for years was my guess—and very soon he was going to run out of patience and do something more drastic than ask to get it.

I think if it had only been that, I might have caught some sleep, but while he'd morphed into the restless animal on the other side of the bars, I was still locked in with the rabid one.

Greene's reaction had been about as telling as my own. No one seemed to doubt that I hadn't had a clue what Project Destiny was about, while he'd managed to talk himself into more and more trouble as he attempted to do damage control. Nate had listened to him ramble with a stony face, then had pretty much lost it at "but they were all just hobos and drug addicts, anyway." I'd looked away, but the sounds his fist had made as it landed on Greene's face and torso would likely follow me into my nightmares for years. That reaction had definitely been personal, no question. Greene's self-preservation had kicked in then and he'd pretty much folded instead of playing the tough guy, which made him a potential time bomb at my back now. He'd been all moans and whines since then, letting others dote on him, but when he'd been sure that everyone else was asleep, he'd shown surprising alacrity of movement as he'd tangoed with the bucket.

I figured my main problem wasn't who I thought was more ready to do me harm, but it was simply a matter of who would get to me first.

So I spent an endless night huddled in my corner, afraid and sorry for myself, while acid kept churning in the broiling pit of my stomach.

Eventually, I must have dozed off despite everything else, because it took me a moment to remember where I was when I startled awake again. While my mind was still sluggishly evading touching down on any of the glaring subjects, the primitive part of my brain was suddenly wide awake. Something was going on, and it wasn't going to be good. Maybe some long neglected part of my senses picked up sound or motion, or I just had an overactive imagination, but I had a single moment of clarity in which I knew that the shit was about to hit the fan, and it was going to hit hard.

Then a large hand clamped down over my mouth and nose, stifling any noise I might have made. My mind screamed at me to fight, but I was frozen, unable to react even when I felt warm breath ghost over the side of my neck before Greene cooed into my ear.

"I am so going to enjoy this, but I doubt that the feeling will be mutual."

Then he yanked me back with surprising strength and I toppled over, the back of my skull smashing against the floor hard enough to make me see stars. The impact was somewhat muffled by my hair, barely making a sound, but pain exploded through my head and stunned me for another second. That was all Greene needed to wrap his hands around my throat and squeeze. Hard.

Fear sent my heart galloping, but Greene was quick to straddle me, putting his entire weight into crushing my trachea—or simply waiting until I'd suffocate. My fingers instinctively went to my neck, trying to pry his off, but even sinking my nails into them didn't yield any results. They were simply too short—kept that way because I worked with latex gloves on every day—to be used as weapons. With my lungs already burning, panic kicked into overdrive and I went for the only target I could reach—Greene's face.

He tried to jerk his head away as my nails raked his cheek, lessening the pressure on my throat, but not enough to let me gulp for breath. My arms were a little too short to go for his eyes, so I hooked my fingers into the corner of his mouth and jerked as hard as I could. That didn't lessen his grip, either, but he shifted his weight farther off my body as he leaned away. My field of vision was narrowing already and I started feeling light-headed—not a good sign. I tried punching him in the face next, but lying on the floor like that, I just couldn't get a good swing in.

I needed a better solution—any solution, really!—and just flailing around wasn't going to get me very far. Yet trying to order my thoughts and come up with something got increasingly more impossible as the seconds ticked on.

What is most vulnerable about the human body? Eyes and face I had already ruled out, and there was no way that I'd get to his throat. Pretty much the only part of his body that was close enough for me to reach were his arms as he used the advantage in reach he had over me perfectly.

Arms… arms… joints!

The moment my increasingly more sluggish brain caught on to that, I grabbed Greene's elbows and started digging my thumbs in, trying to close my hands into fists right through flesh and bones between them. He didn't let go immediately, but I heard him wince over the all-consuming whooshing sound of my pulse racing in my ears.

Something gave under my right thumb, making Greene curse under his breath, and the pressure on my throat lessened. Realizing that this was my last chance, I threw my entire body into that side, making me roll over partially underneath him, which dislodged his weight on me. I felt him fight for balance, then shift, just as I managed to pull my left knee up, wedging it between my body and his thigh. My lungs were burning so painfully that they drowned out the agony that was splitting my head, but I forced myself to keep digging with my fingers, right as I shoved my knee upward.

Greene's hold slipped, and for a split second I managed to pull air into my lungs. It hurt like hell but was the sweetest breath I'd ever taken. Triumph blazed through me, but it was short-lived as he only let go to pry my right hand off his elbow—and punched me in the face hard enough that I blacked out for a moment. Pain blossomed all over my nose and I felt hot blood run down the back of my throat, making me splutter when it came into my airways with my next ragged inhale.

That probably saved my life, as my body was wracked with a series of coughs so hard that Greene didn't manage to tighten his hands around my throat again. I ended up on my side, my body protecting my more vulnerable front momentarily—at least until

Greene grabbed the back of my head and smashed it face-first into the floor.

A bright starburst of agony bloomed all over the right side of my face where it connected with the hard marble, my jaw and cheekbone taking the brunt. Precious air rushed out of my lungs and I tried to draw another breath, but it hurt so fucking much that my chest simply wouldn't expand. My brain was screaming at me to roll into a ball and protect my face with my hands, but instead I pulled my legs to my chest, kicking out as soon as I felt tension in my thighs. It was probably only luck that made me hit something, but at least I got a grunt out of him. He tried shoving my face into the cool marble again, but this time I managed to cushion the blow with my arm pulled underneath me, which ended up giving me enough leverage to throw myself onto my other side and finally dislodge him from above me.

Our struggle couldn't have taken more than a minute, but I felt ready to keel over and die right there. Casting around frantically, I tried to find something to use as a weapon, but Nate and his posse had been rather efficient in divesting us of that. Then my eyes latched on to the bucket, and as soon as random information condensed to thought, I threw my body in that direction, going for a mix between rolling and twisting forward.

I was almost close enough to reach it with my extended hand when strong fingers grabbed my shoulder and heaved me onto my back again as Greene tried to go with what had worked the best so far—strangling me. I had only a moment to decide what to do—try to fend him off, or go for the bucket. Instinct screamed at me to protect my throat, but I forced myself to not even hunch my shoulders, but do everything to stretch just that little bit farther and wrap my fingers around the plastic brim just as Greene's closed around my throat.

I didn't even think, I just reacted—grabbing the bucket so I could hurl it up and smash it against the side of Greene's head and torso, wherever I'd hit.

A deluge of cold liquid came down on us both, and if I'd had enough processing power left to think, I might have been glad that I couldn't breathe right now and was consequently spared the foul smell—but really, I didn't care. The pressure around my throat was suddenly gone and the weight above me lessened, making me kick and flail at whatever I could reach, then scramble back as soon as my legs were free. My back hit the glass wall hard, strong enough that I could feel the vibrations it caused throughout my entire body. Gasping for breath, I used the solid wall at my back to push myself up onto my legs, trying to ignore what was soaking my hair and shirt through and through.

Greene came at me before I was fully standing, but this time I was better prepared. His body collided with mine just as my knee went up, hitting him right in the junk. I knew it was a hit because he went still just as he barreled into me, giving me just enough time to grab my left fist with my right hand and bash them forward, hitting the middle of his face with what strength I had left. The knee probably did more damage, but as that had made him hunch over, the force of my blow made him stagger back, and he went down when I aimed a last, hard kick against the front of his left kneecap.

Supporting myself against the wall, I gulped another lungful of air, ready for the next round, but Greene stayed down, one hand clutching his balls, the other digging into his knee. And because I was not going to give him another chance, I slammed my foot into his side hard enough to hurt my ankle, making him moan out and roll over protectively.

The lights came on, the blaze momentarily blinding me, making me stagger back against the glass wall instinctively. Raising one arm to my face, I tried to shield my eyes, barely able to make out the hunched figures sitting against the other walls of the cube, huddled together to give us all the space we needed. My fellow hostages, none of whom had raised hand nor voice to help me defend myself. Disgust so thick that it made me taste bile welled up inside of me, but

I did my best to swallow it down as the telltale drum of boots on the stone floors put a definite end to this charade of a fight. I sagged back against the wall, and suddenly, just drawing breath and remaining on my feet demanded strength that was quickly leaking out of my body.

A sharp, female voice was issuing commands, then the Ice Queen stepped into my hazy field of vision. Her presence didn't exactly calm me, but right then no one was touching me, and I felt somewhat less vulnerable in the corner they'd backed me into. Her normally hard, cold eyes held a look I hadn't seen in them yet, one that surprised me. I'd expected sympathy, or worse yet, pity, but after a few moments I recognized it as appreciation.

She held my gaze a moment longer, and whatever she must have seen on my face made her give a curt nod. Then she raised her arm to her shoulder and curled her fingers over her thumb, but the motion was so slow that my frayed mind didn't even perceive it as a threat.

"Next time you throw a punch, do it like this. And put your entire body weight into it—you don't have the strength yet to do damage otherwise. No uncontrolled swings. You only do damage with controlled punches and good aim."

I continued to stare at her wide-eyed before my brain unfroze and I managed a jerky nod. She gave me a pleased smile that was the greatest show of emotion that I'd seen from her yet, then turned around so that she was facing the room. I noticed that she had positioned herself so that she was partly blocking my way out of the corner, but, if anything, it made me feel protected. The day the presence of what I presumed was a former KGB agent or similar could kindle that warmth inside my chest was not something I wanted to relive.

And I wasn't deluding myself that it would get much better from here on out. Then again, it could hardly get worse.

With adrenaline slowly leaking out of my blood, I was able to do a brief damage assessment. Breathing still hurt and was harder than that one time I'd had a terribly sore throat after a strep infection;

even without checking with my fingers, I could tell that the side of my face was swelling, and the back of my head felt like one pulsing, open wound to me. But I was alive, and breathing, so it could have been worse.

In the meantime, at least ten mercenaries had crowded into the room, not counting the Ice Queen. All had their weapons drawn but not pointed at anyone in particular, yet the way they had positioned themselves in a loose circle around Greene forced the other hostages to plaster themselves against the walls of the cube unless they wanted a boot heel in the face.

Nate was standing just inside the door of the cube, a look of disgust on his face. He glanced over the Ice Queen's shoulder at me, holding my gaze with an actual, faint smile on his face. With my head pounding like mad, it was hard to think, but I forced myself not to look away, my jaw flaming up with pain as I gnashed my teeth. Then I pushed away from my corner and stepped up to him, the Ice Queen keeping her distance now.

"I think I'm ready to talk now," I croaked out, the few words hurting so much that I almost didn't finish.

"Good," was all Nate said as he turned around, gesturing for me to lead the way. I walked out of the cube without looking back—neither at Greene, nor at the others. They had clearly made their choice—now it was time for me to make mine.

Chapter 15

We didn't go far, only to the side of the atrium that led from the glass cathedral into the warren of labs, where Nate pushed me through the first door on the left. It was the women's changing room, but that didn't deter him one bit as he put a hand between my shoulder blades and gave me a decisive nudge toward the door at the other end that led to the showers.

I stumbled but didn't protest, at least not until I was standing on the tiled floor in front of the community showers and he came in after me.

"Uh, a little privacy maybe?" I asked, or tried to. My throat felt like it was lined with sandpaper, and every sound that I made came out husky and deep.

He gave me a wide yet humorless grin as he leaned against the tiled wall next to the door.

"Now you get self-conscious because of a little nudity? Nothing I haven't seen before." I opened my mouth to protest while inadvertently hugging myself harder, but he didn't let me speak. "Besides, you're smelling like a public toilet that no one has cleaned for months, and you have so much fecal-matter-stained urine in your hair that it completely obscures the charming red color modern day chemistry lent it. My brain might be wired a little differently than most people's, but not that differently."

Normally, his words might have made me self-conscious for real, but Greene had pretty much beaten that right out of me. Setting my jaw stubbornly—softly—I turned around and started shrugging out of my clothes. I could feel his gaze on my back, a sensation that should have felt like nails scraping over a chalkboard but was everything but, yet I did my best to ignore it. He obviously wasn't going to leave, and with the battles I figured I still had ahead of me, this one seemed like the least important to fight.

I still hugged myself with one arm as I turned on the shower. The water was cold at first, but quickly heated up. I stepped under the spray and just stood there, letting the water do the ground work before I got down to business.

It must have taken me the better part of twenty minutes to clean myself as properly as my shaking, aching hands would let me. The industrial-strength soap from the dispensers would do terrible things to my hair, but considering the state it was already in, I couldn't find it in me to care.

As the suds were washed off my body, I felt my mind slowly grind into gear. Now that the last of the fright from my fight had dwindled, it was a deeper-seated kind of terror that made breathing even harder than it already was. I could have died in there. That Greene had only tried to strangle me without raping me first was no consolation whatsoever. I really hadn't thought him capable of that. All I really wanted to do was wrap my arms around my knees and rock back and forth, crying softly to myself. Catching the occasional look from Nate where he still leaned against the wall helped. Not because his presence made me feel comforted or safe, but what little dignity was still intact deep down inside of me wouldn't let me lose it in front of him.

When I couldn't stand to stay under the spray of water any longer, I shut it off, then turned to face Nate. He held out a white, not exactly fluffy towel to me, and I took it without a word of thanks. His lip curled a little as if he noticed the omission and found it somehow cute. He probably did. Who could tell with someone like him?

The towel wasn't large enough to wrap myself in once I had patted myself as dry as I was going to get, presenting me with a new dilemma. I could try to hold it over the front of my body and cover what modesty dictated me to, or not bother and maybe spare myself the ridicule I was going to get for my troubles.

I dropped the towel, making it end up like a weird kind of demarcation line between us.

I wasn't surprised that he completely ignored it as he stepped up to me, and I drew in a sharp breath when he raised one hand to my cheek, his eyes intent on my face. What might have looked like a tender gesture was far from it, I realized, when he prodded first my cheekbone, then my temple, nose, and jaw. I'd dimly been aware of the discomfort and early swelling, but the moment he touched me, pain flared up, making me wince whenever pressure was applied.

"I don't think you need stitches, but I should patch you up," he remarked, taking a step back and glancing down my glaringly naked body. "Raise your arms."

I really didn't want to—and not just because I was stark naked, right in front of him. His gaze zoomed back up to catch mine, and now it was real laughter that I saw dancing in his eyes.

"How many times do I have to tell you this? I'm not going to throw you down on the floor and have my wicked way with you. Right now I wouldn't even do it if you begged me to. You have scrapes and bruises all over your ribs and hips. You're the biologist. You tell me how well soap cleans bacteria from open wounds."

I blinked, then looked down at myself. He was right, of course, and the moment I saw my defensive wounds, they started to ache. I knew that it should have bothered me that my body was acting like this, but I couldn't quite bring myself to care. He raised his brows in askance, and I took another step back but brought my arms up to lace my fingers behind my neck. They seemed to weigh a ton each.

He set to work with some cotton balls and a bottle of antiseptic, moving fast and meticulous. The only positive thing about it was that he didn't touch me anywhere not strictly required, although he had ample opportunity to. He also cut the ruined bandages off my hand, and after cleaning it again left it as it was.

Once finished, he picked up his tools and walked back into the locker room, and with nothing better to do I trailed after him. I stopped abruptly inside the door when I saw a stack of scrubs, complete with white, knee-high socks, resting on the bench in the middle of the room. Next to it was a smaller stack, consisting of the washed-out cotton panties and bra I kept in my locker for emergencies. On top of it rested a picture of Sam and me, both of us smiling at the camera.

Of course he knew about her. He probably knew every little detail of my entire life. That sense of betrayal was back in full force now, making me feel not only stupid, but raging mad.

Trying to shove away my ire, I focused on the clothes instead. I always kept several T-shirts and pants in my locker; that whoever had fetched my other stuff from there hadn't brought them sent me a message that I really didn't want to hear right now.

Nate looked from my clothes to me, then raised his brows in silence once more. Apparently we were beyond the stage where he used words to order me around.

Taking the hint, I dressed quickly. Routine had me pull up the socks over the scrubs legs, but when I caught myself, I stopped. In a show of likely juvenile protest I reached for the hem of the pant legs and tore through the part of them that clung to my ankles, then pulled the socks up underneath.

Then there was only the photo left on the bench, and my fingers shook as I picked it up slowly. Was this a warning? A reminder? A weird kind of peace offering to comfort me?

He only glanced at it briefly, then turned to dump the used cotton balls into the trash by the sink. "Cute," was all he said, but it still made me glare at the back of his head as I hastily pushed the picture into the back pocket of the scrubs.

Only then did I notice that the overhead lights were on, and belatedly I wondered why the water had been warm. My exaggerated look around must have given my thoughts away again, and this time he was only too happy to supply an answer.

"We've restored electricity to this part of the floor for convenience. There's even a coffee machine plugged in, if you want another cup?"

My eyes zipped back to his face, and although I knew that hostility on my part was nothing if not suicidal, I couldn't keep the acid out of the rasp that left my aching throat.

"Thank you, but if I never drink another cup of coffee again, it will be too soon."

Why was I even surprised that my remark made him offer me one of those genuine smiles?

"Suit yourself. But you should drink something before the swelling in your throat makes it even harder to swallow."

I had avoided looking into the bank of mirrors over the sinks, but as his words registered, my eyes were inadvertently drawn to them. I couldn't say what I'd expected, but I looked a lot worse. The side of my face that had been smashed repeatedly into the floor was already darkening with subcutaneous hematomas, same as my throat. I was a long shot from vain, but seeing my own face like that made me want to shrink back. Then I remembered how I'd sustained all those bruises and that I hadn't needed anyone else to save myself, and even managed a semblance of a proud smile. That hurt like hell, too, but I didn't really give a damn about it.

"I'll get you some ice packs to reduce the swelling. Come on," he said, reaching for the door handle.

My smile died.

"I'm not leaving here before I get some answers."

My tone was laced with confidence that I didn't know I still had within me, but when Nate turned to glare at me, I didn't even feel the need to shrink back. Much.

"And what exactly gives you the insane idea that you're in any position to make demands?" he asked.

If anything, the challenge in his tone hardened my newfound backbone.

"I'm not asking for anything unreasonable, just some information. You want my cooperation, right? I can't help you if I don't know what you might need help with."

I'd expected him not to give in so easily, but he relaxed and sank back against the door, successfully shutting me in as a by-product. Glancing at his watch briefly, he then looked at me with a blank face.

"I have fifteen minutes to spare. What do you want to know?"

My heart sped up a little with triumph, although I was reasonably sure that this wasn't really anything I should be happy about.

A million questions burned on my tongue, but I forced myself to start with the two things that made acid churn in my stomach.

"How long were you watching that cube before you turned on the lights and marched in?"

A look of genuine surprise crossed his face, but it disappeared after a moment. His gaze turned almost shrewd, and I wondered if I'd somehow earned a few points for asking about that.

"We had the entire bunch of you under surveillance all night, but as everything seemed to have calmed down over the last hour, we got a little lax. If you mean to insinuate whether I was watching Greene make his move on you and waited for whatever unfathomable reason to see what the outcome would be, no. I wasn't in the atrium at the time the shit hit the fan, or, more correctly, the walls, floor, and everyone inside, but followed my men as they stepped in to secure the situation."

I couldn't suppress a shudder running through me, but did my best to let my crossed arms look like a show of defiance rather than protectiveness.

"It never crossed your mind that I'd be twice as susceptible to your, let's call them suggestions, if you let him rough me up first?"

Now he looked pissed off, and he didn't try to keep that out of his tone.

"Why should it? I gain absolutely nothing from jeopardizing your physical and mental health. You obviously put up a good fight, but if he had succeeded to completely subdue you, I'm sure that you would have been incapable of any kind of controlled movement by the time he let off you again. You're of no use to me if you're dead or unconscious."

"Then why did you throw me into the cube again? You warned me before that he would come after me, and you didn't exactly help by beating him up. In fact, I think that was the last straw that made him unhinged enough to come after me once he thought he had a good chance at not getting interrupted. Does that even bother you?"

I had no idea why I added the last, and I hated just how much emotion there was in my voice. Nate pursed his lips as if he had to think about his answer. That infuriated me enough to take a step toward him, but only one. His slight smile returned, but his voice held no mirth now.

"That was a calculated risk I was willing to take. It is good to see that you've finally shed some of that naiveté and start seeing things as they really are."

Now it was my turn to consider my reply carefully. He seemed as non-threatening as I'd ever seen him—which wasn't saying much—

but I didn't doubt that if I physically assaulted him, he would stop acting so damn civil in a heartbeat.

"Trust me when I say that I have no delusions about what you're capable of. You proved that point enough times now. You can stop. I'm convinced. You're a deranged bastard who won't shy away from anything to get what he wants."

"Few things, not anything," he corrected me, but it came with that dangerous glint in his eyes that made it twice as hard to swallow as it already was.

Taking a deep breath, I forced myself to calm down again.

"Good that that's settled. Speaking of which, what exactly is it you want me to do?" I really didn't want to add the next part, but as we were already on such candid speaking terms, I might as well forge on and spare myself any useless beating around the bush that might just prolong the inevitable. Besides, if I had learned anything, it was that he wouldn't appreciate it if I tried to play dumb. "I'm not stupid, I get hints when they are slammed in my face. The scrubs and socks I'm wearing are from the hot labs, and since you pretty much aided in Thecla's untimely demise, I'm the only one of your hostages who has both clearance and experience working under biosafety level four conditions." Fixing him with what I hoped was a dauntless stare, I went on. "If you're here because of whatever fucked-up virus they've supposedly been cooking up and testing on humans down there, you can forget it. I'm not going to help you get your grubby hands on it so you can sell it to the highest bidder or use it yourself to endanger millions of lives. You've made your point that there are many terrible things you can do to me and I can't stop you, but nothing you can think of will make me compromise myself on this."

He took that all in with not a muscle moving in his entire body, and waited an endless five seconds after I'd fallen silent before he replied.

"I'm not here to set that virus free on the world. I'm here to destroy it and tear down the company that is responsible for creating it, one single brick at a time."

Considering how they'd started their operation, the ending of his statement wasn't just a figure of speech, and he sounded utterly serious. He had no reason to lie to me, either; he'd said so before that he didn't absolutely need me, and if he simply wanted to blow up the entire facility, I was sure he knew better than I did where to place the charges.

"So it is real?" I asked, my voice a lot fainter than before. Righteousness had carried me so far, but with the mind-numbing idea of endangering millions of people out of the way, it was hard not to let the horror of it catch up to me now.

Nate considered me for a moment. When he inclined his head, there was a look in his eyes that came as close to sympathy as I'd seen from him.

"I would love nothing more than to tell you that the clip I showed you was a hoax, for whatever sadistic reason you can insert here yourself, but that's sadly not the case."

"Is there more?"

Probably the most inane question possible, but it was the only thing that my mind could come up with. Nate held my gaze as he replied.

"We haven't managed to drag up anything on the company servers or hard drives that we got from the labs in the main building. By now it's obvious that they've stored the data off-site. My guess is somewhere down in the BSL-4 lab, likely in the part where they conducted their experiments."

Licking my lips, I tried to quell the panic quickly rising inside my chest.

"I can't—"

He interrupted me before I could go any further.

"No more excuses. Either you're in, or you're out."

I did my best to quench the panic that wanted to spread and take over my mind, and even with my loyalty now frayed at the edges because of what had just happened that was cause for all the cuts and bruises on my face and body, it was hard to come to a final decision.

"It's not that easy," I offered.

"But it is," he replied, shaking his head as I opened my mouth to protest. "I know that you'll probably not believe me, but I don't actually want to drag you through hell. Can you really back down and fall in line with all the other sheep after learning what you know now? I'm not asking you to point a gun at anyone and pull the trigger. I can go down into the hot lab alone and try to find and retrieve the data myself, but I'm standing a much better chance of doing so and getting out of there alive if you help me. You've worked there for months. You still know the drill, even if it's been a while. You don't have to actually do anything except walk in there with me and get me back out with whatever I find."

I hadn't expected something that sounded so close to a peace offering from him. And it wasn't like I couldn't see the silent "or else" written plainly across his features. One time I had managed to get the better of Greene and keep him from ending my life. I was pretty sure that if I ever stepped into that cube again, the outcome would be quite different.

Didn't look like I had that much of a choice.

"I'm in," I whispered, feeling my heart speed up with a different kind of apprehension now.

Nate smiled, and that didn't make it better one bit.

Chapter 16

B ack in the atrium, Nate escorted me over to the bank of monitors, right to where the techie and the Ice Queen were quietly chatting but fell silent as we drew close. The Ice Queen looked me over with a critical eye, then thrust a bottle of neon green energy drink into my hand before she left without saying a single word. I looked after her with a measure of bewilderment and opened the bottle. I normally hated that chemical sweetness, but I didn't need to be reprimanded that I couldn't even take care of myself right now. Nate watched me finish the entire bottle in a few gulps, then handed me another one. This one was blue and tasted just as vile, but

I didn't care. The flood lights were shut off again, leaving most of the atrium in perpetual gloom, which was fine with me. Just seeing that damn glass cube at the other end made my gorge rise, and that had nothing to do with my energy drink guzzling.

Halfway through that bottle I stopped, partly because I felt like my stomach simply couldn't take any more, but also because something else occurred to me.

"Does helping you maybe come with bathroom privileges?"

He gave me what I interpreted as a suffering look, but I didn't miss the amused twinkle in his eyes.

"Under supervision, yes."

I made a face and took another, if much smaller, sip.

"Why, do you get your rocks off watching me urinate?"

"Our conversations keep taking such mature turns," he remarked, a light lilt in his voice. "But after the air duct stunt you pulled, I'm not going to make the same mistake twice. You're going nowhere without constant supervision—that includes the bathroom. If that's beneath you, you can strip and piss in the shower, too, whichever you prefer."

I glared at him and did my best to make my next swallow a show of defiance. That made me feel so ridiculous that I almost smiled. Almost.

"Thanks, but I think I can stand using the toilet with the stall door open."

"How mature of you. Do you have to go now, or is this just a discussion on general principle?"

I thought about it, then finished off the second bottle.

"I'm so dehydrated, I think my kidneys are about to go on strike. I doubt that my body will be ready to let precious water go to waste any time soon." Looking around, I exhaled slowly, feeling a little better now that my blood sugar levels were slowly normalizing, and I didn't feel like I was living in constant terror. "So, exactly what do you want me to do now?"

"First things first." He avoided answering me, which must have been a first. "How are you feeling?"

I blinked, irritation quickly swimming to the surface of my already non-existent calm exterior.

"What do you think? I'm feeling like the warmed up cross between awful and morgue gurney." He gave me a critical look, but I didn't get the sense that he was taking me particularly seriously, so I went with the most abused word people my age used. "What?"

His grin in return was definitely amused now as he leaned back against a console and crossed his arms over his chest, making the tendons stand out in his forearms. He'd ditched the suit jacket between throwing me into the cube and getting me out again, and with the shirt sleeves rolled up, there was lots of tanned skin visible that drew my gaze. Great, because I needed one more thing to obsess about.

"Let's pick up where we left off. Where were we? Ah, right. You were just about to throw a hissy fit about how you'll never enter a BSL-4 lab, and I told you to shut the fuck up and get over it."

"I remember," I pointed out. "You already said you're doing all this to take Green Fields Biotech down. If this super virus is real, and I'm still not completely convinced that it is—"

"It is," he interrupted, his voice deceptively soft.

"With proof supposedly stored in a secret room in the hot labs. That's the first thing I have problems with. I've been working down there for months, and I never noticed a suspicious, unmarked door leading into nowhere."

Nate pursed his lips, then looked over to where the techie was making no pretense of not eavesdropping on us.

"Can you bring up the floor plans on the screen?"

"Sure."

A few strokes on her keyboard later, the security camera feeds rearranged themselves, clearing one screen to show the familiar floor plan of the hot lab.

"That's the diagram that's in all the instruction material and prominently displayed next to the sign-in sheet downstairs," I confirmed, probably needlessly. "Now tell me where that room is supposed to be?"

"That's the floor plan they sent to the CDC when they got the L4 level certified. This is the actual blueprint the construction crew used," he explained.

The screen split in half, adding a color inverted image on the right side that looked just the same at first glance, but I quickly found the difference.

"That's right behind Biomolecule Production. There is no secret room there. I've been working in there the entire time. I would have noticed something."

"Can you zoom in?"

At his direction, the techie worked her magic and the entire screen filled with the section in question. I squinted at the slightly grainy image, then felt a frown come to my forehead.

"There's a maintenance panel behind the wall there, but it's just a few inches deep—not even deep enough to step into."

"Ever checked it out yourself?" he wanted to know.

I shook my head, feeling my stomach sink. That was happening a lot these days, and I had a good idea that it would get worse—yet again—very soon.

"Nope."

"Then you know already where we have to go."

Pressing my lips together, I did my best to quell the rising terror that was crawling up my spine.

"I still don't understand why you're doing all this." Looking at the big screen and its scrolling numbers, I finally understood what that was all about. "You're selling our entire research. Why?"

Nate shrugged, looking vaguely disappointed that I had to ask.

"An operation like this requires a lot of money. A lot more than I would have been able to acquire myself. About an hour ago we broke even. Now we can pay everyone's promised salary. Maybe there'll be bonuses."

I couldn't help but frown at this.

"Who's buying all that information? Whatever you do, the patents remain with the company. No one else can use them until the licenses expire."

"People are nevertheless interested in the exact details of how those patents came to be. The real money's in what didn't make it into the papers. And there's of course the current, unpublished research."

"And you're okay with likely funding terrorism with this?"

He snorted.

"What do you think this operation will be classified as? Come on, you're smarter than that."

I gave him the blankest stare I could manage, but it was the techie who supplied the answer I was looking for.

"I'm part of a hacktivist group. We screen all the prospective buyers. They might think that they can hide behind screen names and a VPN, but it's easy for us to keep tabs on who's after what. Most of this stuff goes straight into the archives of similar corporations, with the odd eccentric billionaire looking around. It's lucrative business, but mostly harmless. Pays well to be a part of, too." She looked from me to Nate. "Have you tried offering her money? Because with student loan rates these days many people get driven into desperate situations."

The smile he gave her was almost fond, although he showed too many teeth.

"Don't bother. She's one of those people who do things because they're right. Or have I judged you wrong?"

There was a lot of condescension in his eyes as he looked at me, but I didn't take the bait.

"Whatever your reason for this wretched crusade, don't make me a part of it. I'm not helping you out of the goodness of my heart or because I'm such a wonderful human being, and you know it."

"There you have it," he told the techie, who shrugged as if to say that it was fine with her if I wanted to have it my way.

This conversation was quickly turning weird, so I decided to hone in on the part I really wanted to avoid, but knew I had to face eventually.

"This is personal for you. Until you showed me that video I figured this was just another job, but your reaction wasn't what I'd expected."

"My reaction?" he asked.

I focused on him for a moment, trying to weigh my options.

"You're like this finely tuned, precise machine, or so I thought. You plan, you plot, you execute, it all falls in line. But when you were having Greene and me out here, that mask slipped and underneath is lurking a beast—wild, untamed, tired of being bound. I'm honestly surprised that you didn't kill Greene right there when he slipped up about that project, Destiny?"

Even thinking of the name made me shudder. Nate didn't react; in fact, he was regarding me as if he saw me in a completely new light.

"Go on."

"Well, not much more to say. It was like something just broke through the sleek veneer, something wild and primal. You've above average level intellect, you likely have some kind of personality disorder, but as much as I'd love to call you a full-blown psychopath to your face, you clearly empathize, so you're much more dangerous than one of those. You choose what you do. Everything is calculated, planned. Your entire operation, dragging me into it, but also the small details. You clearly get what you want because you know how to make people get you what you want. But there's this one trigger you have that you can't completely control because it cuts too deep, is too painful to let intellect tide you over the moment. The only thing that can cause that in a person is grief and loss. My guess is that they hurt someone very close to you." Having already doomed myself so far, judging from the way he kept staring at me, I might as well finish that thought. "Not just hurt, they killed that person in one of their sick experiments, and now you're here because you seek vengeance."

Silence fell, and it was one of those really uncomfortable ones. More than at any other moment when I'd been around him, I was aware that he was not only physically, but psychologically capable of doing all kinds of terrible things to me. And still, in some twisted, fucked-up way, I realized that he wouldn't.

I wondered what exactly was wrong with me that on some level, deep down and until-recently buried, that entire dichotomy was a turn-on for me.

The moment didn't pass as much as he shook it off. Life returned to his eyes, and after another couple of seconds he gave a brief bark of laughter.

"I think I could get used to this kind of surprise," he remarked dryly.

"Like what?"

I wasn't even playing dumb. That was not the reaction I'd anticipated.

"Someone having the guts to face me down, and going about it in a smart manner, too. But I guess it makes sense. I wouldn't have screwed up my policy of not screwing with a potential ally just for anyone." He let that hang between us, a twist coming to his lips that made me want to roll my eyes. Somehow, the air between us had gotten a lot more relaxed since he'd watched me beat the shit out of Greene. He only underlined that as he continued. "It often takes guts to say the truth. I think that deserves a reward."

I wasn't sure I would like where this was going.

"Such as?"

"The truth," he offered.

I licked my lips but remained silent, and did my best not to back up when he came out of his casual pose leaning against the console and advanced on me until he could lean in and whisper into my ear.

"They did not just kill him, they murdered him. And his name was Raleigh Miller."

I had expected a lot of things, but not this. For what felt like a small eternity, I could just stare at him while my brain was unable to come up with any kind of reply, let alone a coherent one.

Shit.

At this point I should probably explain who Raleigh Miller is—or, more precisely, was.

Raleigh Miller was on the fast track to becoming something like the Steve Jobs of virology. Young, dynamic, insanely bright, and a true visionary. It didn't hurt that he was quite the looker, but after five minutes of listening to him talk it was hard to focus on anything but his intellect and charisma.

I met him three times in my life.

The first time was when I was in grad school, and he was a guest lecturer in one of my optional seminars. Until then, I'd still been torn—did I want to go into cancer research or virology? He made that decision easy. Two hours I listened to him talk, and then I was sold. And I wasn't the only one, but maybe a little more consistent with my hero worship.

Three years later I met him at a conference. I'd been citing two of his papers in my PhD thesis, and I wanted to hear his opinion of my conclusions firsthand. I could have done that via email, but I wanted to look into his eyes while we discussed this.

I must have left some kind of impression on him, because when I sent in my application for a job at Green Fields Biotech—the corporation whose headhunter had snatched him up six years ago— he wrote a recommendation letter for me, ultimately landing me the job. I met him the day of my final interview, and I was ecstatic when I found out that I'd be working as one of his research assistants.

The following weekend an accident happened in the hot lab, and he died right before my first day of work.

Looking up at Nate now, I felt a last puzzle piece click in my head. Not what kind of "accident" that must have been—that was pretty obvious. No, for hours now—and possibly longer, but I'd been missing the context completely—something had been nagging at my mind, but with all the horror and stress, I'd been unable to find the time to sort it out. But now I realized what had been bothering me.

"You're his brother. You're—"

His full name was burning on my tongue, but before I could say it, he put a finger over my lips in a terribly intimate gesture.

"Don't."

Holding his gaze, I gave the barest of nods, then counted the seconds until he dropped his hand. Five. Way too long to only make a point, not long enough to mean something.

He looked different, but then the picture that was the basis of my epiphany had to be fifteen years old by now. He'd been younger, a lot more carefree, and back then the family resemblance had been obvious as he and his brother had shared the same eyes and wheat-yellow hair. They'd been goofing around in it, playing ball or something, and Raleigh had had his brother in a head lock, both of them laughing. They couldn't have been more than eighteen or twenty back then.

Not much of that boy on the cusp of adulthood was left anymore. Of course he was older, and there was the dark hair color that obviously stemmed from the same source as my riot red curls. But now there was steel and calculation where happiness and laughter had been. A lot had happened since then, and I could only guess that Raleigh's death had been just one event in a million that had shaped him. Maybe a part of me, buried deep down, had recognized him that day in the park—a much better explanation than instant animalistic attraction.

What really terrified me was that it wasn't really the resemblance to his brother—now that I'd seen it so glaringly obvious—that drew me to him. No, it had been those few glances at the beast lurking underneath the steel armor that still made me want to wrap myself around him and forget that there was anything in the world besides us.

How I knew this, I couldn't say. It shouldn't have made any sense, and it should have troubled me deeply, but the opposite was the case. Some twisted, dark, deeply buried part of me welcomed him, stretched out her claws and found like where only difference should have been.

And with the way he was looking at me just now, outwardly composed but with that beast lurking in his eyes, I was sure that he knew exactly what I was thinking.

I was obviously only a hairbreadth away from a psychotic break; either that, or Greene had bashed my head into the floor one time too many.

"The question is, where does that leave us now?" he asked, his voice deceptively calm.

I couldn't say exactly why that revelation changed something for me. Maybe because I'd always wondered what had really happened to Raleigh because I worked in the same field. Maybe it was the last dregs of my hero worship. Maybe it gave all that horror I'd been through a personal component that my mind needed to latch on to.

I really didn't know why, but when Nate asked me, I knew what my answer would be.

"I'll do it. I'll go into the L4 lab with you."

He held my gaze for another moment, then turned away.

"No sense in burning daylight then. Unless you have anything better to do right now?"

I shook my head, refraining from noting that it was in the middle of the night. That my stomach was sinking with a familiar feeling of dread kept my mirth at the backburner.

"No, my calendar is completely free for some obscure reason."

The grin I got for my effort was grim rather than humorous, and I didn't feel like returning it when he made a sweeping gesture toward the back of the atrium, where hallways would lead us down into the lower levels of the building.

"After you."

Chapter 17

G iven the circumstances, I'd expected two things to happen—a full-blown panic attack on my part, and that in front of a large audience of guards. I was surprised when Nate only brought Andrej and one other guard with him, and while that didn't make me feel much better as we headed for the connective tunnel that would bring us inside the concrete shell that housed the hot lab, I didn't completely lose it, either.

Through most of the complex, the mercenaries used flashlights when needed, but once we reached the tunnel, the way was illuminated by dim emergency lighting. I remembered from my safety training that the entire BSL-4 lab complex was supplied with two generator units that could each power the entire lab for four days straight, so shutting off the electricity in the rest of the building hadn't had that much influence here. I still would have felt better knowing that the air filtration system was running on something other than giant fuel tanks, but if I'd learned anything about Nate and his mission, it was that he had thought about everything that could be prepared for.

My hands started to shake a little when we reached the bottom end of the tunnel and stepped into the wide hallway that ran around the lab complex itself.

During the construction of the building, they'd built the lab complex as an entire autonomous unit inside the extended basement of the main building, like a reinforced concrete cube sitting on top of the foundations of the rest. I remembered that it encompassed three levels—the main lab floor plus air and electricity maintenance above, and liquid waste management below. The lab level itself didn't look that different except for the obvious reinforcements of walls and windows that made up the labs. In reality, it was a bunker that could withstand earthquakes and other natural disasters, and everything else short of an atomic bomb being dropped onto the levels above. It was the safest place inside the entire building, and the last place I wanted to be.

Nate stopped once we reached the main door to the lab and turned to his men. While they conferred in hushed tones, I gravitated toward the blackboard and sign-in sheet. It seemed ludicrous to follow normal procedures, but I had the sudden, irrational feeling that if I didn't, I would jinx this. And if you go into an L4 lab where pretty much everything inside kills ninety percent of what it infects, you don't want to jinx it.

Glancing at the others, I bit my lip, but then reached for the felt tip marker and wrote my initials onto the field that indicated who was currently working inside. After a moment of hesitation, I added an "NM" for him.

Whatever he and his men had to sort out was done quickly, and a few moments later Nate joined me at the board. He looked faintly amused at my antics but didn't call me out on them.

"Still following protocol?"

I gave a noncommittal grunt. "Can we go in now?"

"That eager?"

I shrugged.

"The sooner we get this over with, the sooner I'm out again, and that sounds freaking awesome to me right now."

He gave me a "have it your way" kind of look and repeated his previous direction.

"After you."

My hand still shook as I reached for the handle, but my grip was strong, and I even felt a hint of vindication as I pushed open the door and stepped inside. My very special guest followed me, while the others remained outside.

Exhaling slowly, I let routine guide me when I felt my mind wanting to go into overdrive. With limited space down here, there was only one changing room instead of two, but then the shower thing had proven that something as simple as convention didn't keep him out of designated female-only spaces. And it wasn't like he'd never seen me naked before.

I ignored the lockers and went straight to the cabinet where the scrubs were kept. Reaching up, I got pants and a shirt for him first, then added some for me, leaving the socks for last. Upstairs it had been a nice moment of rebellion to rip the scrubs he'd provided for me once my clothes were no longer fit for wear, but no way was I going to use them inside the lab.

Turning back to him, I divided the heap of blue and white into two stacks and handed him his.

"Have you had any training at all concerning biosafety regulations?"

The right corner of his mouth quirked up as he tried not to grin. He did seem a little tense, now that I looked at him more closely. Understandably, considering what we were about to do, but it was still strange after the last few hours to see him react so... predictably normal.

"I think I can manage donning scrubs," he retorted, taking the offered clothes.

As he started unbuttoning his shirt without turning around—of course he didn't—I chose to take the high road and turned my back on him. I only had to shed one layer of rather uncomplicated clothes, so I was in fresh scrubs well ahead of him.

It seemed utterly girlish to play coy now, but then remaining standing there with my back turned on him wasn't much better. I did my best to imitate the casual leaning pose he liked to strike as I settled against the lockers and got a good eyeful of what lurked underneath those dress clothes.

His upper body was mostly lean but well-defined muscle, but now the amount of scars, under and around the tattoos that marched up one upper arm and a good portion of his back, made a lot more sense to me. I'd never bothered to ask, just assumed that he'd been in the army or something. I had no experience with the marks wounds left behind, but there was more than one roundish, puckered scar that looked like a gunshot wound, and the white, fine lines had to be from a knife. There were also a few darker patches that I realized must have been still-embedded shrapnel.

He thankfully didn't go commando and also kept on the tight, black boxer briefs, and while part of me wanted to look, I averted my eyes before they could get really curious. It was bad enough that my fingers were itching to reacquaint themselves with every pane and curve of his body.

"See something you like?" he asked, a playful lilt in his voice as he started pulling on the socks.

"Do you care?" I shot back, hoping that my increasing anxiety would bleach my face of any color that might have been rising in my cheeks under different circumstances.

"Every man cares what an attractive woman thinks of his physique."

Touching the bruised and battered side of my face gingerly, I winced.

"Not feeling so attractive right now. And not that gossipy, either."

He paused, grinning as he put his foot off the bench he'd used to pull the stockings on over the scrub pant legs, following regulations to a T. I silently handed him the roll of tape, then got my own socks rolled up and securely taped into place over my calves. Nothing worse than wandering socks when you're already in a space suit and can't adjust them for the next couple of hours.

"You still haven't answered my question," I reminded him.

"Neither have you," he observed.

I snorted.

"Because unraveling the mystery of whether I still have the hots for you or not is on the same scale as the question of whether or not you have any clue about putting on a positive pressure personnel suit?"

"Well, I know your answer already," he teased, but then got serious. "I'm familiar with the safety regulations. I've worn a space suit before, but I'd be much obliged if you'd give me another rundown of the proceedings. As much as I don't mind dying for the cause, I don't want it to happen because of avoidable mistakes."

I glared at him for another moment, then decided that I really had something more pressing to worry about than his cockiness.

"I have to check my suit anyway, so I'll do the checks on yours, too. Mind if I take point on this from here on until we leave the lab again?"

He shook his head and motioned for me to go ahead.

Exhaling slowly, I walked back out into the foyer, then continued on into the suit room. It was eerie seeing the entire rack of suits without vacancies, but then it didn't come as a surprise. Fetching some gloves, I told him to select a pair that fit him well, then taped them down and let him do mine over the standard latex gloves. His touch was deft but gentle, and entirely too distracting. I was glad when he was done and I could get our communicators, briefly explaining the functionality, but as they would be on the entire time, I didn't go into too much detail.

While I taped the first blue suit for the pressure check, I rattled off the explanations of what I was doing. Talking along while going through the motions was more soothing than I expected.

First, visual check for holes, paying special attention to the hazard zones of the gloves, feet, and visor seams. Next, tape the vents shut and connect the suit to pressurized air to inflate it enough to check for the hiss of air escaping through a previously missed leak. There was none, so I opened the suit back up, removed the tape, and handed it to him.

"Step into it one foot at a time. I'll help you with the rest."

He gave me a long-suffering look as if I was treating him like a child, so I didn't feel the least bit guilty when I let him figure out for himself how to wriggle his feet properly in place, then get the upper half of the suit on without banging his head or wrenching a shoulder. This obviously wasn't the first time he'd donned similar gear, but there was still that amount of uncertainty in his motions that came with lack of familiarity. I'd suffered the same when I got used to the whole procedure.

Once he was all zipped up, I helped him with the boots, then unhooked one of the red spiral air hoses and handed it to him, explaining how to connect and disconnect it from the suit. I had him practice it while I got my own gear ready, then watched him take a few experimental steps as I pulled on the suit.

The room seemed to close in on me as I pulled the zipper up and connected a hose to properly inflate the suit. Panic clawed at the back of my throat, poisoning my veins with adrenaline and locking muscles all over my body. Screwing my eyes shut, I forced myself to take a few even, deep breaths while the air hissed loudly in my ears.

I was safe. Nothing was going to happen to me. We were not going to handle anything that could kill me. The suits were precaution only. This was just like a training run. I knew that I simply had to get lost in the close comfort of the plastic encasing me and let the steady stream of air that rushed around me soothe me into the routine, and I would be fine.

"You really weren't kidding about the claustrophobia, eh?" came his mocking voice over the speakers of my com unit. Close as we were standing, I could still hear him directly, too, but using communicators made that entire "unhook yourself from the air supply so you can talk" hassle a thing of the past.

Turning slowly so that I faced him, I glared at him, wondering just how ridiculous the move must look.

"I'm really not in the mood for taunts right now."

"I was just observing," he amended. Not that he sounded chagrined, but he waved his hand in what might have been a mitigating gesture. "There's no need for you to freak out. The labs have been out of order for more than a day now, and I ran a full decontamination round last evening."

"You did what?"

He flashed me a grin.

"Told you I have some experience with this. I'm really not keen on catching anything down here, so I checked the logs and initiated a full decontamination cycle in all rooms. Even if anyone left anything out in the open, we're good. Feeling better now?"

I considered that, but shook my head. "No, the fact that the leader of the terrorists who have taken over the building knows his way around the hot lab does not alleviate all my fears."

He gave me a deadpan stare but broke it off when I just kept glaring back at him.

"I get it. You're scared shitless. That's why you think it's a good idea to get in my face. That's okay, I can handle you not worshiping the ground I tread on. But now that we're already here, all suited up, we might as well do what we came here for and get this over with."

He unhooked his hose and swayed over to the door we'd entered through to pick up a small black device. I'd noticed him putting it there earlier but hadn't really paid any attention to it until now.

"What's that? We're not supposed to take anything into the lab with us without proper decontamination. And no electronics."

Turning enough so that he could see me through the side of his visor, he offered me a small smile.

"I think I'll ignore those regulations. It's some kind of routing device that's cued into our main tech station. If we find a computer down here, I just need to plug it in and Dolores will be able to get all the files stored on there in no time. Or would you prefer it if we dismantled the hard drive and then somehow tried to decontaminate it without destroying all the data? Would make our endeavor here quite pointless, wouldn't you say?"

I swallowed the remark that I didn't really care, but then told myself that antagonizing him was the last thing I wanted to do while we were in here. Unhooking my own hose, I headed for the door that would lead us into the central corridor behind the air lock. He followed me without another word.

Logically, I knew that once the suit was fully prepped, there was clean air for six to eight minutes for me to breathe before I even had to think about hooking myself to the next hose, but the moment we'd cleared the airlock I threw myself at the next red lifeline and connected it to my suit. The familiar hiss of air rushing in didn't relax me, but it kept my panic at bay. Nate imitated my maneuver—if at a more measured pace—and patiently waited until I'd gotten myself under control enough to proceed.

Walking through the empty lab was eerie in itself. I was used to working alone at weird hours in my cell culture lab, but down here there'd always been a coordinated bustle of activity. Unlike in all other labs, the hot lab was run by specialists who did only what they were specialists for, not entire experiment runs from planning to finishing up. That usually meant that at any given time, there were at least five if not ten people around for any experiment that was being conducted.

How Thecla and whoever else had been involved in that ominous Project Destiny had managed to hide it from the rest of the staff was beyond me.

That was, if they hadn't been involved, too. Somehow that didn't make me feel any better.

Trying my best to ignore my galloping pulse, I turned to face the central hallway rather than stare at the wall like a caged animal.

"Okay, let's do this. Biomolecule Production is the third door on the left. Stay with me, but I'll go in first and check that everything is where it's supposed to be."

Nate could have added a scathing remark there but kept his tongue. At his nod, I disconnected the air hose and started walking down the hallway, trying to let routine take over. Even with fourteen months between now and the last time I'd been down here, it was deceptively easy to fall into my old rhythms.

My heart ached thinking back to that time. I'd felt so at home down here, finally part of a team where most of my eccentricities were valued as virtues, where people kept track of each other, cared... and killed innocent human beings behind a door I was now supposed to find. That thought was sobering, but did its own to disband the ghosts—and panic—of events past.

Just before we reached the door to my previous lab, I hooked up again and waited for him to do the same. He was still the picture of patience, making me wonder how nervous he must be.

Mostly to distract myself, I asked, "Where did you get your suit training?"

"Not anywhere you would have heard of," he replied.

"As ominous as it sounds?" I ventured a guess.

He moved a little in what I presumed should have been a shrug.

"I had eighteen months to get this operation going, from the first bit of concrete information to acquiring special training, recruiting people, and gathering all the intel I could. I'm good, but I'm not good enough to get into a BSL-4 safety training course with only basic school chemistry for my main qualification."

I considered asking him more about this, but right now wasn't the time to obsess over how many drug lords funded labs that could rival the CDC's in equipment.

"Fair enough."

With that, I disconnected the hose once more, turned to the door, and opened it.

Beyond, the lab looked exactly as I remembered.

This was rather anticlimactic. There should have been flashing lights, ominous stains on the walls, or at least an unscrewed container open in one of the hoods. Reality was your typical neat and clean, boring lab setup, with all clutter stored away and the hoods shut for the vaporized hydrogen peroxide to kill anything that might have been of organic origin once.

After a brief look around, I walked back to the door and signaled Nate to follow me. He surveyed the room with interest, and before I could ask what he planned to do next, he singled out the small maintenance panel half hidden next to one of the cabinets.

"That's the door?"

I nodded, feeling my throat constrict with something else than the panic that had been upsetting my equilibrium for the last half hour.

"It is."

He nodded and made a beeline for it, taking a moment to grab a hose even when he seemed driven to get this over with fast. I was a lot more reluctant to follow him, but did when standing around uselessly didn't sound like a good alternative.

Unused to working with several sets of gloves—even though they were surprisingly manipulable—made him fumble, so I stepped up to help. Together we got the panel pried loose quickly, but behind it was the same old crawlspace I remembered.

"Maybe your plans were outdated?" I suggested, but shut up when he gave me the stink-eye. Seeing as with him it had a definitely homicidal quality, I figured it was for the best to let him see for himself.

My heart sank when the back wall of the maintenance cabinet swung into the adjacent room not twenty seconds later.

At first glance, the room looked like a cross between the lab we were standing in and a hospital room. The far wall was taken up by a one-way mirror that looked like a dark window, with a workstation and hood beside it. Closer to the door were two hospital beds, facing each other, bare except for the multiple leather straps dangling from the frame.

Nate walked through the door with determination, and with curiosity surpassing trepidation, I followed.

He ignored me as he made his way over to the workstation and table-mounted terminal, connecting his nifty black box that would hopefully do the work for us. That left me with either inspecting the beds or checking the hood and adjacent cabinet. For obvious reasons, I chose the latter.

More boring, everyday lab equipment waited for me there— boxes of autoclaved pipette tips, empty 15 and 50 milliliter tubes— and medical supplies that I didn't want to second-guess what they were for. There was also a small fridge and freezer, but they were both empty and turned off. The lack of ice and condensation buildup made me guess that they hadn't been in use in quite some time.

"Find anything useful?" I asked when I'd exhausted all my resources.

"That I can't type in these gloves," came his surprisingly dry answer.

I sent him a pointed look that he missed as he was still staring at the keyboard with frustration.

"Maybe I can find a way around that," I offered.

He ignored me, so I shrugged and went to the blank panel I'd seen set into the wall next to the hospital beds. Two taps with my index finger were enough to make the screen come alive. It didn't display the company logo as all touch screens inside the building normally did, but went straight to a folder full of video files. They were labeled in ascending order of numbers and short abbreviations—sample series.

There were no ports on this terminal so I figured he was better off with the other. I wondered if I should warn him, but then clicked on one of the files at random.

Thecla's face behind the visor of a blue suit appeared, and she started reading numbers and facts off a sheet she held somewhere off screen. Nate looked up briefly, but otherwise continued ignoring me. I figured he'd found the same—and likely a lot more—at the computer. Judging from the consistency in labeling, I figured that all of the files were Thecla's personal logs.

Listening to her confirm that the video they'd shown me before wasn't a fake was making me sick, but thankfully not yet in a way that would compromise the integrity—or at least comfort—of my suit. Until yesterday I'd had the joy of never having to deal with betrayal. Being forced to face it not once—with Nate—but twice now hurt on an even deeper level.

After about five minutes I shut the video off and checked some of the others. They were just more of the same—a chaotic log system not supposed to be seen by anyone but the woman who'd recorded it, and not just because of the horrible things she'd done. Bringing a personal recorder into the hot lab was impossible, and this terminal had clearly been the next best thing she could come up with.

"I think I got what we came for," Nate let me know from across the room. I nodded absently and closed the video I'd been watching, but then paused when I saw that somewhere near the bottom of the second row of files one had a different title. It was also longer, fifteen minutes instead of the briefer other files.

My curiosity piqued, I tapped the screen to activate it, expecting more of the same.

Raleigh Miller's face appeared on the screen, unobscured by any suit or face shield, close enough to the camera to give it focusing troubles, his eyes narrowed and anger plain on his usually charming face.

"Thecla, you miserable bitch! If I get my hands around your throat I will choke you to death, then reanimate you, and choke you again."

I shied away from the screen, not because of his threat, but seeing a ghost wasn't the most reassuring thing when I already felt leagues off my game. Common sense had me hit the screen again so that the video turned off, but before I could even look around and check whether Nate had noticed anything, he was right behind me, one hand touching my upper arm lightly. Fear zoomed through me, sharp and acute; there was no guessing what he would do if he found not only proof of what had happened to his brother, but his first-hand log recount.

He looked surprisingly calm and composed, but his eyes were filled with a sadness that was so profound that it cut right through my terror and made me want to lessen his grief somehow. Giving someone a hug in a space suit was a bad idea, so I touched his hand where it was still resting on my arm. He looked from the screen to me, then back, before he used his other hand to reactivate the video.

It started from the beginning again and wasn't much better the second time around. After hissing into the camera, Raleigh moved back enough to let the autofocus do its thing while he pushed his fingers through his sweaty, disarrayed hair. Now that I knew that he was Nate's brother, it was impossible for me not to see the family resemblance.

"This is your log, eh? Guess it will be my log for the next fifty hours or so. Oh, right, if that was version eight point four you stuck me with, it will be closer to forty, because by then I will have lost all coordination and will be unable to operate this fucking terminal."

The camera shook briefly as he moved, and I realized that he must have punched the wall beside the terminal. If I hadn't met his brother in the meantime, I would have been surprised to see him get himself under control in less than the blink of an eye, but that trait seemed to run in the family.

"I've looked through some of your logs. I hope you don't expect me to keep a timetable. Finding myself on the other side leaves me somewhat disinclined to give you any useful data." He went silent for a moment, looking away as if he was considering something. Then his eyes were back on the camera. "No, I think I'll use this entirely for self-gratification, seeing as you'll likely not let me have a last phone call to my relatives. What are you planning on telling them—that I was too stupid to follow the safety regulations I helped establish in this lab? That I was overworked and tired, making me infect myself? If you're stupid enough to use that excuse, you deserve what you have coming for you. But then you do anyway, after sticking a fucking needle into the side of my neck!"

Nate let go of me, but only to assume a more comfortable position. I did the same, seeing as we were clearly bound to stay until the video was over.

Raleigh paced up and down for a few seconds, then went back to glaring at the camera as if it was a video conference and he had his adversary right in front of him.

"You better hope that Nate never learns of this, or God help you, and I'm saying that as an atheist. Find it peculiar that I'm painting a target on my own brother's head? You don't know shit about him, and if you're smart you'll make sure that stays that way."

I couldn't help but shoot a sidelong glance at the man in question. He looked away from the screen long enough to stare back, but didn't say anything. Raleigh went on in the meantime.

"If anyone doesn't need my protection, it's him. Shit, I don't even know where he is right now, and I'm not sure I would want to if I wasn't trapped down in this hellhole. We're not exactly on speaking terms, but that won't hinder him from tearing this entire fucking corporation apart, one brick at a time."

That phrase sounded awfully familiar, but as Raleigh was ranting on without pause, I filed it away for later consideration.

"Unlike other little brothers, that sucker never needed my protection. He made a habit out of beating up schoolyard bullies when he was five, and if our mother hadn't been a psychologist, they would have thrown him into therapy when he was seven. I decided to go into biology when I found him vivisecting our neighbor's cat one day, just so we could claim that he was just imitating me and avoid being put on heavy medication. I bet the United fucking States of America are grateful to me now because I didn't shove him off the fast-track to becoming a full-blown psychopath."

Now it was much harder not to speak up, but another glance revealed that Nate was smiling fondly. Of course he would. The things you learn about the people you fuck…

The video cut off there but went on after a few seconds. I checked the time stamp in the corner when Raleigh looked much worse for wear, with sweat covering his flushed face, his eyes too bright, the dark circles underneath more evident now. Two hours had passed.

"You're really going to watch me die down here, aren't you? You fucking bitch."

He was obviously ranting at Thecla again. He let out a sigh of frustration as he wrenched a hand through his hair, making it stand even more on end.

"Why are you doing this? Whatever's your beef with me, we could have resolved it peacefully. Is it envy? I know you're always going after everyone in your team who could one day outshine you, but, shit, kill me? Just a reminder, I was here first. I built this fucking project from scratch. They just let you have the stage three test runs when I balked."

He hesitated and settled back as if he was trying to get more comfortable on his perch at the foot-end rail of the bed.

"Or did they order you to? You've always been such a trooper. So determined, so loyal. What did they offer you to instill that belief in them? Sure, we get to do some insanely fucked-up shit down here that we wouldn't get away with otherwise, and the pay's good, but at the end of the day it's still just a job. It's not like we're trying to save the world or something." He smiled humorlessly as if that was an inside joke. "Now you killed a friend just because the company asked you to? That's fucked up. Just fucked up."

The video cut off again and resumed five hours later.

The change was so drastic that I checked not just the time but date of the time stamp. Yup, just five hours later, but the progression of his physical deterioration was so advanced that I would have figured it being closer to thirty hours.

His face was sunken, the skin a sallow color typical of prolonged illness. His eyes had taken on a yellow tint, likely caused by renal failure, with bright red veins in them. He was sweating heavily now, his hair plastered to his face, and there were lesions covering his jaw, neck, and one arm that I could see. There was also a vivid rash all over his hand. If it had been Ebola or another hemorrhagic fever, it would have taken days to cause that much damage, not hours.

When he started talking, his voice was hoarse and lacking the energy that I'd always associated with him.

"Guess I deserve this, on some level. A karmic bitch-slap, if you will. I helped build this fucking virus, why not die from it, too? The revolution eats its own children."

He then started rattling off symptoms that weren't visible, but just as bad. His tone was clinical, detached, but there was panic lurking in his eyes now—a doomed man clutching at any straws available.

I was glad when the video cut off, but it came back on one last time at the twelve-hour mark.

Raleigh was barely able to hold himself upright anymore and remained leaning against the wall right next to the terminal, giving a good view of the blood slowly leaking from his ear. My heart twisted in anguish, and I could only guess how his brother must be feeling seeing him like that.

"I guess this will be the last rant of famous Raleigh Miller tonight," he opened with, his voice low and cracking, making it hard to understand. He had to stop there and coughed, his hand coming away speckled with blood.

"I'm pissing blood, shitting blood, breathing blood... this stopped feeling like a fucking vacation hours ago," he summarized, then stared blankly into the camera for almost a minute. "Nate, I know you'll never see this, but, man, I fucking love you. You're like the dysfunctional copy of me that somehow always ends up making what I fuck up right. No wonder Nana wanted you to have her knife, because she knew that I'd just do something stupid, like slice up the fucking bitch who did this to me!"

He tried to raise his voice at the end, but succumbed to a coughing fit instead. It took him over two minutes to gather himself enough to go on. He didn't appear quite lucid anymore.

"Want to know what the funny thing is? I had this grand plan of how to get out of this. I'm too much of an egotistical chickenshit to be a whistle-blower, but somewhere between watching mice convulse in so much pain that they cracked their own spine and reading your first report of how it wasn't much different in homo sapiens, I realized that this is the most fucked-up shit I've ever done, and that I can't live with this guilt anymore. Any decent human being would have just offed himself, but, noooo, I had to keep going for five fucking years, tweaking and streamlining this beast of a virus to finally stabilize it enough that we'd get an antidote. And why? Because it was my fucking creation, and I couldn't let anyone have it until it was perfect. Safe. See, I deserve this."

He trailed off as if he'd lost his train of thought, but then his eyes focused on the camera again.

"Shit. It's so damn hard to concentrate on anything I'm saying when I feel like my fucking brain is coming out through my eyes!"

Raleigh seemed to notice then that his ear was bleeding, but he only stared at the blood on his fingers before looking back at the camera. A string of expletives followed but was abruptly ended by more coughing, and this time it took him a small eternity to return to the camera. Every second of it hurt me deep down, and although the tape was months old, it still made me feel like I could see his ghost standing hunched over where we were right now.

"Shit, I think I need to lie down, and I'm not gonna get up again if I do. Nate, don't do anything stupid, bro. But if you do, make sure you drag them all down with you, every fucking one of them. No idea how far up this shit goes, but I'm sure that Greene's not involved. Walter Greene, I mean. His son's a fucking cocksucker who'd sell his soul for half of what I make each month thanks to this shit. If you tear down the whole house of cards, make sure you don't hurt too many innocents. Most of the people who work here have no fucking clue what's going on. I wish I didn't. But I couldn't let this go on, know what I mean? You know better than me that it's out. And what it does. Fuck."

More coughing followed, giving me plenty of time for the knot in my stomach to solidify at the words "it" and "out." But what did he mean about Nate knowing more about that virus?

"I can't do this anymore. I love you, bro. Don't ever forget that."

He stared into the camera for another second, then the screen went black, and at Nate's repeated tap reverted back to the file directory view.

To say I was shaken didn't quite cut it. More like someone had pulled the rug from under my feet and I was still falling, not having hit rock bottom yet.

There were so many things my mind clung to that it was hard to sort through the trivialities to get to the important stuff. Like that Nate had quoted what his brother had said at least twice. From the utter lack of emotion on his face, I gathered that this had been the first time he'd seen the video, but he'd known what was on it, word by word.

He'd known exactly where to look for what, and had clearly figured out who to turn to for help.

The rational thing would have been to hate Raleigh right now— he certainly deserved it for what he'd confessed to—but even having all this information presented on a silver platter, it was impossible. True, I'd given him quite the mouthful, but he'd been quirky and sarcastic as he'd defended himself at that conference, and I'd always had a good feeling around him. He had made a couple of fundamentally bad decisions in his life and had ultimately paid the price for it, but that didn't negate that he was one of the good guys. Even with the video evidence pointing in a different direction, I just knew that there was more to this than just a young scientist going on the ego trip of his life, ignoring all possible consequences.

And with that came the realization that I didn't feel much different about his brother, even though he had dumped enough shit on me to hate him for ten lifetimes.

Today was shaping up to make me feel even less mentally stable than the day before.

Chapter 18

"Come on, let's get out of here," Nate prompted. When I didn't react, he made as if to reach for me, but didn't finish the motion. Now he was getting hesitant? One thing was for sure. I had no clue what was going on inside his head—but judging from his brother's assessment, no one did. I hadn't forgotten that tidbit about the cat.

Turning toward the door, I unhooked my air hose, deposited it on the hanger, and with deliberate movements made my way out of the room.

Whether it was because Raleigh's vid had overloaded whatever psychological pressure sensors my mind had, or because I still felt like everything that was going on around me was just unreal, my panic from before was completely gone. I felt like I was moving inside a bubble as I walked out of my old lab, then down the central hallway. Nate followed me—likely hard-pressed to keep up with my pace—but he didn't complain.

At the exit I stopped and half turned to face him, but chose to look at somewhere between his shoulder and the wall.

"We have to go through the decontamination showers to get out. It's a four minute chemical shower followed by a four minute rinse, then the doors will open on the other side and it's out of the scrubs for another round of thorough cleaning, three minutes with shampoo and soap in hot water. We normally do this one by one, but I get the feeling you're not yet done with your constant supervision routine?"

He gave something that sounded like a snort over the com.

"Get in there."

"Thought so," I grumbled as he followed me.

I waited until the door had sealed itself, then hit the button that started the chemical shower. The room was large enough to house five people easily at once, but I still made sure to retreat into the opposite corner from him so that we'd both get sprayed with the maximum amount of chemicals and water from all sides.

The shower came on with its usual blast of liquids I never wanted anywhere near my skin, and I shut my eyes instinctively. Decontamination used to be the part of the hot lab routine that made me relax, but now depriving my mind of stimulus and leaving it to stew on its own was not a very calming experience.

Eight minutes later, the showers turned off and the display by the door informed me that it was okay to leave now. I waited until Nate had followed me out and closed the door, then unzipped my suit and laboriously climbed out of it. My hair and scrubs were plastered to my skin. Being out of the hot suit was heaven, but it barely registered right now. Regulations dictated that I should dry and hang up my suit, but I simply left it on the floor and trudged on into the showers.

I shucked the scrubs, socks, and gloves in the basket by the door, then turned on the shower right next to me. The water was too hot, but I didn't care. Right then I didn't give much of a shit that I was naked in a shower room with a guy who was also getting very unclothed this very second, but just screwed my eyes shut and started to wash myself, facing the corner.

I had to hand it to him, he left me to my own devices until I was ready to vacate the hot comfort of the shower, towel myself dry, and don my other set of scrubs. It felt like years since he'd given them to me in the shower room upstairs, not just a few hours.

While I tucked up the pants, the photo inside the back pocket seemed to burn a hole into my skin. I glanced over to where he was busy dressing himself, and figured that the shoes alone would take him another minute. Turning my back on him, I got the picture out and ran a gentle finger down the side of Sam's face. Tears burned in my eyes, but I refused to let them fall; if I lost it now, there was no telling what I'd scream or do until I got a grip on myself again. It didn't really matter in the end—those were tears of grief and frustration, not longing and fear.

Everything that I'd been ignoring for the past years—not just the last ten hours—came crashing down on me. Anger swept through the bleakness, speeding my pulse up and making it hard to draw even breaths. My muscles locked up and started to shake, but it was no longer that fear-driven tremor from before. Within seconds my mind cleared—gone was the stupor brought on by my epiphany. My fingers convulsed around the photo, crumbling it into a ball, and it took all my strength to smooth it back out and put it into my pocket again.

"You've been awfully quiet," Nate remarked from much closer than I was comfortable with.

Whipping around, I glared at him, then took another step forward that put me right in his face.

"What do you expect me to say, huh?"

His eyes scanned my expression briefly before meeting my gaze, once again calm and collected.

"Expect? Nothing specific, but I don't need mind-reading abilities to know that right now you're yearning to punch me in the face."

Was I? I couldn't say for sure, but the anger simmering in my gut was all for physical violence.

"What the hell is wrong with you both that you think you have the right to just storm into my life and ruin it?"

My voice was surprisingly even, but I was sure that he didn't miss any of the rage interlaced with my words.

"Both?"

"Don't sound so surprised," I hissed, my outward calm falling away. "Yes, I might have been your brother's fangirl number one, and yes, getting the job as his assistant was a dream come true, but he clearly wouldn't have hesitated a second to drag me into this! Without thinking for a moment that it would end my career, my relationship, everything I've worked for and dreamed of!"

Nate didn't look impressed, but he also didn't make fun of me.

"And your point is?"

The muscles in my right arm contracted on their own volition, and it cost me a lot to not just slap him right there. I briefly wondered if he'd let me, and what might happen afterward. As angry as I was, I wasn't ready to find out, so I forced myself to relax again, grasping for the next available rational straw.

"The way you looked at the screen, I figure you hadn't seen the video until then, but you damn well knew what was on it. That's why you chatted me up all those weeks ago in the park. Seduced me. Screwed me. Because you needed an ally!"

He didn't deny my accusation, just offered a curt nod at the second part.

"I had a transcript, yes."

I waited for more, but when it didn't come, I had to grind my teeth not to scream at him. My frustration was so palpable that it left a bad taste on my tongue.

"And?"

His lips quivered, but he didn't let the smile appear fully. When I kept staring at him, he folded.

"Eighteen months ago someone put a lot of effort into delivering a transcript of the video we just watched while trying to stay anonymous. It took me two weeks to find someone to verify that it was genuine, five and a half months to drag up enough background information to plan the mission, four months to recruit the right people, and another couple of weeks to get substantial funding. The second thing I did, after asking Dolores to hack into the company servers and find me evidence that something was going on in the L4 lab that was outside of the company's mission statement, was to find out more about you. It took me less than three days to case your routines, read your personal files, and ascertain that you were in fact in a position where you might be of use to me later."

My skin started to itch with unease at the described invasion of my privacy, but that was not the part that my mind snagged on to.

"When exactly was that?"

His stare became a tad more intense, as if he knew already why I was asking.

"About two months before your freak-out."

My mind went haywire with possibilities, but I shut down my paranoia before it could run rampant.

"Did you have anything to do with that?"

He looked at me as if I'd asked him if the sky was green, but after a second he shrugged.

"You were only of use to me if you had access to the L4 lab; if anything, seeing you barred from it was a step back, not forward. I only gathered enough information to be able to judge how useful you'd be, then turned to more important things."

For whatever crazy reason it stung to be disregarded like that, but I told myself not to be so fucking stupid.

"And that I ran into you in the park last month was no coincidence, obviously."

His mouth quirked up into the hint of a smile.

"Of course it wasn't."

Swallowing became hard for a second, but I forced myself to keep my gaze locked with his.

"So, you figured you'd do what, fuck me into compliance?"

His broadening smile let me know that he'd greatly enjoyed himself along the way, but he surprised me by shaking his head.

"The plan was to get to know you, yes. Or, more importantly, for you to get to know me. Build some trust, a loose friendship, if you will. You had a dog as a kid, so I borrowed one from a friend. You often lingered in that park after work, so I figured it was the ideal place to run into you. You're addicted to coffee, so taking you to get some was a no-brainer."

"And the rest?" I gritted out when he didn't go on.

"Well," he started, cutting off with a snort. "If you need me to repeat what happened after that coffee in that alley right behind the coffee shop, I didn't really do as good a job at it as I remember."

I kept glaring at him, trying hard to swallow the resurfacing betrayal that wanted to clog my throat.

"You know, it takes a special kind of asshole to pull that number on a woman and gloat about it, too."

Was that irritation that crossed his face?

"My intention was to be friendly, never to lie to you," Nate insisted.

"Then why did you?" I asked, happy that I sounded more pissed than hurt.

"I didn't."

"But you—"

He cut me off by leaning into me, and when I took a step back, he followed, until my spine ended up pressed against the locker with him hovering over me.

"Trust me, that was pure, unadulterated chemistry. I never, not in a million years, thought I'd find you attractive, let alone wouldn't be able to keep it in my pants for even half an hour after meeting you. And don't pretend that it wasn't mutual."

Denial burned on my tongue, but I swallowed it when my mind just wouldn't let me utter that lie.

"So it was what, a bonus?"

His shrug was a slap in the face in its own way, but the way he kept staring at me—need and hunger so plain in his gaze that they were impossible to ignore—gave me the answer that I kind of needed to hear.

"Actually, it sucks, because now you hate me and feel betrayed, and I had to fuck up the one connection I've made to anyone in years that really meant something to me, and all for this fucking mission. Happy now?"

Not really, but I did feel a little vindicated—even if the fact that his cause meant more to him than I did rankled. Which it shouldn't. I was so screwed.

Nate glowered at me for another second, then pulled away, giving me much-needed space to breathe.

"Did you ever find out who leaked that transcript to you?" I asked, trying to change tracks, my voice still a little hoarse with emotion.

"Mike Jenkins," he replied, his tone stating that, of course, he had followed up on that.

That was a revelation that hit me like a slap in the face.

"Jenkins?"

Nate frowned as if my disbelief irked him.

"He was one of the people working down here. It can't be that much of a surprise that he was the one who set things in motion."

"Not because of that," I started, then trailed off as another piece of the puzzle whizzed through my mind. "That fucking tea!" He shot me a look that wasn't even asking for an explanation but plain demanded it, and I was only too happy to oblige him. "The morning of my breakdown, Thecla, Mike, and I were having breakfast and coffee in the kitchen down the corridor outside the lab before going in. Thecla got all mysterious, hinting that she had something she wanted to show me." Now it was easy to guess what. "Anyway, she left early, because according to her work ethics, she had to be on site at least fifteen minutes before the set work time, while I lingered over my mug of coffee. It was early, and taking another five minutes seemed like a good idea."

He cleared his throat, prompting me to get to the important part, and after a slight shake of my head I forced myself to go on.

"Mike and I usually didn't talk much, but I knew that his wife had been sick for a while then."

"Terminal stage cancer," Nate helpfully supplied. That made my heart sink, but I chose to ignore that for now.

"He told me she'd made a batch of kombucha the weekend before. You know, that fermented tea? When he offered me some, I couldn't decline. It was more a service to his wife than him to drink it. It tasted dreadful, but I figured that was part of the deal. And, lo and behold, an hour later I saw miniature unicorns and dragons chasing each other through the lab, then get inside my suit as they turned into scorpions, which made me want to tear it off right in the middle of the hot zone." Swallowing bile, I snorted. "Guess it wasn't that much of a coincidence that Mike dropped by just in time to drag me back out of the airlock into the decontamination shower to keep me from killing myself."

"He likely saved your life in more ways than one," came Nate's succinct reply.

I mulled that over for a moment. It wasn't hard to guess what he meant. I doubted that I would still be standing here if I'd been in cahoots with Thecla. Then again, the more I thought about the last minutes of her life, the more it seemed to me that he really hadn't intended to kill her, just talk. I had to admit, if she'd been responsible for killing my brother, demanding answers would have been the least I'd have wanted to do.

"I would like to hope that I would have had too much integrity to let her drag me into that fucked-up project of hers," I offered.

His intense stare made me start to sweat, but when I didn't back down, he let it slide.

"If it interests you, Jenkins sold all his assets the week after he quit working here, which I think coincided with his attempt to get you out of the line of fire. I was able to trace him back to a rental boat and cabin on a small island in Indonesia that he only left three times to get provisions and fill his wife's prescription. The trail went cold five months later, long before I had the knowledge or means to reach out to him to gather more information."

"You think he was a part of it?"

He gave a noncommittal grunt.

"So far, I've only been able to directly implicate four people. My brother did the groundwork; Thecla the human trials and further development after his death; Elena Glover likely got her current job as head of the HR department because she used her previous employment as a social worker to find the perfect test subjects. Gabriel Greene knew about the project and it is likely that he was responsible for funding at least the later stages of it, but I don't have a signature, and he only got involved with his father's corporation three years ago, so someone must have financed Raleigh's earliest endeavors. I have no evidence about Mike Jenkins's involvement. My guess is that he either stumbled over the files or the experiment himself, or Raleigh confided in him. As former head of animal handling, either is possible. Maybe you can fill in those blanks if you take a look at the files stored on the lab terminal."

"If?"

"When?" he asked in return, cocking one eyebrow.

"What makes you think that I have any motivation to continue helping you?"

His answering smile held just enough mirth to make me want to punch myself for phrasing it like that, but for once he didn't use the opening I'd offered him on a silver platter to tease me.

"Your reaction to seeing my brother's video log was quite telling. The fact that you've talked yourself down from both a nervous breakdown and a fit of anger just underlines that."

"Quite telling, huh?"

During our talk we'd slowly regained some distance, but now he leaned close, forcing me to steel my spine to keep from backing away.

"Unlike most people who know you, I do think you can be ruthless, particularly under the wrong kind of stress and bolstered by the right kind of motivation. You try so very hard to be a nice, compassionate team player, but you're like a rabid honey badger when you get all riled up. You may not agree with my methods, but you're curious by nature, and I know that you want to find out what exactly Raleigh was working on, and why. Either to exonerate him, or find out where he went wrong, maybe even learn from his mistakes. I have no delusions about you wanting to help me, but if it will work out for you, you'd be happy to compromise your superficial loyalty to your employer—again."

My sputtering indignation was an instantaneous reaction, but it came with a sinking feeling in my gut.

"I have no fucking clue what you're talking about!"

"You don't? I thought you were smarter than that," he taunted, then settled back into a relaxed stance. "Want me to elaborate, to dissect the thin slices of your life that were enough for me to come to this conclusion?"

"No!"

"Well, too bad, I don't believe in coddling people I think deserve more honesty." His smile grew as I kept glowering at him, and he seemed to take my silence as demand for him to explain himself.

"Just take the last eleven hours. When we took over, you hid, you took care of yourself first. Once we threw you in with the others, you didn't try to socialize, just chatted with the only person you were familiar with. Your attempt to come to her aid might have been genuine, but after so many years of deceiving yourself into acting like a good little girl, that is to be expected. Your claws definitely came out when you kicked the living shit out of Greene. Since you walked out of that cube, you don't seem to have had a care in the world for how your former compatriots are doing, and you needed no convincing at all to help yourself by helping me. When you were confronted with what is almost irrefutable evidence of what happened to my brother coming out of his own mouth, it was not simple horror or compassion that was etched into the lines of your face, but conviction. You may not agree with my methods, but then it's been a while since you balked at them. Who knows? Either way, you now understand what I'm doing, and deep down you agree with me that it needs to be done. The logical conclusion of that is that you will continue helping me, and your knowledge of virology and my brother's other work predestines you to be the one to look through his files and reconstruct any details that are not obvious to us already."

It was quite the speech that he delivered, and while I could have found excuses for every point he made, none of them wanted to trip over my lips when I opened my mouth to defend myself. His words made me uncomfortable, and not just because they painted me in a different light than I wanted to see. No—what shut me up was that the woman he was talking about sounded a lot more self-sufficient than I thought myself capable of.

"Convinced, or shall I go on?" Nate asked.

He had me there, and he knew it, judging from the smug look on his face.

"Considering how much you obviously love to hear yourself talk, please, indulge yourself," I shot back, at a loss for what else to say.

Nate snorted, but did oblige me after a brief pause.

"The one mistake my brother made was trusting in the wrong people. I guess you could also say that it was a mistake that he clearly misjudged Thecla Soudekis, which ultimately led to his demise, but it is in the end just a consequence of the other."

"That's rather fatalistic," I offered.

"You think? You saw what that virus does to people," he pointed out. "And he helped develop it. I have a good idea why, but that doesn't make it any less reprehensible. My brother was a self-serving, narcissistic asshole on a mission."

"Sounds like someone else I know," I pointed out.

The grin he flashed me was a real one.

"Whatever. Fact is, he probably had it coming. None of the people who have been working on this are around anymore, and with the exception of Jenkins, they more or less died for the cause. Does this look like the kind of project any scientist would embark on who still had a working moral compass?"

I couldn't help it. His words just rubbed me the wrong way.

"He mentioned an antidote."

"To something that should never have existed in the first place," Nate replied, but the complete lack of anger in his voice didn't go by me unnoticed. There definitely was more to this than he wanted to admit.

"So it's his fault that he got killed?"

His shrug was pretty much confirmation.

"As I said, he trusted the wrong people. I don't intend to make that same mistake. That's why I picked you from the pile of possible candidates whose help I could recruit. And don't glare at me like that. I already told you that how that actually happened wasn't according to plan."

"And that should make me feel better about it now?" I huffed.

"And there I thought most women would feel at least vindicated at the knowledge that they're irresistible?"

I held his gaze until he broke it as he turned away, unable to keep a certain smugness from surfacing.

"And where does this leave us now?" Nate mused, striking a mock-considering pose. "Ah, right. Are you going to help me finish this? Or would you rather curl up somewhere and pretend that nothing I said got through to you?"

My first reaction was to deny that his words had struck a chord deep inside of me, but honestly, I couldn't. If anything, what had happened during the last hours rather than our talk had made me weary of continuing the way my life had played out over the last couple of years. Realizing now how different things could have been just added to my conviction.

"I may regret this later, but I'm going to help you."

He cocked his head to the side, a hint of bewilderment on his face, but it was quickly replaced by what I'd come to think of as a genuine grin from him.

"Excellent."

With that, he turned around and walked over to the door, like before holding it open for me to step out before him. I wondered if he thought of that as a gentlemanly gesture, or still didn't trust me enough not to run off first chance I got. Even with what I'd just committed myself to, I wouldn't have trusted myself, either.

Andrej and the other guard were gone, but that didn't seem to alarm Nate in the least. He set out for the connective tunnel as he got his radio out, sounding calm and almost bored as he asked for a status report. The rest of the trip to the atrium we passed in silence.

Chapter 19

Just outside the double doors that led into the glass cathedral of the atrium, the techie—Dolores, I reminded myself—was waiting for us.

"Get her a copy of the files from the off-site computer," Nate told her before he turned back to me. "You have two hours. After that, we have to get this party wrapped up. I wish I could give you more time, but we already hit a lucky streak that they've let us hunker down here so long undisturbed."

"They?"

He shrugged.

"Police, national guard, you name it. I honestly didn't think we'd manage to stay under their radar for so long."

I had to admit, now that he mentioned it, it made sense.

"So you haven't completely infiltrated them?" I mocked.

"Only key personnel," he replied, smirking.

"Guess the flu epidemic is playing into your hands?"

He paused for a moment, but then shook his head as if to disband the thought that had occurred to him.

"In theory, we should manage to be out of here before anyone notices. Then, of course, they will notice, but Friday afternoon to Saturday morning is a good window to remain under cover. People leave early, they go out for drinks, so they don't show up before late morning again. Don't worry about it." He glanced at the techie, then back to me. "Let me know if you need anything."

"Something to write on would be useful," I offered.

"I think that can be arranged."

I still waited until he had left the atrium through one of the back doors before I sank into one of the swivel chairs by the workstation. Then I let out a loud sigh, waiting for a weight to lift off my chest, but I only got a twinge from my nose and cheek for my bother. In the hot lab, I had been able to ignore how the bruises on my face were doing, but now that I could prod at them, they got increasingly harder to ignore.

"Electronic format works for you? The data is mostly in pdfs and text files, and you should be able to play the vids on this, too," the techie said as she held out a state-of-the-art tablet to me. I looked at the offering for a moment before accepting it. My fingers were steady and my grip firm yet not convulsive, and if not for the cuts in my palm I might have deluded myself into thinking that the last day hadn't happened.

The screen was set to show a folder containing a huge amount of the aforementioned documents, making me wonder how anyone should be able to make sense of it all in just two hours. Some of them were labeled in ascending numbers, others looked like dates, and none had the telltale "start here, incriminating evidence inside" tag that such things always had in movies.

"He likes you, you know?" the techie remarked, briefly looking from her screens to me.

Her tone was just casual enough to tip me off that she was fishing for information even if it sounded like random small talk, but her face looked open and trustworthy, making me wonder if it maybe was simple curiosity. Unlike the Ice Queen and Nate himself, I had a terribly hard time getting a reading from her.

"You think?" I offered when I couldn't come up with anything more intelligent.

She grinned, obviously understanding where I came from. I couldn't say why my alarm bells didn't go off around her—she was as much a part of the operation as everyone else, and I was sure that she was armed, too. But something about her demeanor made her appear less hostile. I just couldn't put a finger on it.

"I do. And it's obvious that the feeling is mutual, even though you must really hate yourself for that right now. Don't bother continuing to beat yourself up over it. Nate has that effect on some people."

That was when I remembered that all of the rooms in the hot lab had security cameras, and even though Green Fields Biotech had always claimed that they didn't have one in the changing rooms, I was sure that she'd followed our every move and listened in on our every word exchanged.

"He does?" I shot back dryly. "So it's what, his MO to stalk prospective future collaborators and screw them?" She gave me a blank stare that could have meant anything, so I dropped the subject. But considering she was ready to dish... "You sound like you've known him for a long time."

"Since after college, so, yeah, pretty much half of my life," she confirmed. I did the math in my head, frowning. She looked a few years younger than I was, and even if she rocked good genes, that would have made her my junior by half a decade. "Child prodigy. I graduated high school when I was fourteen," she offered, clearly getting where my mind had gone. "We had a rocky start, but things changed quickly. Which I guess is normal, considering the circumstances."

"Circumstances?"

"When you're locked in a bunker for three days without food or water you either kill each other, or you become friends for life. Guess which it was for us?"

"Chums."

"You bet."

Not knowing where to go from there, or whether I even wanted to keep chatting, I looked down at my tablet but got interrupted when Nate returned, bearing some provisions. I still sent him a dirty look even though I was quite happy to see a sandwich and bottle of water in my very near future, which he, of course, ignored. While I was busy digging into the food, he grabbed a stack of white paper from another desk, and lastly handed me a pen that he'd had clipped inside the pocket of his shirt. It was one of the Green Fields Biotech pens that the company handed out in their promo packages for visitors, quite ironically—or not.

"Anything specific you want me to look for?" I asked, not even sure that I could deliver on the offer.

"Just how committed to helping us are you?" he wanted to know in turn.

I pointedly sniffed through my now nicely swollen nose, glad when the resulting ache was barely more than a nuisance.

"Still a little conflicted, I guess you'll understand? Most of all, now I really want to know what is going on here."

The wry grin he answered me with looked quite like a taunt.

"I don't really give a shit about your motivation, or how long you plan on feeling guilty for it afterward. Just answer the question." I raised my brows at him, which seemed answer enough. "There are two things you can help me with, if you're so inclined. Our plan is to upload everything we've been able to scavenge from the company servers and the off-site computer about my brother's work. It will take only a couple of days for experts of all flavors to dissect everything, but it would lend the raw data a lot more credibility if we had a statement made by someone familiar with the material. You."

That made me snort.

"I'm not sure how credible I am, considering that people will either believe that I'm talking at gunpoint, or that I've switched sides."

The sound he made could have been a noncommittal grunt.

"Doesn't really matter, but the 'at gunpoint' part can be arranged, if that lessens your unease about being mistaken for an aggressor rather than a victim." He said that as if it was something impossibly hilarious to him. I kept looking back at him blankly, eventually making him tone down his grin somewhat. "Just look through the files, then coordinate with Dolores here to get a few images together that we can splice into the video feed. It doesn't have to be on point with your dissertation defense, just say a few things about the who, what, where, and why it is so damn important not to let this virus out of its vault. The news stations will pick up the video as it is and lead everyone else to the road you're going to pave with it, whether to discredit you or underline your arguments. Doesn't matter which."

I hated the idea of sitting in front of a camera, but I could see where he was going with it, and even agreed that it was a good point. It was the only thing so far that I felt I was even remotely qualified to do.

"And the second thing?"

That sardonic grin of his took on a slightly different tint.

"After we've wrapped up the video, you're coming down with me into the hot lab again so we can place remotely detonated explosives everywhere inside the concrete cocoon of the BSL-4 zone, and make sure we vaporize every single molecule stored down there when we blow up the building later."

Chapter 20

Almost exactly two hours later I found myself perched on a barstool—scavenged from the visitor waiting area—in front of a camera that looked like it belonged in a studio, making me wonder if Nate would have let me decline his offer of "cooperation." I sat awfully close to where Thecla had found her grisly end. The charred remains had been cleared away since then, but I could still tell where it had been; that image would forever be burned into my mind. In my hand I had two print-outs and three pages of hastily scrawled notes, and my heart rate was climbing steadily as I waited for the techie to give me the "go." But it wasn't stage fright, or the extenuating circumstances that gave me jitters. No, it was what I had found in Raleigh's notes that had my heart seizing with anxiety.

It had taken surprisingly little time to find actual information within the files. I couldn't shake the suspicion that Thecla had been a very conflicted woman in the last months of her life, because she could have easily erased everything of Raleigh's that incriminated her. Yet all of his files had remained untouched since the week after his death, as Dolores had confirmed after a brief analysis. Thecla had continued to catalog the progress of the experiments, but the additional notes accompanying the raw data had dwindled to a bare minimum as more time passed. As had progress and success. Clearly, he had been the mastermind behind the work, and she barely more than the executing hand, pun intended.

In the context of her reactions during what had turned out to be her last hours, I couldn't help but feel like she'd known that her end had come, and maybe even felt that she deserved it. She must have recognized Raleigh's brother sooner than I did—likely instantly—and considering the message from the log, the conclusions she had to have drawn must have been grim. Once they'd dragged me into the cube, there was no way she hadn't realized that she'd just become obsolete, except for paying for her crimes. The longer I thought about it, the less I understood her reaction. Sure, Nate didn't seem to have any inhibitions where beating the shit out of someone was concerned, but I doubted that he would have actually tortured her. That gave her death a somewhat uncomfortable connotation. Had she died to save herself—or someone else?

Considering that I'd likely never find out, it was easier to concentrate on what information I actually could come up with.

A few months before his death, Raleigh had compiled an overview of his work and progress so far, yielding what I suspected was some kind of status update. It not only sounded like thousands of reviews in scientific journals that I'd read over the years, it was even formatted like one, including an extensive list of references. That file alone would have been enough to condemn him and Green Fields Biotech, no questions asked—if not for the conclusions that he had drawn.

He hadn't mentioned anyone but him working on the project, but another file had held endless columns of work hours, marked with two recurring initials—RM and TS. I doubted that he and Thecla had been the only ones involved as there were massive amounts of data to be sifted through, but it was unlikely that the lab techs who had done the actual work outside of the hot lab had known exactly where the samples had come from that they were analyzing. Heck, I'd even spent a couple of minutes checking that none of my research had turned up on there.

I'd found a few other lists, but no new names. Mike Jenkins wasn't mentioned anywhere so I remained with my suspicion that Raleigh had confided in him, maybe even as a backup plan should things go wrong. I hadn't known him well enough to say for sure, but if his last video log had been any indication, the thought of siccing his brother on the people who were responsible for his death must have given him at least a hint of satisfaction.

And somehow, I just couldn't shake the suspicion that I was still missing one integral piece of data that would tie all this together. The longer I watched Nate's operation unfold, the less it looked like the terrorist takeover I figured it was supposed to seem like.

Once I'd started reading through files, I'd pretty much blocked out everything else around me, but even so I could tell that things had been suspiciously quiet. Most of the guards in the atrium were positioned so that they weren't easily visible from the outside, but except the door to the cube, there wasn't really anything to guard—in or outside of the building. Apparently, Nate's prediction about the optimal time frame had turned out to be true. The techie had confirmed my suspicion that all the exits—barred by the explosions that had caved them in—were also guarded by both mercenaries and an array of mines, but that still left the better part of thirty people unoccupied within the building. From time to time I thought I heard high-pitched, whining noises echo through the hallways, but that could have been my imagination.

The only real disturbance had—oh wonder—come from Gabriel Greene when he'd gotten up and started pounding on the wall of the glass cube closest to me, screeching profanities and threats that were only bothering me insofar as they dragged my attention away from my task. The Ice Queen had eventually shut him up by firing twice at the glass between them with a hand gun. The reinforced glass had splintered yet kept the bullets from their intended target, but still managed to shut Greene up for good. He'd looked scared shitless as he'd sunk down at his customary place next to the door, but I still couldn't find it in me to feel sorry for him.

As I sat there on my stool and waited for my signal, I wondered if what I was about to do made me a bad person. From my perch in the spotlight, I could hardly see anything besides the silhouette of the camera in front of me, but I knew that Greene must be watching me like a hawk. Deep down I was still unnerved by what he'd almost accomplished, but it was easier now to ignore that until later. Maybe that was because I had a task now and a definite end in sight. Maybe it was just my mind protecting what was left of my sanity. Either way, I really didn't give a shit anymore what happened to Greene, but I could sympathize with Raleigh on some level. If any of my actions yielded further grief to befall Greene, I would feel satisfaction, even if my finger wasn't pulling the trigger.

"Ready when you are," Nate said from somewhere beside the camera, forcing my attention back to the here and now. I gave a jerky nod, trying to quell the bout of anxiety gripping me. His instructions had been curt and to the point, and I doubted that I could fuck this up whatever I said, but my stomach clenched nevertheless. I knew that if I survived this, I'd forever be associated with this video.

"Okay, going live in three, two, one, go!" the techie counted down for me, and I saw a bright red light flash on at the bottom of the camera.

Taking a deep breath, I cast a last glance down at my notes, then did my best to appear calmer and more composed than I'd felt since this whole mess had started. Donning a fresh, crisp white lab coat over my scrubs had helped a little with that.

"My name is Dr. Brianna Lewis. I've been working for Green Fields Biotech for two years now, in the immunology department. My specialty is highly infectious viral diseases, particularly coronavirus. You can easily view my credentials online and on the company website."

I felt rather stupid rattling that off, but Dolores had agreed that it was important to stress that I knew what I was talking about.

The next part was all me.

"I don't know when you will see this video, but I expect that it will be after the accompanying data package has been made available to the press and everyone else with an internet connection. Feel free to make of the data what you wish, but this is my take on it. Several of my own publications have been cited in one of the files; I think I'm as close to an expert on hand as there is still left in this building."

I cleared my throat and nodded at where I figured the techie was standing, ready to work her computer magic.

"This file is a sort of review of the unsanctioned work conducted in the biosafety level four lab during the last approximately six years. The project was started by Dr. Raleigh Miller and conducted further by Dr. Thecla Soudekis, who took over after his death." I had to pause again, my throat suddenly parched. "After she murdered him, that is, with the very killer virus that he helped develop. As far as I know, Dr. Soudekis did not confess to this, but in the package you will find the unedited version of Dr. Miller's last video log in which he personally incriminates her."

The rapid progression of his illness flashed through my mind as I went on, trying to stay as objective as possible.

"Dr. Miller was one of the leading virologists in the field, and he got tempted to play God. He was working on a virus made up of the combined genetic material and proteins of three of the most deadly viruses known to mankind. In its last, stable iteration this virus appears to have been lethal within forty-eight hours of infection.

"Movies always make it appear as if that is a normal, maybe even slow progress, but most viruses, even those causing hemorrhagic fevers like Ebola, take up to two weeks to kill, and several days for the symptoms to appear. If this virus was ever set free on the population of a large city, millions of people would die before anything could be done. Because of the short time frame, I doubt that it would spread to become a pandemic, but in the hands of terrorists, it would be a weapon of mass destruction."

This time my pause was for dramatic reasons.

"This is why such a virus cannot be allowed to exist, even sealed away in a vault. It is my conviction that any means necessary are acceptable to ensure that it is destroyed. And I think Raleigh Miller held the same conviction, because his research shows that he was working on an antidote." Another pause, this one because the jitters made my throat close up. "A vaccine. Dr. Soudekis did not continue to develop it, so we will never know if it would have been effective, but that doesn't change the fact that this virus, if ever set free, would cause a devastating loss of life."

Now I could only hope that no one had the brilliant idea of leaking this video before we were out of the building, or there might be some problems with whatever exit strategy Nate had up his sleeve.

After another nod to Dolores, I went on.

"As you can see here, and on figure two in the review, the molecular structure of..."

I kept droning on through my notes, hashing over most facts but trying to speak in layman's terms where I could stress what was really important. How exactly Raleigh had built the virus, the vaccine, a progress graph of the earlier versus later versions, a time-lapsed view of one of the victims.

My voice sounded hollow in my own ears, but I figured that was just as well. The more I'd read about Raleigh's progress, the more the reasoning behind his brother's actions had become clear. I hated to admit it, but even now, knowing what I did, there was a part of me that was so fascinated by the project that it was hard to justify destroying it all. I stood by my conviction that it could not be left in active form, but it was a shame to completely destroy everything except for the files. At least the vaccine should have been developed to later stages, and for that, eventually, testing would have been necessary—

Nate was right, and he was doing the only morally acceptable thing. If not for Raleigh's death, I would have ended up with the potential blood of millions on my hands. Only that now he was making sure that would never happen.

After about ten minutes I reached the end of my notes, and there was only one thing left for me to say. Taking a moment to collect my thoughts, I did my best to stare into the camera, unblinking.

"Raleigh Miller and Thecla Soudekis have both played God, and they have died for their sins. Some things are not meant to be done even if they are possible. As scientists, we so often forget that."

I allowed myself a brief pause before I launched into the last bit of hopefully damning information.

"Evidence of who has been involved in this Project Destiny, as it was called, is scarce, and I'm afraid that with Thecla, the last person who knew about everyone's involvement has died without being able to offer a confession first. What we know is that Raleigh Miller finalized the current version of the virus, and he was working on a vaccine. Thecla Soudekis took over when he got squeamish, and was project leader until she died yesterday. Records indicate that Elena Glover, head of the Green Fields Biotech human resources department, was responsible for rounding up the victims. I personally don't know about her qualifications, but the fact that she got this job after Project Destiny started the first round of human trials is condemning. Concrete evidence of who provided the finances has not been included in the data, but information has been found that directly incriminates Gabriel Greene. As much as I would love to put the sole blame on that son of a bitch, his involvement in his father's company doesn't reach back long enough. We have no information on who helped Miller start the project in the first place. I don't believe that anyone else was involved; the amount of data gathered is indicative of a small team, one to three people, working part time over the space of years."

When I fell silent this time, my throat raw from talking so much at once, it had a feeling of finality to it. I thought about what else I should tell the world, but nothing came to mind.

"I do not condone the actions of terrorists. I do not think that violence is a solution for anything. I have no idea how many people have been killed in this attack so far, and I cannot predict how many more will die before it is over. Until yesterday midnight, I'd never heard of this virus, but the evidence I've just shared with you is compelling. I personally, as a virologist, as a human being, cannot let anyone use this virus as a weapon, not even as a means of defense."

The red light on the camera went out ten seconds later, and with it I felt part of the conviction I'd tried to put into my words leave my body. What was left was a mixture of confusion and fear, but also hope. Hope that, come what may, this nightmare would end today, once and for all.

Don't they say that there are some things out there worth dying for? I might have just found mine.

Chapter 21

"Guess that's a wrap?" I heard Nate say just as they turned off the lights, casting me in momentary darkness until my tortured eyes got used to the absence of several megawatts burning into my retinas.

"I'll edit in the graphs and check everything else again, but yes, it's a wrap," Dolores confirmed.

"Good," he muttered, nodding at the techie to do her thing now. He and the Ice Queen exchanged a few words, then he stepped up to where I was still perched on my stool. Amusement was back on his face, but without the mockery I'd expected.

"Very inspired speech. Even inspiring, some might say."

Cocking my head to the side, I cleared my throat to make my strained vocal cords work again. Turned out that being partly strangled hours before didn't work so well with speeches of all kinds.

"Anything you feel I should have added?"

"It's your speech. That's for you to decide."

I wondered if that was a hint, but then I'd long since gotten the feeling that we were beyond playing games.

"Shall we go then?" he prompted, pretty much confirming my guess.

"Just give me something to drink first, and I'm game."

"You're so easy to please," he teased, but diligently fetched me an unopened bottle of water as we made our way across the atrium. Yet when he held out a chocolate bar to me, I shied back, my pulse slamming into overdrive even before the rational part of my mind caught up. Nate looked from me to the sweet treat, his eyes narrowing slightly. "Something wrong?"

"You ask me that after one of your people went all rabid cannibal after eating one of those?" I shot back, my voice wavering with fear.

It was definitely calculation in his gaze now, making me wonder if I'd just passed some kind of test.

"You sure about that?"

"Positive," I agreed. "Watching Thecla blow herself up is one thing, but I'm not oblivious to what triggered her reaction. Besides, you know, threat of torture from you."

He ignored that last jibe as he threw the chocolate bar into a trash can that we passed.

"Anything about that unfortunate incident that you'd like to add?" he asked.

"You mean Thecla?"

He shook his head. "No, my guy."

I couldn't help but feel instantly suspicious. "Why would I?"

He shrugged. "You're a virologist, right? If it actually was rabies—" He let that hang in the air between us.

I wondered for a second if he was yanking my chain, but he looked serious enough to give me the creeps. "It's not like I can get a better look at the body now. Considering you burned all of them. Inside the building."

My accusation—as expected—had no effect on him.

"I did what was necessary. Would you have preferred to look at dead people the better half of the night? Not ideal for morale, you know?"

Again I got the sense that there was something he wasn't telling me.

"So you went out of your way to make us all comfortable? How sweet."

He pursed his lips but let it go.

"Ever seen or read about something like that happening? Instant rabies by means of chocolate?"

I shook my head. "Nope. But the fact that you pretty much confirmed that you think it was what he ate that made him go ballistic is kind of unnerving."

"I confirmed nothing."

"Did, too," I insisted, holding his gaze as he glanced at me. "Wanna tell me what is going on?"

"Wanna guess?" he shot back.

As a matter of fact, I did, but mostly because talking kept my mind off what we had set out to do.

"My guess? Steroids, or some other kind of uppers. You know, the shit that fighter pilots take to remain awake for extended missions? You and your guys have likely been popping that stuff like candy. It was just coincidence that he was having the munchies before that chemical cocktail fried his brain."

Nate's lips curled up, but I wouldn't have gone as far as calling that a smile.

"And still you refused to eat that chocolate bar."

"I'm doing low carb," I lied.

"Humor me."

"I wouldn't know how?" I replied, giving him a toothy smile of my own. "But seriously, what was it?"

A look passed his features that I'd glimpsed before, only this time he didn't try to hide it immediately.

"It's better if you don't know."

"Because otherwise you'd have to kill me?" I joked—or hoped that it was a joke.

"Me? No. But others might have other plans. Then again, the fact that you're helping me might do the trick already, so, yeah. Either way, you're kind of fucked."

"So nice of you to put my mind at ease just before we're about to go into the hot lab. With explosives, because just being exposed to lethal microorganisms isn't fun enough on its own?" I jeered.

"If you really want to know, ask me again when we're inside the lab," he replied, sounding way too cheery for such a cryptic message. I left it at that, because, really? What else could I have done?

The rest of our descent into the bowels of the complex went unsupervised, and for the most part in silence. There wasn't really anything I felt like saying until we reached the corridor outside the hot lab, where four gym bags sat waiting for us.

"That's it?" I asked, a new kind of unease clenching my stomach.

"Enough explosives to bring down half the building," Nate confirmed. When he saw me hesitate, he stopped in mid-motion of picking two of the bags up, and instead unzipped one so he could show me the gray slabs stored inside.

"You know basic chemistry, right? Without the detonator, the charge is only so much flammable play dough. The detonators are remote controlled and cannot be set off accidentally. They are stored in this bag, and you won't get anywhere near them." He indicated his other, unopened bag.

That wasn't exactly soothing, but I nodded anyway. Reluctance had me move extra carefully as I picked up the remaining bags, then had to fight hard not to drop them when their full weight yanked on my weary muscles.

We went through the same ritual of changing into scrubs and getting ready before stepping into the suit room as before, although I hesitated in front of the mirror for a moment to check my nose. It had stopped swelling, but was still tender. Next to the darkening bruises on my jaw and cheek, it looked almost normal.

"You're not getting vain now, are you?" Nate remarked dryly as he walked by behind me, then held the door to the suit room for me. I gave him a level look.

"Not vain, just concerned."

"About your good looks? Don't worry, a week from now none of that will be visible any longer. And you're still pretty, if more in a tough-chick kind of way."

I hesitated, about to close my mouth and let it slide, but it was just one more comment in a line of others that irked me too much to let me smooth my ruffled feathers.

"In the past, I've been barred from going into the hot lab because I've had a cut on my finger or a light case of the sniffles. Now I'm looking like a road map made of scrapes, cuts, and bruises, all of them barely scabbed over. I shouldn't be anywhere near this."

"And you only notice that now?" he continued to taunt me.

That was exactly the reason why I'd tried to shut myself up, and having that rubbed in my face didn't make me feel any better.

"Yeah, but last time I still had the excuse of not being here of my own free will."

"I haven't forced you to do anything," he pointed out.

Instead of answering right away, I pulled on two layers of gloves—the thicker, blue nitrile gloves because my paranoia kept telling me that flimsy latex just wouldn't cut it to keep my nerves at bay—and I started prepping two new suits, ignoring our discarded ones from the first venture into the lab. If my motions were a little jerky, there was nothing I could do about that now.

"No, you just set everything up so that the alternative was even more of a nightmare."

He didn't reply, so I looked up to gauge his reaction. His face was blank, but there was something lurking in his eyes that was part exasperation, part something that I couldn't decipher. Could it be regret? Guilt?

"I know," he admitted, startling me. "I wish there'd been another way, but even pissed off as you are, you have to admit that it was the easiest route to take."

"Like I care," I shot back, feeling my anger resurface.

"Frankly, I don't give a shit about your hurt feelings."

"Again, like I care," I repeated, turning my head away to hide a stupid grin that came out of nowhere. Why did bantering with him have to be so much fun? I really must have gone nuts.

"Ah, but you do. Are you really stupid enough to romanticize this situation?"

My guffaw in reply made him smile just a little.

"Trust me, I'm not romanticizing anything. I'd even go as far as saying that if I hadn't been of use to you, you might have let Greene strangle me. I'm well aware of that."

A muscle jumped in his jaw, proving that I'd landed a hit. Yet his voice was light as he replied. "And still you can't extricate yourself from the gravitational pull of my charm."

His grin was way too bright to be healthy as he took the suit from me, then started the laborious task of getting into it. This time I didn't lift a finger to help.

"You're so full of shit, you know that?"

Pausing, he looked at me, still obviously amused.

"Oh, I do, but that doesn't make my observation any less keen."

Kicking myself in the head sounded like a good idea right then, but instead I plugged in the hose to inflate the second suit to check for ruptures.

"Then you've clearly realized that whatever this is between us started under false pretenses before you brought down the building and set my heart up for premature cardiac arrest, not quite incidentally killing any chances of a continuation of 'us' in whatever definition. So your point is invalid," I replied.

"Liar," was all he said, making me hate the fact that he saw right through me.

Instead of stoking the flames of his argumentation, I started donning my own suit. Childish as it was, I was tempted not to turn on my com unit before zipping myself up, but we were working with explosives, and I didn't want to accidentally kill myself just out of spite.

Carrying the gym bags through the air locks and into the main zone of the L4 lab irked me immensely, simply because it had been drilled into me that nothing, absolutely nothing got into the lab without proper cleaning first. And now it happened the second time in a row on my watch. Just perfect. Nate either ignored my baleful glances, or, more likely, wasn't even aware of them as he preceded me into the lab proper.

"How are we going to do this?" I asked once the air lock had closed behind us and the constant hiss of the connected air hose droned out even my galloping heartbeat. In a way I was even happy to be as mad as I was right now—it helped keep the panic at bay.

"Easy. First I mark where all the explosives go. Then we glue them to the walls, arm the detonators, and get the hell out of here."

He got out a fat, red sharpie from one of his bags and started down the corridor, painting four huge Xs onto the walls in even intervals. I followed him at a sedate pace, not entirely comfortable with leaving the bags full of C4 or thermite or whatever by the air lock doors, but I didn't want to give him a chance to order me to follow him like a dog. Like before, it was obvious to me that he still had a little trouble navigating the lab in the suit, but less so than most people after their first couple of weeks.

"Remind me again why you need me along for this? You're doing quite well for yourself."

He halted after marking the back wall of the now deserted animal holding facility and turned his head comically slowly to glance back at me.

"I didn't explain it before, so what's with the repetition?"

"Feel free to attribute that to my level of annoyance," I ground out.

I thought that made him grin, but couldn't be sure with the lights hitting his visor just so.

"You'll see."

And I did, once we had completed the slow circuit and returned to the exit. With careful, deliberate motions he unzipped the bags, then got out one of the explosive bricks, and, much to my surprise, something that looked like a large tube of glue.

"You really weren't kidding when you said that we'd stick them to the walls, eh?"

He shook his head, holding out the tube to me.

"You're better with fine motor control wearing the space suits, so you do the fine motor control work. Yes, I could do this alone, but it's much less nerve-wracking as a two-man job."

I accepted the tube with apprehension, studying the instructions before I unscrewed the stopper and gingerly broke the safety seal with the back of it, making sure that nothing leaked out onto my gloves.

"It's a strong adhesive, but it's not corrosive. Even if you get something onto your gloves, you should be fine."

"Should be," I echoed, staring at the unwrapped brick he held out to me. "I'm more concerned about accidentally gluing myself to something, then tearing the glove when I pull it free."

He shrugged as if he hadn't considered that, and told me to apply a liberal amount to the brick. I did, then watched with fascination as he slapped the explosive onto the wall and held it there for maybe twenty seconds. When he removed his hand, the brick stayed firmly in place, even when he pulled on it sideways. Next, he got out what I presumed was the detonator, which looked disappointingly like a pen connected to a small control unit with a bunch of cables. The explosives brick yielded easily as he pushed the detonator in. Last, he pulled something off the back of the small, attached control unit and stuck it to the wall beside the brick.

We moved on to the next red cross marking, where the same procedure began anew.

"I take it you know what you're doing?" I asked.

"Doesn't look too hard, now, does it?" he shot back.

"You know that's not what I meant."

Holding the next brick out to me, he gave a noncommittal grunt. "In a storage facility far, far away, there's a diploma that has my name on it and states that I'm qualified to do this shit, yes. Satisfied?"

"So you have a degree in engineering?" I ventured a guess. No idea why I was doing small talk now of all times, but it was better than to dwell on the obvious.

"Ballistics and Explosives Engineering, yes," he agreed.

"College?"

Fitting another piece of the puzzle that was Nate Miller in place was strangely satisfying.

"Yes, but I actually learned it all on the job. Later, someone thought they should commemorate it on a plaque."

"Sounds nifty."

"Says the woman with a longer tail of academic titles to her name than her actual name itself. You're not getting all uppity on me now, are you? I spent time defending my country. That takes away from academic pursuits."

I ignored his jibe.

"Army?"

I tried to remember if that was what he'd told me about his family in the past, if that had even been the truth. As much as I wanted to doubt it, I somehow couldn't disband the suspicion that—except for the obvious—Nate had been surprisingly candid with me from the start.

"Rangers, at first. After that, not an institution you've ever heard of, or ever will. Until I dropped out, that is."

"So you were some kind of black ops operative?"

He scrunched up his face, but after a second replied.

"I should probably say 'that's classified,' but considering that the report about my return to civilian life must look as if the file got soaked in tar, I think I can just admit it."

We moved on to a new mark where he stopped and started unwrapping the next brick.

"And why did you quit? Not that I know the first thing about black ops, but in the movies they always look like they don't really have the same moral code as your stereotypical good guys. Sounds practically made for you."

"I had my reasons," he replied

"I bet," I muttered, not sure I even wanted him to hear that remark. Judging from the slight grin on his face, he had.

"Just my luck that I got my new mission only a week after," he offered, sounding pensive.

"So you didn't plan on avenging Raleigh right away?"

Nate studied me intently for a moment as he considered his reply. "Remember the first time we met?"

"You mean in the park?"

He shook his head. "No, the first time. At my brother's funeral?"

Now that he mentioned it, I remembered, if vaguely. It had felt weird to attend when I hadn't known the deceased personally, not really, and I'd barely remained long enough to pay my respects. Except—

"We talked briefly," I said, memories returning now that I focused on them. And with that came a different realization. "I told you that I didn't understand how it could have happened. With Raleigh being a trained professional, and all the fail-safes in place and all." Meaning, I'd likely doomed myself.

The way Nate looked back at me pretty much confirmed that guess.

"Shit," I muttered under my breath.

"You were the only one who doubted that it was an accident," he explained, his voice soft, contemplative. "At the time, I chalked that up to you being some kind of lovesick puppy or admirer, but over the course of the following months, your words just wouldn't let me go. And when I got the transcript of the vid we watched, it all came back to me. Now who would I rather believe—the company who considered everything settled after handing my mother a check, or the woman who was familiar with my brother's work and work environment, and who had nothing whatsoever to lose with her accusations?"

"I never accused anyone of anything," I interjected.

"Wasn't necessary. Your doubt was accusation enough. And Raleigh confirmed it all."

I didn't know what to add to that, so I remained silent. Nate finished setting up the next bomb before he continued to speak.

"Be that as it may, I guess the fact that soon we'll reduce an entire city block to just so much dust means that from now on it won't be smooth sailing anymore."

That made me look up sharply. "You call the last hours smooth sailing?"

His shrug was nothing if not nonchalant. "No casualties on my side, and almost no civilian. We scrounged together enough money so that I won't have unsavory drug lords breathing down my neck for a decade, and I'm here with you, doing what I came here to do. How is that not unfolding perfectly?"

Viewed like that, he was right. Only my personal perspective was somewhat different. It was impossible not to let that sour my mood. So instead of chatting on, I resigned myself to playing my part in his perfect little game, resenting him—and myself— just a little more.

Over the course of what felt like a small eternity but was likely closer to half an hour, I went through six tubes of adhesive, and we left a trail of empty gym bags and explosive wrappers behind. I'd kind of expected him to keep the last explosive for the room his brother died in, but we passed through that midway. There were still four explosives left in the last bag when he told me to use the remainder of the glue on the brick that he then stuck to the door of the room the viral stocks were kept in.

"Why not put that onto the walls inside the vault?" I asked, feeling a little stupid.

Nate finished setting up the detonator, then turned so he was looking at me.

"Because we can't get inside. This is the best we can do."

He put the remaining bricks, complete with the blasting caps, at the foot of the wall left and right of that door.

"Why can't you get inside?" I asked. So far, none of the doors that usually required authentication via retina scanners had been barred to them.

"Because the vault is controlled by a different set of security measures. It was easy enough to blast through the others, but this one was too tricky for the limited time frame that we had. I've planned for that eventuality; with the strategically positioned explosives around the room, the walls should cave in. They are not reinforced."

I still didn't quite get it.

"What's so different about this door?"

Even through the perpetual background noise of the hissing air hoses, the condescension in his voice was obvious.

"Have you ever been inside?" he inquired.

I shrugged, wondering how much the gesture was visible with the suit.

"Yes, a couple of times."

For a moment he looked at me sharply, but then his enthusiasm muted.

"Alone?"

"No, always with Thecla. I'm not authorized to... oh."

"Oh, indeed," he agreed, mimicking the sound I'd made as my epiphany struck. "Only very few people are allowed to open the vault, and you're not one of them. Dolores cracked the general security override by allowing any valid ID in the general system to be accepted by the lab complex database, but the same didn't work on this door. Something about being unable to add any new entries without the right verification key. Don't ask me for the specifics; I know how to blow up a building, not its computer system."

This time it wasn't fright exactly that made the fine hairs at the back of my neck stand on end. For a few seconds it was overwhelmingly hard to keep my mouth shut, but somehow, I managed. Why I did, I had no idea, but with my thoughts suddenly racing, that was nothing I wanted to concern myself with.

"So there was one more thing you wanted to show me?" I asked, referring back to our conversation on the way down here.

"It's probably nothing," he said—but the way he said it made me twice as suspicious about the entire thing as I'd already been.

"Yeah, right."

His snort sent dissonant static over the com.

"Then I'll let you be the judge of that," he replied as he unhooked the air hose and started down the hall again—back to the secret room hidden behind my old workspace.

"Something on the terminal?" I ventured a guess—and stopped in my tracks as my mind zoomed to the next conclusion. "What exactly does one of your guys losing it have to do with whatever fucked-up things your brother was doing down here?"

Nate stopped and turned, and this time his smile couldn't have been described as anything except sardonic. "You'll see."

I really didn't like the sound of that. Not. At. All.

It took us only a minute to make it back there, and we stopped in front of the terminal. Like last time, the screen activated as soon as Nate touched it. He briefly scanned the list of files until he tapped the one showing Raleigh's last hours. I wondered if he expected me to watch the entirety of it yet again, but instead he swished around with his fingers until he managed to activate the time control. He dragged his finger to about the last third of the bar and let go, making the video resume just as Raleigh said his last goodbye to his brother, again.

There were still five minutes remaining when the screen went black. I had a really bad feeling about this all of a sudden.

The screen remained dark for about ten seconds before it switched back to camera view, if of a different angle. The entire room was visible, shown from what looked like a camera that had been installed in the corner above the observation lounge window. The lab furniture and the two hospital beds were recognizable, with Raleigh's body unmoving on the one to the right. The clock in the upper corner showed ten minutes and fifty hours—a little over two hours after Raleigh's catalogued demise. With the different angle and more distance, it was hard to judge how extensive his physical deterioration had become by the end, but there were rivulets of blood dried from his nose, eyes, and ears, and I could make out several dark splotches of subdermal hematomas and lesions on his cheek, neck, and exposed arms. His scrubs likely covered more, judging from their soiled state. It was hard to watch, but nothing unexpected.

"Why are you showing me this?" I asked, turning partly so I could catch the look on Nate's face. The impassive mask from before was back in place, but now he was quick to shush me.

"Just watch."

"I don't know—"

"Watch," he interrupted my protest, his voice coming out pressed over the com. One hand settled securely between my shoulders—the worst show of support in history, if it was supposed to be that. More to oblige him than anything, I looked back to the screen—

And let out a shout and took an instinctive step back, or would have if not for the hand pressing harder against my spine now.

Raleigh was up and moving, but I wasn't sure if I'd have called what he did "walking," exactly. There was something fundamentally wrong about the way he moved, jerky and kind of uncoordinated. I had seen my share of sick people rise after their musculature had been partly atrophied, but this looked nothing like it. His limbs seemed to weigh a ton, judging from how much momentum he needed to gather for each motion. Yet his face remained impassive, not a muscle moving in his cheeks although he should have been scowling or frowning from exertion. If he would just look up…

Then I got my wish, and immediately rued my curiosity. His eyes—they weren't empty, far from it. Mindless rage shone from them, and as if the camera catching that look was a clue, he screamed—a sound so primal that it made hair all over my body stand on end despite the perpetual overheating that always happened in the suit. That first scream was followed by a second, then a low moan that was even worse before Raleigh whipped around, grabbed the foot-end railing of the bed, and wrenched it away from the wall as if it weighed nothing. Metal groaned as it crashed into formica hard enough to leave a dent—which, considering the security standards the lab was built to should have been impossible. The thing on screen—it was hard to continue to think of it as my almost-mentor—wrenched the bed around again and into the other direction, this time succeeding in tearing the rail off completely. It wailed in triumph before it ran toward the only part not covered by the view—the observation window. The rail, wielded like a club, was smashed repeatedly into the glass, each dull impact making my body jerk with tension. Another scream that barely sounded like an animal's, and I heard the glass splinter.

The sprinkler system engaged, automatically flooding the room with the hydrogen peroxide and formaldehyde vapor used for disinfection, the first fail-safe should any kind of contamination happen. Even tense with fright as I was, my heart went out to the creature, as nothing—macro nor microorganism—could survive that.

Yet instead of dropping dead within the first few seconds of inhalation, it continued to rage on, until two minutes later it staggered back as the body started shutting down with hypoxia and systemic shock. More moaning and clawing at the air and floor followed until—finally—it remained motionless on the floor, dead for good now.

Neither of us moved as the video rolled on for another minute, and I wasn't sure that I took more than a breath or two. I certainly welcomed the darkness of the screen when it finally came before it reverted to the file menu.

It was only when he removed his hand that I realized just how much pressure Nate had had to put up to keep me in place, making me stagger with the sudden missing support. Inhaling deeply, I turned to look at him, feeling cold sweat trickle down my neck and face.

"What the fuck was that?"

The look in Nate's eyes was impassive, but even through the distortion of the visor I could see the line of his jaw stand out as he gnashed his teeth.

"That was the effect XLC34 has on one out of ten people exposed to it."

"XLC34?"

He gave a quick jerk of a nod.

"The lab designation the virus has. At least I presume that Thecla infected Raleigh with the initial strain, because the one he'd been developing further to stabilize kills in less than a day after infection."

I knew that this wasn't the part of the information that my mind should have latched on to, but I couldn't help myself. "What happens to the other nine?" I asked, my voice shaking slightly.

"They die."

In a way, that answer felt like it was the lesser of two evils, but my mind wasn't quite up to judging that yet correctly.

"Just… how is this even possible? He was too weak to remain upright just half a day into the infection. And then he just got up and…" I trailed off there, not sure how to go on.

Nate offered me a sardonic smile completely void of humor.

"I'm neither a doctor nor a scientist, so I can't really give you an answer. But the official version is something along the lines of the virus attacking the central nervous system along with the brain, which shuts down one system after the other. Most die of cardiac arrest or pulmonary failure."

Having a heart attack or suffocating didn't sound pleasant, but considering what Raleigh had turned into… and my mind was so not ready to finish that thought yet. If ever.

"And the unofficial version?"

I got a snort for again jumping at the least obvious clue.

"I don't know. What would you call something that appears to be dead for an hour or two, then suddenly attacks everything in sight, all teeth and claws?"

I opened my mouth, but closed it without anything coming out. My mind was in overdrive right now, panic making racing thoughts blow up before they'd led to the right connections—or not.

"Your guy, the one with the chocolate bar," I started, my voice gaining strength as I went on. "That's exactly what happened to him. I'm right, aren't I?" Just seeing the jaded look in his eyes was confirmation enough—and kicked my fear up another notch or two. "But that's fucking—"

"Impossible?" Nate supplied helpfully.

"Insane!" I finished, then frowned when something else occurred to me. "Wait. You knew. You knew that this could happen. You didn't even hesitate to shoot him. And Thecla knew it, too. That's what she meant with 'it's out there,' right?"

He did me the courtesy not to play dumb.

"She saw this video, right? And was likely the one who had to dispose of the body and repair the damage by herself. Plus, I find it highly unlikely that she wasn't aware of exactly what she had been working on."

That was not the part that had my teeth on edge.

"Are you shitting me? Please tell me that this is not spreading out there, right fucking now?"

Just the fact that Nate seemed relatively unperturbed even in the face of my panicked interrogation should have been answer enough, but I needed to hear it from him like nothing before in my entire life.

"No. The virus remains stable once it has infected a host, and transmission hasn't occurred in situ as far as I know."

"As far as you know?!" I echoed, still on the verge of screaming. If not for the suits, I would have grabbed his shoulders and physically shaken him, whatever good that would have done me.

"It has been engineered to remain that way. Infection has to occur through injection. You're the virologist, you tell me exactly how you people do it, but it has a built-in off-switch. As soon as it has infected a host, it deactivates the infection vectors, or some shit. Like with a vaccine, you can't transfer it to another person. Not even a full blood transfusion would have that effect. Some kind of integration into the host's DNA," he explained, followed by a snort. "You'll probably understand that a hell of a lot better than I do."

There were viruses that worked that way, but I had yet to encounter one that wasn't out to jump from host to host at the earliest convenience. Unlike bacteria or larger critters, viruses never turned parasitic. They were always a "in for the whole pot or nothing" kind of gamble.

"They engineered it like that?" I asked when I finally got a grip on my racing heart and managed to clear my mind a bit. "Whoever actually built this thing? Because Raleigh didn't. He was working on the vaccine." The more I'd scanned his research, the more obvious that had become—at least now, in hindsight. He certainly seemed to have made the already deadly virus a lot faster in its killing time—which might have been a small grace had it replicated freely and jumped from host to host, as fast-replicating viruses were usually the inefficient ones, killing their host long before effective spread to new hosts could occur. Just one of the reasons why everyone and their mother caught the common cold—virtually no deaths and a long window of contagion guaranteed a maximum of exposure potential.

And that I was rattling off these facts in the back of my mind bothered me on a different level.

Nate's reply was a welcome reminder that I had more important things to focus on than the underlying biology of whatever it was that had killed his brother.

"The most commonly used strain, yes."

Just like that, whatever calm I had managed to hold on to evaporated.

"So there are more?" I asked, back in the throes of my rising panic attack.

"Several. But that's the only one I know of that anyone ever turned into a weaponized form." With stats like what he'd told me—and I'd seen for myself, in action—I didn't know if that was a relief. That the very thing existed was beyond mind-boggling.

"Does the CDC know of this?"

Nate shrugged, and even with the bulky suit it looked kind of smug. "Who do you think funded Raleigh's research?"

It made sense, of course... but also didn't. And the more I thought about this, the more questions came up in my mind—but first things first.

"So let me get this straight. You came here to destroy a CDC-funded operation that was trying to find a vaccine against some kind of supervirus? And you needed my help for that, telling me that it was the right thing to do?"

Thankfully, he refrained from pointing out that his exact words had been different, but that didn't mean that he didn't sound condescending as hell.

"I came here, and recruited your help, to find out what exactly happened to my brother, and put an end to it. Whatever his ideas or plans were, they died with him, as did his research. Or did you find any further files on this? Because we sure didn't. That bitch killed him, and while I would have loved to put the fear of her life into her before she died, I'm not regretting that she's gone."

Judging from the way she had looked when she'd gone for the grenade, I figured he'd gotten that wish either way.

"But this makes no sense! If she knew what he'd been working on, why kill him? Why?!" I shouted.

Nate remained mute at my outburst, his silence speaking louder than words.

"Hell if I know," he admitted, defeat seeping back into his tone. "And that's by far not the only hole in this story. As much as I'd like to have all the answers, I don't, and with Raleigh and Thecla both dead, I doubt we'll ever know."

"You don't have a lead on who financed this? Who at the CDC signed off on a billion-dollar check?" Suddenly, the very existence of Green Fields Biotech seemed so arbitrary. Two brilliant scientists banding together to build up their company that focused on basic research—the part of the field that paid the least, except for the patents, if they could sell them—and earned out within a decade, without ever developing some ground-breaking compound or procedure? "It's all a front, isn't it?"

This time every second he took to answer grated on my nerves. When he finally gave his reply, a hint of sympathy was plain in the look he gave me.

"Every scientist they ever employed was carefully vetted and selected for their skills and previous accomplishments. Meticulous work ethics, out-of-the-box thinking, a deeper understanding in the right fields that was perfectly suited for their goals. I doubt that more than a fraction of the people who worked here knew what they actually worked on. Have you never wondered why all the papers that came from basic research here could have been done by any grad student at any publicly funded university lab, while the company blew billions of dollars into research each year?"

That implication hurt, but then it made sense. To keep a low profile, they'd had to employ a number of pipetting monkeys to lead everyone who might have gone looking on quite the merry chase. That I'd been degraded to that stung on so many levels—and might just have saved my life, considering that it could easily have been me who drew Thecla's ire, for whatever reason it had been directed at Raleigh Miller in the first place.

"That still doesn't explain your guy," I pointed out when mulling over the implications just got too painful. "He didn't go full-on raving lunatic from one second to the next over nothing." At least I hoped that there had been a well-balanced trigger for that built in. "And how come he was infected in the first place? He didn't bleed or look like he was running a fever." Even a lighter case might have yielded the same end result, but there should have been some symptoms.

Exhaling slowly, Nate shrugged.

"He didn't catch it in here, if that's what you mean. He was a carrier for many years."

Right when my mind was ready to leave crap-your-pants territory, he had to pull me right back to square one.

"Carrier? Are you fucking kidding me? There's a dormant version of this shit out there, too?"

"Only the dormant version, as you call it," he replied, a little too unperturbed to put me back at ease.

"How so?" And where did that little tidbit come from?

"It is what the virus was initially developed as, or at least the first and only useful application."

"Excuse me?" I didn't need to shout to convey just how insane that concept was. Nate had clearly anticipated that reaction, judging from the almost lazy way he tried to cross his arms over his chest, greatly hindered by the suit.

"In the dormant, inactivated form, the progression of the outbreak is much more controlled, and the symptoms less severe."

"Define 'less severe'?" I interrupted him.

"Only one in two dies, and those who survive don't turn into raving monsters. There are even benefits."

That anyone could willfully infect someone with anything like this was simply beyond me—but at the same time, my curiosity was piqued.

"What benefits?"

"To name only a few—increased stamina and strength, better healing, and an almost perfect immunity to most diseases and many poisons."

"Because the immune system is active and on high alert, eliminating everything else that might intrude into the closed system," I murmured, earning myself a sharp look from Nate. "Like worms and allergies. In those places in the third world where people still suffer from the usual parasites that our standards of hygiene have eradicated, people don't have allergies. Their immune system is too busy to auto-activate."

I just got a shrug in return. As he'd said, he wasn't the scientist.

"But what about the physical perks?" I asked, unable to explain that.

"Light neural damage," he provided. "You can drive yourself harder and ignore pain better when you don't actually feel your muscles hurt. As for the healing capabilities, it's probably a mix of both. You're asking the wrong guy about the 'hows' here."

I thought about that for a moment. "So your guy was infected with this, what, super soldier thing?" It was the logical conclusion, particularly considering what I figured had been his military background. Not that I liked that implication one bit.

Nate rightly guessed the lines my thoughts had followed.

"They called it a serum," he provided succinctly, as if that made anything better.

"Did all of you guys get dosed with that?" My heart sped up painfully at the very idea, but he shook his head without hesitating for a second.

"No. I didn't even know that Jones got it. And no, I have no fucking idea what triggered the change. For all I know, he could have been a ticking time bomb for years and McManus was one unlucky bastard to be standing right next to him at the wrong time."

It wasn't a satisfying answer, but at least one that was a lot more plausible than insta-rabies from sugar overload.

Silence fell, and after letting out a long breath, Nate glanced at the exit to this hidden chamber of morbidity, but looked back to me instead of leaving immediately.

"I thought you deserved to know, particularly as you're one observant tough cookie. We didn't include the last part of the vid in the transmission that we're going to send out, and I didn't want to show you upstairs because I'm generally not a fan of making everyone I need to rely on paranoid that they are going to get chomped on any moment now for whatever reason. Maybe once this is over and we get out of here alive and in one piece, you can help me track down the missing answers. But this here," he gestured at the room around us, "is a dead end. We've secured what we could from the company servers, maybe we'll find more answers there. Maybe what we caused here creates enough of a stir to make another whistle-blower come out of hiding, if only to let me continue to do their dirty work for them. But after seeing that video, after learning what you know now, can you honestly condemn me for my actions?

"We didn't kill a single employee of this company, even if some might have had it coming. Your friend killed herself, likely because she was too petty to give me the satisfaction of finally knowing why my brother had to die. If you ask me, it's likely that she was jealous of him, or some shit. She certainly didn't pursue world domination after she killed him. I'm just a trained monkey with a gun who's good at motivating people and getting shit done. I need someone on my team who can be the brain to my brawn. The conclusions you jumped to from what little I know by heart and could tell you were what I needed weeks to work out for myself, months even in some places. You were smart enough that they wanted you on board for their project, even if that might be a double-edged sword for you now. Be smart enough with me to uncover just how deep this goes. If for no other reason, then because you'll have a target on your back the moment anyone finds out that you got wind of this project here."

I hadn't expected that rousing speech, but that last part slammed me right back onto the bottom of reality.

"Which is entirely your fault because you made me pretty much confirm that in front of that damn camera!" I accused.

He shrugged. "All's fair in love and war. Might as well enjoy yourself while you follow up on the inevitable." That came with such a sappy, completely out-of-place grin that it made me laugh in spite of myself.

"You're such an ass!"

"No objections there," Nate admitted, looking over to the exit again. "Why not discuss all my short-comings after we're out of here? I have a lot of faith in my calculations, but I'd rather not spend any more time right next to a shit-ton of explosives in one of the most hostile environments man has ever built."

I had a lot of objections, but that was not one of them.

"Lead the way," I offered, already reaching for my air hose. With all the knowledge that was now weighing heavily on me, being blown up sounded almost rudimentary, but now that my mind had been reminded of this much less abstract danger, I already felt that underlying nausea return that had been riding shotgun the entire time in the hot lab. Nate agreed and preceded me back into the lab proper before he turned toward the central corridor.

Mostly to combat that rising sense of dread, I let my thoughts come freely as they ran to my head. "So this is not the first time you've done something like this?" I asked, nodding toward the stack of explosives as we passed the viral vault—which reminded me of something else, making my pulse spike for an entirely different reason that suddenly sent alarms of urgency to go off in my mind.

Taking the next step as slowly and deliberately as the last one was a feat.

Nate sent me a bright smile that worked well even through the visor of his suit.

"I have both the academic and practical qualifications to blow stuff up, and have done it many times before. As for this lab in particular, we've built a similar setup using materials as closely resembling what we knew are in use here, and we blew that up twice for practice. Does that answer your question?"

"In more detail than I ever needed to know."

He laughed, taking a last look around before he zeroed in on the door to the chemical showers.

"Then let's get out of here, unless you need another moment? Getting sentimental all of a sudden?"

That last comment made me go still for a second when I felt like a deer caught in the headlights, but then I realized that he was joking. Shaking my head, I tried to mentally relax and keep my galloping heart in check before stepping up to the air lock doors.

"Nope, I can't wait to get into the shower with you. Those minutes have proven to be the highlight of my completely screwed-up day."

He laughed again, and when I looked back, I saw that now he had a slight swagger in his gait. Relaxed, happy to have the worst of the work behind him, at ease to continue bantering with me. Perfect. I wished I could manage that.

"I bet they are."

The air lock door swung open easily enough, and I paused just inside it.

"I guess there's not a chance in hell that you'll let me do this alone?"

"Nope. Wouldn't want to deprive you." He shook his head, already moving toward the door as I stepped to the side to let him through.

The voice at the back of my mind screamed for me to stand down and let his plan unfold, trust in the one thing that he clearly was an expert in—planning. But with what he'd revealed to me in the hidden lab, I just couldn't. His plan was good, but not good enough.

For the past fifteen hours I had done nothing but be a passive, if somewhat elusive at times, victim. I'd run, I'd hidden, I'd only fought back as a last resort. I'd let myself be bullied and intimidated, and I was so sick of it that it made me physically ill. There was still some doubt remaining in me about his mission, but not in the knowledge he'd shared with me. I didn't need to know every minute detail to know enough.

"Why didn't you just ask me?" I demanded, my voice hollow. For a moment I wondered if I'd said too much, but he took my question for exactly what it sounded like.

"To join us, help us, before we took over?" Nate guessed. I nodded. He caught my gaze and held it. "It might sound sentimental, but I figured that I owed it to my brother's last message to the world to leave you with the one saving grace that will let you walk out of this unscathed, if you can lie just a little bit about what exactly you found in his data. How you said it in the video might just be enough to throw them off your trail. Plausible deniability."

His brows drew together when I just kept staring back at him. I didn't know how to reply. It was the last thing I'd expected, but knowing about him what I did now, it made perfect sense. It also underscored that the insane idea brewing inside my head that almost petrified me with fear had me on the right track.

"What, disappointed?" he jibed, then added a nasty chuckle. "Trust me, it will be the only thing I ever do to incidentally protect you if you choose not to side with me."

"I guess I should be thanking you now?" I replied, then took two steps forward, bringing me to a stop between him and the door.

He snorted, but the sound held only a little derision and a lot of humor.

"No. Actually, don't, or that last remaining shred of decency deep down inside of me will make me feel an iota of guilt."

"Well, then I won't."

He smirked, which turned into a very typical male grin when I stepped even closer to him, my gaze holding his.

Then I punched both hands into his shoulders, making him lose his balance and stagger back, so I could whip around and launch myself through the still open air lock, back into the lab. My searching hand found the heavy steel door blindly and I wrenched hard on it, forcing the metal to move much faster than it had been intended to. His angry scream made static reverberate through the com, but I did my best to ignore it as I slammed the door shut just as he came after me.

The dull "thunk" when he hit the door made me take an involuntary step back, even though I knew I was safe—or as safe as one could be locked inside a corridor with explosive charges set every couple of yards. It was then that I felt something tug on my left glove. Looking down, I realized that I'd managed to snag it inside the frame of the air lock, just a bit at the tip of my third finger. Bringing it up to my face now, I saw the tiniest sliver of blue peeking through the thick, white outer glove.

Panic instantly clawed at the back of my throat, making breathing almost impossible, but I stomped down on it with the same conviction that had made me start this idiotic maneuver. Now there was no going back, and I would finish this, come what may.

"What the fuck are you doing?" Nate screamed at me, the effect kind of warped as I heard him all too clearly over the com system but could barely see his face through the reinforced window in the door.

"The chemical shower will automatically come on any second now. The cycle takes exactly eight minutes. That's the earliest you can get out of that room. I'd advise against returning to the corridor afterward as I intend to be ready to exit the lab by the time the shower shuts off, and it would be just another wasted eight minutes to wait until you are back outside after I'm already finished."

My voice was still sounding hollow but surprisingly firm, just me relaying facts. I tried to breathe evenly but that was impossible, same as I couldn't unclench my left hand. Objectively, I knew that the positive pressure of the suit would keep me safe, and it wasn't like I intended to dip my hand into anything that could kill me, but rationality wasn't my strong suit right now.

"I repeat, what the fuck are you doing? All the detonators are activated. I've told Dolores to remotely trigger them if anything goes wrong, right fucking now."

Blinking through the layers of plastic and glass separating us, I still managed to catch his gaze.

"I don't give a shit about your detonators. You asked the wrong question, or answered the wrong one. When I asked you just now why you didn't ask me, I meant why you didn't ask me about the vault."

He paused, but I could still hear his fast, angry breaths well enough.

"We checked your clearance. You are not authorized to go into the vault."

I hoped that my answering smile was more serene, and not as insane as I felt right then.

"Your brother did a lot more than rant on that log. He already had all the papers I'd need to take over compiled. Did I mention that I was supposed to work as his assistant? Yes, you knew that already. Well, guess what? I might not be authorized to go into the vault, but I'm damn sure I know his access code."

Just then the shower came on, obscuring him completely except for a blue blob inside the white tiled room.

"You could have told me that five minutes ago," he grated out. There was still a lot of anger in his voice, but it had dimmed somewhat—or maybe that was just the background static caused by the drone of the chemicals pelting down on him.

"Yes, I could have."

With that, I raised my right hand and pushed down at my hip until I found the off-switch of the com through the suit, and turned off my unit.

For several seconds my mind was just blank, fear hanging like a heavy cloud over me.

Closing my eyes, I counted down from five.

As the numbers kept echoing through my head, I admitted—at least to myself—why I was really doing this.

Nate had been right with every single accusation he'd thrown in my face, or only implied. He was right—I was the right woman for his mission, to sift through the data and maybe find the next rung in the ladder that might lead us to who was responsible for all this in the first place. But anyone with my knowledge could do that, anywhere in the world. But only I was here, right now, and I felt that it was my obligation to put things right.

Taking a last, deep breath, I turned around and started walking toward the vault.

Chapter 22

For the last two years, I'd always marveled at one thing—why was my access code for the hot lab the birth date of a dead man?

Of course I could have changed it at any time, but I kept it that way out of some strange kind of sentimentality. Maybe it was the remnants of my hero worship for Raleigh Miller. Maybe it was plain laziness to memorize one more ten-digit number. But it had never even occurred to me that it was anything other than what he'd filled out in the application for my security profile. He should have been my supervisor—of course it had fallen to him to choose my code. And apparently, no one had realized that it was a date—the digits for the year split apart to accommodate those for month and day between them, and a 76 for his name at the beginning.

My right hand shook almost too hard to hit the numbers on the pad, but after the first two, it steadied.

This was just a wild guess, likely an idiotic one. But still. People were lazy. There was a chance that he'd simply used his code, intent on telling me to choose my own once I could change it myself. Only that he'd never survived that day.

The display flashed green, and the door lock disengaged.

Part of me wished that I'd been wrong. Part of me wanted to punch my fist in the air and do a victory dance.

What I actually did was exhale slowly before I opened the door and walked inside.

I'd been in the vault a few times to help Thecla remove stocks from the tanks. Access was restricted to five people—that I'd known of—and few things were as tightly controlled as the access logs. Because the system was so restrictive, I'd hoped that no one had bothered removing a dead man from the roster.

Time was ticking, and not just because of my torn glove. In less than six minutes the chemical shower would turn off, and I didn't doubt that if it took me much longer than that to get out of here, Nate would come after me, and that was something I wanted even less than being locked in here when the detonators went off. I was well aware that I was risking my life right now—but I didn't want to risk his. Not like this.

My opinion of Thecla had been smudged over the course of the last day, but one of her quirks I still held in high regard—like few other people I'd known, she had been highly organized. Counting on that to also hold up where clandestine experiments were concerned, I walked over to the binder that held the protocol of the viral stocks. The sheets were all manually filled in and often updated, whenever someone removed or added something to the tanks, but virtually indecipherable for anyone not knowing what to look for.

I'd not just worked in Particle Production and Processing, thus becoming innately acquainted with anything anyone wanted to handle down here, but also as her right hand, intimately familiar with her abbreviations and cataloging systems. It took me less than forty seconds to find the section in a box in tank five that I was looking for. Thirty-five vials out of the hundred stored in the third box from the bottom were labeled with the abbreviations Raleigh had used in his review paper of their experiments—and evenly distributed among them seven more that held the "XLC" moniker Nate had been talking about, four with a thirty-four, three with a twenty-two attached.

Bingo.

I didn't bother with hooking up an air hose to my suit as I walked across the room to where the tanks were lined up against the wall. The air depot inside my suit would last me another couple of minutes—even with a steady stream leaving through the tear in the glove—and time was of the essence right now. What I did bother with was donning a pair of thick, padded gloves we always used for getting anything in or out of the tanks.

Tank five was partly hidden between four and seven, so I had to pull them aside first to get to my prize. The lid came off with some brute strength, a cloud of frozen air greeting me. I forced myself to slow down as I reached for the metal handle of the rack that held the boxes suspended in liquid nitrogen.

Moving slowly, I pulled the rack out, making sure to tilt it so that the liquid that had run in between the boxes could go right back into the tank, and not slosh all over me instead. Even through the thick, hot suit and gloves, I felt the cold radiating from the tank and rack.

Once I had hoisted the metal contraption that held the compartments out completely, I put the bottom onto the rim of the tank and pulled out the box I was looking for. Through the see-through container top, I could just get a glimpse of the right vial designation inside before the box hazed over.

More out of habit than thought, I carefully put the rack back into the tank, but left it open as I turned around and started my trek out of the vault and over to Biomolecule Production—not because it was the lab I was most familiar with, but because it was the closest.

The explosive charges plastered to the wall right opposite of the biosafety cabinet were ominous at my back as I pushed the box inside, then turned on the hood for good measure. Working under sterile conditions was no longer of any concern, but the directed airflow might help keep what I intended to do now to a lower risk.

Of course there were protocols for how to handle liquid and solid waste in the hot lab, but all of that involved hours of well-calibrated machines working under ideal conditions, and I had no idea when Nate planned to blow the lab up exactly. Simply putting the box into the autoclave had been my first impulse, but the machine might actually shield the contents and vaporize the still frozen virus without inactivating it first. This was one thing I really didn't need free in aerosol form if the explosions damaged the banks of HEPA filters that kept the lab air from contaminating the outside world.

So hands-on decontamination it was, even if the thought alone made the skin on my entire body crawl.

I didn't hesitate long but simply walked over to one of the supply cabinets and got out two open containers and a bottle of hydrogen peroxide. Back at the hood, I put everything inside and finally hooked up to one of the air hoses, just to shut up the voice clamoring inside of my head. Sitting down gingerly, I made sure that I had enough freedom of movement, then shucked the thick freezer gloves and went to work.

Pouring hydrogen peroxide into the two containers went well enough, but my right hand shook so badly that I dropped the pipette twice before I got a good grip on it. With the ruptured glove, everything inside of me screamed for me to keep that hand as far away from the vials as possible, but I was used to handling the pipette with my right and vials with my left, and now was not the time for experimentation.

Taking another shaky, supposedly steadying breath, I pushed the lid off the box, then took out the first vial of the seventh row, marked in handwriting I wasn't familiar with—Raleigh's most likely. Using careful, deliberate motions, I one-handedly unscrewed the cap, then dropped hydrogen peroxide inside until the meniscus of the liquid reached the upper rim. Then I dumped the vial into the second container, refilled the pipette tip from the other, and reached for the second vial.

I doubted that I inhaled more than five times until I had put all the opened, topped-up vials into the other container.

Allowing myself a moment to ease up but not completely lose it, I pushed my chair back and got up, leaving the open containers where they were but taking the box with me into the vault. It was probably stupid to put it back where it belonged, but that would keep the other virus stocks frozen solid, at least for a while. Back outside, I picked up three of the four explosive packs as carefully as I could, and brought them into the vault one by one, to rest at the foot of the tanks now. The last one I deposited inside the still running hood, right next to the container with the now flushed-out vials.

Without hesitating another second, I walked out of the lab, across the main corridor, and into the shower, then hit the button inside to immediately unleash the torrent of chemicals onto me.

The first ten seconds I felt as if an immense weight had been lifted off me, making me light-headed and almost giddy. Then reality caught up with me.

I'd just handled a virus that, as far as I knew, had killed everyone it had come in contact with. Inside a hood that hadn't been sterilized beforehand, that needed a good fifteen minutes for the airflow to stabilize, with my outer glove torn.

Sure, nitrile gloves were also used when handling highly carcinogenic substances like ethidium bromide for DNA tagging in gel electrophoresis because they were durable and virtually impervious to most substances, but I couldn't remember how they'd do with hydrogen peroxide, and all the intellectual reassurance in the world couldn't help me right now. Looking at my left hand, I forced my fingers to splay apart, then started rubbing at them vigorously, as if that could do anything helpful.

The eight minutes until the water shut off were the longest in my life, which, under different circumstances, might have cracked me the hell up, seeing as they came seamlessly after the shortest ten minutes I'd ever whizzed through.

The sign by the door went green just as the last droplets rained down on me, and I was out of the shower before I could even consciously will my muscles into action. I barely noticed the discarded blue suit on the floor next to the hulking, scrub-clad figure waiting for me in the next room before I started tearing my own suit off, already staggering to the sink and engaging the sanitizer flow before I'd completely stepped out of it. My motions were so frantic that I almost didn't get the gloves and tape off. I kept on scrubbing until my skin was a bright, vivid red.

"You have sixty seconds to explain to me what exactly you just did, or I swear, I will make you rue every single of those twenty minutes until your last breath."

His voice came from much too close to me, and it was so full of anger that it was only a hint away from a gravelly growl, but right then I didn't give a shit.

His words made me go still, inside and out, and the first deliberate thing I did was shut off the sanitizer and switch to normal water to rinse off the chemicals that would likely eat away all flesh until only the bones of my hand remained if I kept going like that.

The next thing I did was turn around, which put me face to face with Nate as he was hovering right behind me, our bodies only inches apart. His eyes were narrowed, the look in them livid, and in turn I felt my own rage, fueled by fear and a little elation, rise.

"Forty seconds left," he ground out. I could feel his warm breath fan over my sweat-soaked face.

"What I did, you want to know?" I started, a little proud of myself that my voice only shook half as much as I'd anticipated, and was a lot stronger than a previously strangulee's had a right to be. "I did your fucking job for you, that's what I did."

He leaned closer until I could feel the heat radiating off his body, but we still weren't touching.

"I'm not screwing around with you. Just because I've mostly treated you humanely before doesn't mean that has to go on. Thirty seconds. What the fuck did you do?"

Part of me wanted to just square my jaw and wait in silence, but self-preservation kicked in before three seconds had passed.

"I went into the vault, found the stocks of the different generations of the experiment Raleigh and Thecla used, including the initial viral stocks, and dumped them into hydrogen peroxide. One of the explosive packs is resting right next to that container, so when they all detonate, there will be nothing left of the virus. I can't guarantee that we won't cause a massive outbreak of all kinds of viruses if we blow up the lab and the containment shell, but at least nothing of what might escape outside will be the virus that killed your brother." Stopping to take a deep breath, I moved even closer until my knees bumped into his shins. "You're welcome."

He kept staring into my eyes without blinking, and several muscles jumped in his cheek and jaw as he gnashed his teeth. I didn't know what to expect, but the prospect of finding a sudden and violent end right where I stood wasn't so frightening anymore. I'd just done the single most stupid thing in my entire life, and nothing in the world could make me regret it now.

Five seconds turned into ten, and it became apparent that his set time limit for my explanation had passed without him losing it. He still looked incredibly angry, but some of the fierceness left his posture, and after another moment or two he relaxed a little, although that still left me with not enough space to breathe freely.

Suddenly I felt increasingly tired of all this shit, though the anger churning in the pit of my stomach hadn't dissipated yet.

"If you don't mind, I'd like to take a shower now." Not waiting for his reply, I eased myself out from between him and the sink, angling for the showers. He didn't make a grab for me but followed right on my heels, positioning himself in front of the closed door while I started shedding my clothes in the opposite corner. Unhindered, I stepped into the cool spray of the water.

The last two times that I'd been forced to shower in front of him, I'd done it with my back turned and my shoulders hunched, trying to minimize what he could see of me. Now, I frankly didn't care anymore. Whatever there had been between us—still was and might yet come—I was done acting like a scared little shit.

That indifference was shaken in its foundations when I opened my eyes after submerging my head fully in the stream of water, and found his face right in front of mine. I inhaled sharply and instinctively shied back, incidentally shutting off the shower when I bumped into the faucet. He copied me and moved forward, then put his hands against the shower tile left and right of my head, practically forming a cage around me with his body.

I tried to tell myself that I was not intimidated by this, and did my very best to appear anything but self-conscious, but it was incredibly hard. That he'd gotten rid of his scrubs and underwear in the meantime didn't help.

"Why?" he asked, as if the last minutes of silence hadn't happened between us, his voice deceptively calm.

For some reason, his insolence made my temper flare, letting me almost forget to be frightened out of my wits.

"Why? You drag me through hell and back, and then you have the audacity to ask me why?" I shouted, feeling on some level validated when my spittle landed on his chin. He made a face but didn't flinch, nor moved to wipe it off.

"Yes, I want to know why, and you better—"

"Stop threatening me!" I interrupted him, then punched my fists up and forward, hitting him—not quite efficiently—in the torso. Of course he didn't budge, but the outburst alone made me feel a little more grounded. "Ever since you walked into the fucking atrium I did nothing to defy or anger you, and you keep dumping more and more shit on me! I'm done with that! You wanted my help, now you got it. Either be grateful or not, I don't give a shit. But leave me the fuck alone!"

My tantrum had no effect on him, except to paint a lazy smile onto his face once I shut up. I yearned to slap that right off, but the angle between us made that move impossible, so I didn't even try. Plus, I simply didn't trust myself with touching him again, because physical violence wasn't the only thing the adrenaline pumping through my veins was screaming for.

"Because asking you for an answer yields such productive results?" he jeered.

"You'd be surprised if you tried, but I bet it hasn't even occurred to you to ask!" I shot back.

Nate kept grinning, pretty much confirming my accusation as true. Unable to contain my fury any longer, I lashed out again. This time I must have gotten lucky because he let out a low grunt and moved back slightly, giving me just enough room to duck out from under the cage of his body. I didn't go far, though, seeing as the shower room wasn't that large, and I only needed enough space to breathe. Then I rounded on him, angrier than before, if that was even possible.

"Plausible deniability, my ass! Nothing you did in the last fifteen hours or thirty-eight days had anything to do with me. You have no regard for my physical or emotional well-being, so at least do me the favor of being honest with me! You're just using me, like everyone else! Shit, I'm so sick of this!"

During my tirade he'd turned around, then leaned casually against the wall, that insufferable look still on his face. And, quite obviously, mocking amusement wasn't the only thing he was feeling toward me. I tried to avert my gaze, but the intent alone drove my temper into an even hotter frenzy, turning my shaky inhales into loud pants.

"And, of course, now you have a fucking hard-on. Isn't that just perfect?"

His smile split into a grin, and I think I would have tried to physically hurt him if he'd thrust his hips forward or some shit now, but he refrained.

"A natural reaction I can't really control. Nothing to be upset about. You should be familiar with it by now."

"I'm not upset!" I screamed, then turned to the side and punched the tiled wall as hard as I could. Pain flared through the knuckles of my right hand, but it did absolutely nothing to calm me down. "I'm not upset about your fucking hard-on," I tried to amend, not much calmer while I shook my hand out. "I frankly don't give a shit about what fucked-up thing your body does or not!"

Clearly I couldn't win, as my continuing tirade just kept raising his… mood.

"You are aware that every time you say 'fuck,' my libido gets this extra little incentive to stay up? Among other things."

"I don't fucking care!" I shouted back, then, because I just couldn't get a handle on my frustration—"Fuck!"

His laugh might have been a nice sound under different circumstances, but now it just kept driving me insane.

"You know, of all the things that happened to you since I handed you that cup of coffee, I didn't expect you to lose it over my dick."

He continued to laugh—clearly at me, not with me—fanning the flames of my frustration even more. My entire body was tense and quivered with rage, and if I'd thought myself capable, I would have wrenched one of the soap dispensers from the wall and hurled it at him.

"I am not—" I started, then gave up. "Shut up! Shut the fuck up!"

"That's really helpful," he supplied, but at least toned it down to a wide, typically male grin. I ground my teeth, not ready to accept that as a victory.

"Why do you even—" I began anew, then gestured in the general vicinity of his genitals to limit the amount of f-bombs I could possibly drop in five minutes. "Are you really that screwed in the head that the sight of a beaten and bruised body gets you going?"

I wondered in passing if I'd simply missed that reaction the last two times he'd seen me without clothes, but it would have been impossible to ignore after our first trip through this room, and while I might have been otherwise occupied scrubbing fecal matter out of my hair, I was a hundred percent sure that he hadn't looked at me like that after the shit with Greene had gone down.

Nate snorted, and I kind of welcomed the derision leaking into his voice.

"Trust me, neither physical nor mental abuse is stimulating to me in any way. But you just did the single bravest thing in your life, on top of standing up to me. I can't help but salute you."

"Gee, thanks," I huffed, but had to admit that his reply mollified me. Not completely, but coming from him in particular, that was a fucking huge compliment. And while he was obviously still out to bait me, I could tell that he really meant it. Which just opened another can of worms, one I really would have loved to keep shut right now. His words—his praise—shouldn't have meant anything to me, but they did.

I felt my stomach drop as fear zinged right through my dissipating anger, but this time I didn't allow myself to give in to it. Breathing deeply, I kept staring at Nate across the room, trying to somehow even out my chaotic emotions.

"Still wanna know why I did it?" I asked. He inclined his head, a look of seriousness on his face now. "I did it because I had to. Sure, I could say that it was the safest thing to do because this way I've made sure that nothing of that virus will remain intact whatever happens to the lab around it, but that's not the whole truth."

"Is that even true?" he offered.

"Oh, it's true, but it's not why I did it." Pausing, I tried to make sense of my scrambled thoughts, but calmness didn't necessarily help with that. Looking away from him, I tried to find the right words, but they simply wouldn't come.

"You were right. Every fucking thing you said about me was true. If Raleigh had offered me a piece of that cake, I would have eaten it with gusto, and not cared for more than a few days about the moral implications. That's why I did it. If there's no virus, there's no possibility that I will ever be tempted to mess around with it. Laugh at me if you wish, but that's why I did it."

He studied me for a moment, then shook his head.

"I don't think that's the truth."

"What, you don't believe me?"

He snorted. "You're not lying. You might even think that's why you did it, on some level, but that's not the driving force behind your actions. Or rather, why you stopped letting everyone push you around and finally did what you wanted to do."

"Huh." Skeptical as I tried to sound, his words resonated with something deep inside of me and brought with it a new wave of emotion. "I'm so sick of all this shit," I muttered, letting my head fall back against the wall behind me. Staring at the ceiling wasn't very enlightening, so I caught his gaze as I went on instead. "I'm so sick of being taken for granted. So sick of being ignored. There's no one out there in the entire fucking world who even knows who I am, who knows what I want or what motivates me, what gets to me."

No one but him.

I wasn't sure if that epiphany made me want to smile or cry, but I knew that, either way, I was screwed.

That didn't stop me from pushing myself away from the wall, and it didn't make my steps falter as I crossed the room. The entire time

I held his gaze, didn't even try to look away or act coy. There was no need for that, and I doubted that as raw as I felt right then, I could have mimed the seductress.

There were a million reasons why I should have stayed on my side of the room, showered, gotten dressed. I was injured, maybe even infected with one of the most gruesome viruses in existence. He was directly responsible for all the shit that had happened to me that had led to those injuries, or had done nothing to prevent them from happening. He hadn't contradicted me once when I ticked off his shortcomings as a decent human being. I wasn't even sure if I liked him, on whatever fucked up level.

None of that mattered.

I did what I did because I chose to—I wanted to—and that was enough.

My breath caught in my throat as I stopped right in front of him, my neck craned slightly to keep eye contact. I was close enough to feel the heat coming off his body, close enough that when I blew out my breath, it stirred an errant strand of hair below his ear. I had to hand it to him, he'd given up taunting me with that grin of his, and what I saw in his eyes was enough to make me forget all those million reasons I'd chosen to ignore.

He saw me.

Me, with all my faults, shortcomings, the mistakes I'd made; all my strengths, my integrity; he saw it, accepted it, wanted it.

"Ah, fuck this," I muttered when I felt my heartbeat start to race. "No. Fuck me."

Reaching up, I threaded the fingers of my still aching hand through his hair and pulled his head down so I could kiss his lips. He responded immediately, his arms coming around me, pulling me close, his mouth eagerly opening to mine. Throwing all pretense of decency overboard, I moaned, pulling myself even harder against him with my free arm wrapping around his lower back.

From there on it was all primal need, no holding back, no tenderness, but every touch made me yearn for more. My shoulder smacked into the wall when he flipped us over, which I rewarded with a sharp rake of my nails down his back. He let out a most delicious groan and nipped my bottom lip before pulling his head back far enough to catch my gaze. His eyes held challenge, but I bet, so did mine.

Reaching down between us, I wrapped my hand around his cock and started stroking him, intent on not looking away. He rewarded me with a fucking sexy grin before he leaned in so he could kiss and bite down on the soft skin at the side of my neck. I couldn't help laughing when he hit a ticklish spot, which he seemed to like, judging from how he thrust into my hand.

Already feeling great but definitely needing more, I shifted my balance to my right side so I could hitch up my left leg. He caught on quickly and moved one hand under my thigh to support me. I squeezed a little harder, then leaned back more firmly into the wall, bracing myself. My breath caught in my throat when I felt his cock rub over my clit, then slide lower to almost where I needed him to be. He moved in to kiss me again, deep and demanding, but suddenly stopped with a wide grin on his face.

I frowned right back. "What? You haven't forgotten how this works, right?"

Still grinning as he held my gaze, he plucked my hand from around him and dropped it on his shoulder instead.

"I just realized I never even took you out to dinner first."

Unable to remain serious, I cracked a smile myself.

"So raiding vending machines together is not your idea of—"

Whatever snide comeback I'd planned on delivering I lost when he thrust forward, sheathing himself inside of me. I tensed, then relaxed, and didn't give a shit whether he laughed at my moan or not.

"Shut up," he whispered into my mouth, then followed up with his tongue, and things got a lot more frantic and raw.

I didn't hold back, didn't even think for a moment how I must look or sound as I moved against him, needing more, exploring, reacquainting, taking. He gave as good as he got, and before long had me forget about the ice cold wall behind me or the water droplets falling off me. With his lips stifling my shout, I came hard around him, which whipped him into even more of a frenzy. It didn't take him much longer to reach his own climax.

For a few seconds, our ragged panting was the only sound in the room, then he reached over to the faucet to my left and turned on the water. I made a face as the spray stung my eyes, but before I could complain, he silenced me with a last, almost tender kiss.

Still breathing hard, I looked back up into his eyes as he moved away, but his arms stayed around me, keeping most of my body melded to his. I wanted for him to say something, but he didn't. He just kept staring at my face as if he was committing it to memory.

"I don't want to die," I whispered, the water almost drowning out the words.

He gave me a sad smile in return, but when he opened his mouth, his voice was strong, reassuring,

"And you're not going to. Not on my watch."

I wished I shared that optimism.

"I was inside the hot lab for twelve minutes with a ruptured glove. And even if it was smooth sailing so far, I doubt that we'll walk out of here just so."

Now his usual grin was back.

"'We?'" he echoed.

The temptation to roll my eyes at him was strong.

"Yes, we. Unless you've changed your mind and discard me like a rag once you're done."

He made a considering face but started to laugh when I poked a finger into his obliques.

"Honestly, I'd rather keep you around. Once you're mad beyond reason you're a lot of fun, and I could use another element full of erratic randomness in my life."

"Aw, so sweet!" I teased, then stretched so I could plant a kiss on his nose. He foiled the maneuver by nudging my face away, but then made up for it with another deep, lingering kiss. When he let go—his hands sliding across my body before losing contact—it felt less like a good-bye, and more like a promise of more later.

My mind swam with a million things that I might have said, and he looked at me for a moment as if he wanted to reply to all of them, but in the end we just turned around and cleaned up. The neurotic part of my brain resurfaced, telling me that scrubbing myself raw was the only sane thing to do, but I kept my motions deliberate and efficient instead.

If my stunt really turned out to be fatal, no amount of disinfectant would change that now.

Chapter 23

I was done dressing well ahead of Nate, with only my underwear and other set of scrubs to don. That left me with a few blissful moments of rest, sitting on the changing room bench with nothing else to do than watch him dress—and feel the photo in my back pocket sear a hole into my conscience. I didn't even reach for it, but the reason for my partial discomfort must have been quite obvious as Nate sent me a rather nasty smirk as he started buttoning up his shirt.

"Regrets already?"

I shook my head, chewing briefly on my chapped bottom lip to find words that didn't want to be found.

"You mean because I technically cheated on my girlfriend? For, what, the tenth time? Twelfth? The only thing that's different is that now I know what you see in me. Kind of."

"Quite literally, I'd say," he offered, then leaned closer, almost as if he wanted to kiss me, but I didn't fall for it. Whatever had happened in the shower, that moment was gone, and while the balance between us had definitely shifted, I couldn't see him necking on the job. "Practically, and quite thoroughly, if I might say so. Remember, I was there."

"How could I forget?" I squeaked, then sent him a withering glare that he, of course, ignored. "I don't regret it. I don't feel guilty."

"Then why are you fidgeting as if you were sitting on a lump of hot coal?"

I shrugged, not quite sure myself.

"Maybe because on some level I feel like I should?"

"I think you're beyond such bullshit," he observed succinctly. "You never looked particularly shaken up in the past."

"Well, it wasn't like I never felt like I didn't do something wrong," I said, probably a little too sharply not to sound defensive. "Besides, that would still make me the much more faithful partner in our relationship."

A look of surprise crossed his face.

"You knew she was cheating on you?"

And obviously I hadn't been the only one.

"I'm not stupid, and I'm not completely oblivious. I was never home, and Sam has always been the more socially needy of the two of us. She always showers the moment she gets home, but I could often still smell them on her hair, or her clothes. And every time, I kind of hoped that she'd finally met the one she'd break up with me for, because then I wouldn't have to do it myself."

He halted in lacing up his combat boots, his knee right next to my head.

"Why didn't you?"

"That's the big question, now isn't it?" I shrugged, not because I didn't know, but because admitting the knowledge behind it to myself made me feel empty inside. Yet if I'd learned anything today, it was that I was done lying to myself. "It's not that I don't love her. Still do. But things change. People change. It was convenient to live together, have someone to share the rent with, to snuggle up to when I got lonely. Do the dishes, groceries, not be the pathetic thirty-something single at the Christmas party."

He regarded me for a moment longer, already losing interest.

"Bullshit."

"But it's true," I surmised, then thought about it. "You know, it kind of started as an act of rebellion on my side. Backfired, too. I mean, sure, the sex was great and I definitely swing that way, too, but I guess it was my attempt to draw a line and emancipate myself from the girl I'd been in high school. Experiment with your lesbian college roommate, so cliché, so daring. Only that everyone was like, 'oh, I'm so happy for you!' and 'this explains so much!', as if not being the most promiscuous being on Earth and out to get a science degree said anything about my sexual preferences. But they wouldn't stop there, no, they went all, 'and she's so good for you!', and suddenly she was the convenient excuse for everything I didn't want to shove into people's faces."

"And then I came along and burst your happy little bubble," he observed.

I met his grin with a bland look.

"Maybe. You certainly shook me hard enough to wake me up from it."

He considered that for a moment, leaning in again, and this time his face was definitely close enough to touch.

"You're not going to fall back asleep again. You may bitch and scream at me all you want, but deep down you love the woman you finally admit you are. That's why you stood up for yourself and kicked the living shit out of Greene. That's why you went back into the vault. And that's why you fucked me again. I don't suffer from any illusions of grandeur that make me believe that I have a magical dick that can just-like-that change your life, but I'm not blind or oblivious, either."

Staring at him from up close, I was sorely tempted to try to engage him in another go, but then left it at a smile.

"I doubt that your ego needs any stroking, but if anyone's cock could change my life, it's yours."

"You say the sweetest things," he remarked, then got up to put on his shoulder holster and check his gun before he put it inside. It still made me uncomfortable so I got up and left the room, ending up in the corridor outside right next to the viewing window of the main hot lab corridor. Except for the explosives, it looked as clean and serene as always, luring the watcher into a false sense of safety.

Nate joined me seconds later, obviously still not ready to let me out of his sight. He got out his radio and spoke into it, but the usual hiss of static didn't reply. He got out his phone next, and a frown appeared on his face.

"You'll likely not get a good signal down here. The shell of the hot lab screws with reception somewhat badly."

He shook his head. "I am getting a signal, which is disconcerting in and of its own."

I didn't know what to reply to that, but just then something in the corridor behind the viewing window caught my attention. Squinting inside, I wasn't sure what it had been, but then I saw it again.

Something flashed red. Something at the detonator controls.

My blood turned to ice.

"Uh, are they supposed to do that?" I asked. Even before I could explain myself so any sentient human being could maybe understand, Nate's head whipped around and he stared straight at the explosives, cutting right to the chase.

"Shit."

Just then his phone chirped with the most annoying message notification tone I'd ever heard, but instead of going for it, Nate hit a button on the side of his watch.

"Did the lights come on just now, or were they on when you got here already?"

"I don't—" I started to say, but then shook my head. "Just now. I'm sure."

He gave a curt nod, then grabbed the sleeve of my scrubs and started dragging me toward the connective tunnel that would bring us back to the main building. I caught myself soon enough and quickened my step so that I was walking next to him. He let go to type something into his phone.

"Care to explain what is going on?"

That something was wrong was clear from his reaction, and when his face darkened after looking at the phone display, I figured it must have been something worse than just a distraction. I really didn't like this.

"We're about to lose control of the atrium."

"You what?"

He gave me a quick grin, likely because he'd caught my switch back to excluding myself in his merry band of murdering miscreants.

"The red lights you saw coming on are the detonators arming themselves. Except for manual dismantling, nothing can stop the countdown now. It was triggered automatically when the power supply to the control station was cut. Seeing as it was both running on generators and leeching off the main building power grid, it means that someone shot the fucking computers into the stone age. Whether we're ready or not, the last phase of the plan has begun."

"Last phase?" I echoed like a deranged parrot.

"Evacuation."

"Shit." Suddenly his brisk pace was like a crawl, and it took me a lot to stop myself from launching into a run. "You said the detonators were remote controlled before? How long do we have?"

He checked his watch.

"Twenty-six minutes and ten seconds."

"Shit!" I said a lot more emphatically, and now I did speed up. He kept up with me easily, and, damn him, was even grinning a little. "That's not funny! Even using the fastest, most direct route it takes almost ten minutes to get to the atrium from here!"

"Nine minutes and thirty-five seconds at a brisk walk, but it's unlikely that we'll be able to maintain that speed. If they're in the atrium, they'll start screening the corridors around it immediately, and we'll run into those outward-expanding search parties before we get there."

"Is there no other way out?"

He shook his head.

"Nope. The only way to ensure that no one could threaten our operation was to turn the entire complex into a one-exit-only affair. Don't worry, I'm not ready to roll over and let them fuck me in the ass just yet."

By then we'd reached the upper end of the corridor, and much to my dismay Nate stopped there. Getting out his knife, he pried open one of the wall panels, revealing a cavity behind it that was full to the brim with weapons. My eyes might have bugged a bit as I skimmed over at least thirty handguns and rifles neatly stacked in a floor-to-ceiling rack built into the wall itself.

"Just how much planning did you put into this operation?" I murmured, more to myself than him.

"Hopefully enough to get us out mostly unscathed," came his blithe reply.

Instead of going for the rifles, as I'd expected, he got a small black box out of the bottom of the panel, which turned out to be another radio. Several lights flashed on it, and after fiddling with the controls, shouts—mixed with the staccato of gunfire and static—came out of the speaker, startling me.

"Status?" Nate barked into the radio—and then we had to wait for endless seconds that I felt we really didn't have until he received a reply, from Pia, it sounded like. The techie couldn't have managed such a bark.

"Incursion. At least fifty troops, more coming in through the secondary entry. We shot their fucking tank to so much scrap metal, but the perimeter is breached. I repeat, we have a breach—"

Whatever else she reported got drowned out by an explosion much closer to us than I was comfortable with, staggering me as the building around me shook, making dust and two ceiling panels come down. With my pulse spiking, I at first thought it must have been the hot lab that had blown way too early, but the epicenter of the explosion seemed to have come from a different direction than behind us. Nate looked over at me briefly, then reached into his pocket to get out a half-full pack of earplugs and offered it to me after taking two differently colored ones out himself. "It's going to get loud either way. You might want to preserve what's left of your hearing, which likely isn't all that much, anyway."

I didn't protest as I accepted the plugs and squeezed two of them into my ear canals.

"What was that? One of yours?" I figured he'd know I was talking about the detonation.

"Nope," he replied, loading up on magazines. "But I'm sure we'll find out very soon."

Breaking eye contact, he got two of the rifles out, and held one out to me. I shied back as if he'd pointed it, muzzle first, in my direction.

"No way! I'm not touching that thing!"

He gave me a sharp look, but then shrugged and slung the straps of both weapons over his chest.

"Then you better hope that they believe in taking prisoners."

Like that, we were on our way again, until we reached the first open door leading to one of the ransacked labs. It was me this time who called for a halt. Ducking inside, I looked around, then grabbed two lab coats from beside the door and tried to hand him the larger one. Nate frowned.

"And what should I do with that?"

"Put it on?" I snarked back as I shrugged into mine. It was too tight, but it would hold up on a brief inspection. "They're looking for terrorists who are armed to the teeth. They likely have instructions to rescue any remaining hostages, and anyone else who might have been hiding inside the building for the last couple of hours. They don't know that you've been through the entire building, but then you can't be sure if you really got everyone in the first place. Took you three hours to drag me in, remember?"

Nate just gave me a blank look. "They're not here to rescue you."

"Well, maybe not me personally—" I started, a little chagrined, but he shook his head.

"Trust me. This is not a rescue operation. They didn't even waste a minute negotiating."

We started walking again, maybe a little slower than before, but still faster than I'd usually traversed these halls.

"You're sure about this?"

He nodded. "I'm starting to have a really bad feeling about this."

"You don't say?" I jeered, but when he continued to give me a blank stare, I felt my stomach seize up. "Define 'bad feeling,' please?"

"I've been part of my fair share of rescue missions. This doesn't feel like one."

Just then, another explosion rocked the building, making me seriously afraid that it was only a question of time, not more explosives, until it would come down on us. A moment of eerie quiet followed, but it was suddenly broken up by the staccato sound of an automatic rifle going off, quickly followed by a few more. Nate stared into the direction the racket was coming from, then pushed me into making a right turn into a crossing corridor, further away from it.

"What do we do if we run into a search party?" I asked after we paused at the next corridor crossing, and Nate signaled me to continue on after checking that the way was clear. We took another turn to the right.

"We try to evade. If that fails, we shoot our way out."

As much as I hated that idea, I didn't put up any protest.

"Couldn't we try to talk our way out of it?"

I never got an answer to that question, as just then a group of three soldiers stepped into the hallway ahead of us, their rifles up as they scanned their surroundings—two in front, one covering their rear. Nate cursed low under his breath as he grabbed my arm, yanking me through the open door we'd just passed. My heart was suddenly in my throat, and I let him lead me through the lab and back the way we had come at a half-crouched run. The lab was a multi-room affair, allowing us to travel from room to room without having to go back outside into the hallway until we were back at the previous intersection. He motioned me to remain behind, sneaking up to the door to peek outside. The tension in his shoulders was enough to tell me that our small evasive maneuver hadn't worked. At his gesture I joined him, crouching low beside him.

"They're scanning the individual rooms, so we have maybe twenty seconds. One of them is guarding the hallway so we can't run across. Besides, they are much too close to the connection to the hot lab. I need to collapse the tunnel to keep them out of there."

"Are you crazy? There can't be that much time left!" I hissed, mangling half of the words as fear made me utter them way too fast.

"They have enough time to simply yank out at least half of the detonators if they are stupid enough to just walk into the lab," he shot back. "Then the explosion pattern will likely only destroy but not cave in the interior of the concrete shell." He looked outside once more, then gave me a pointed look. "I need a diversion."

"Diversion?" I whisper-squeaked, but it was already too late. Taking hold of the lapels of my coat, he pulled me to my feet, then shoved me ahead of him out of the door. Fright and surprise alike made me squeal, then crouch down and raise my arms protectively over my head.

Shouts greeted me as the soldier patrolling the hallway saw me, his rifle now trained steadily on me. His colleagues joined him moments later, and their determined expressions made me freeze all over. I couldn't even look behind me to check whether Nate was still crouching in the lab or had made it outside and into the other hallway. With my pulse thundering in my ears, it was impossible to hear anything but the slow, deliberate steps of the advancing soldiers.

"Please don't shoot me!" I finally got out when my mind kicked in. Peeking through the cage of my arms, I saw that they were only a couple of yards away now. While the middle one still had his full attention on me, the one to his left kept glancing into the labs, while the other had his eyes trained down the corridor. They clearly didn't perceive me as threat enough to engage their entire attention.

"What are you doing here, Miss?" the one still looking at me asked.

"I've been hiding. In the lab." I gestured at the rooms to my right. "Please help me! You're here to rescue us, right?"

He started to nod, but then his brows drew together underneath the brim of his helmet.

"What makes you think that we're not terrorists?"

Maybe it was my paranoia, but my mind immediately skipped to the suspicion that he knew that I'd maneuvered myself into the gray area between the two fronts. I didn't need Nate's skepticism to add to my paranoia, but suddenly it seemed twice as significant as before. But all that was nonsense, of course, and I was quick to tell him.

"Your gear looks different." And it did. While Nate's people were equipped with a more heterogenous mix of camo and black, they all wore dark tan colored clothes with black patches and vests over it. Only then did I realize that they also carried gas masks with a separate rebreather unit at their belts. They definitely knew what might be waiting for them in here—lending even more credibility to what Nate had explained.

The guy who'd been checking the labs had now reached me, and after glancing around the intersection—clearly seeing nothing—he returned to stand beside his comrade. The third still kept his attention on the hallway, but in a more relaxed fashion. The first two exchanged looks, and when the other shrugged, the one who'd been talking to me reached for the radio attached to his shoulder.

"We have a survivor. She says that she's been hiding out here for the entire attack," he said after exchanging whatever codes their operation was running under. I felt relief flood me when he didn't outright call me a liar, but he still sounded wary. I couldn't hear the reply he received via the ear piece in his helmet, but it must have been less enthusiastic.

"Checking now," he confirmed, reaching for something on his belt that looked like a field version of a mobile phone. Briefly glancing up, he asked for my name.

I froze.

Should I give them my real name? The coat I was wearing had an ID tag that was clearly not my name and photo, but I hadn't cared to check it before I'd shrugged it on, and looking at it now would make me twice as suspicious as anything else. Sure, I could have changed coats, but explaining that would sound like lying immediately. Then again, being unable to do something as simple as tell them my name wasn't exactly casting me in a good light, either.

Before I managed to make up my mind, the second soldier, who had been glancing at the device as well let out a curse, immediately training his rifle at me. The one who'd scanned the corridor mirrored him, while the first did a double check between me and the screen. When he spoke up again, his voice had hardened.

"Miss, is your name Brianna Lewis?"

"Y-yes?" I more asked than stated. Shit.

Either I looked guilty as hell, or the sudden increase in tension that hung in the air was just my imagination, but it pushed my pulse into cardiac arrest threat territory. My arms started to shake, and it got increasingly harder to keep them lifted.

"Have you been cooperating with the terrorists?" the soldier bit out, now clearly hostile as he pocketed his phone and joined the other two in aiming straight at me.

"N-no?" I gave equally unconvincing testimony. His eyes narrowed, and words started falling over my lips in a near unintelligible stammer. I didn't even know what they were accusing me of, or what they could possibly know, and in the back of my mind there was still that rapidly decreasing countdown. "They held me at gunpoint, they forced me. They killed my friend, for fuck's sake! I don't know what you think you know, but I didn't do anything!"

A muscle spasm zinged through my left calf from staying crouched for too long, and with a grunt I sank to my knee, trying to shift my balance. That they didn't immediately shoot me was pure luck.

"Stay where you are, Miss! Don't move!"

I was frightened enough to have a panic attack right there, but I'd never been able to cry on command, something that would have been very useful right now. What I could do was stop trying to compose myself. I might have laid it on a little heavy. Having a whimpering, shaking woman kneeling on the floor in front of them clearly did move the soldiers somewhat, even if they were half convinced that she was one of the bad guys. My only chance was to try to capitalize on that.

"Please, you have to help me, you have to believe me! You have to get me out of here! You have no idea how horrible those last hours have been, what they did to me, what—"

A hollow boom sounded from behind and to my right, loud enough to make me scream. I felt the vibrations under my knees, but it wasn't enough to shake the walls around us. I figured it was the detonation Nate had been talking about, and wondered if it had worked. The explosions that had started his operation had been a lot more forceful, same as the ones just minutes ago. Then again, they had done a lot more damage to a far greater area of the building, or so I figured.

The soldiers were on high alert immediately, the one in the middle barking a status report into his radio. Their rifles were still trained in my general direction, but no longer straight at me. I still didn't dare to move, trying not to set them off.

"Sir, what shall we do with her? Response teams four and five are zeroing in on our position." He listened, and the look on his face turned grim. "Acknowledged, Sir. We're not taking any prisoners until the situation has been secured."

That was the moment I lost faith in humanity.

"What? You can't just shoot me!" I shouted, dumbstruck.

While a lie, my cover story was plausible, and even if they knew that I'd been a hostage, I could have managed to flee and hide since then. I wasn't carrying any weapons, nor had I done anything to threaten them. In the soldier's eyes I saw the knowledge of all that, but also the conviction to follow his orders without question.

"Please, don't," I repeated, coming to my feet slowly. This just couldn't be happening. Not like this. Not after—

Coming from the other side of the corridor—the direction the explosions had originated from—I heard the most toe-curling mixture between a howl and a moan.

My head whipped to the side as I felt a deeper kind of fear grip me. This just sounded too much like what that… thing that Raleigh had turned into had sounded like. Just like—

A strong hand came down on my shoulder, making me yelp, but before I could wrench myself away, Nate had pushed me behind him, putting himself between me and the soldiers. That in itself was strange enough—more or less—but while he still held one of the rifles, he hadn't pointed it at the soldiers. He looked tense, but it was a different tension than before.

"Trust me, you don't want to do that," he said, his eyes fixed on the guy in control.

"Says who?" the soldier bit back, adjusting his grip on his weapon.

The howl repeated itself, cutting off when gunfire made me flinch, and resumed—much, much closer. As much as the three rifles trained on us bothered me, the sheer menace in the sound just made me look down the corridor.

A woman was standing there. I'd never seen her before, but she didn't look like she belonged here, wearing a summer dress and cardigan, but no shoes. Why my mind latched on to that detail, I didn't know, but it only took me a moment to take in the rest. Like the fact that dust mixed with blood and what looked like vomit were covering the front of the dress, and there were dark streaks all over her cheeks and neck, down from her eyes and ears. She took a staggering step forward, moving as if her limbs weren't quite under her control—until her gaze fell on me. Immediately, the vacant stare turned to one of boiling rage, and she let out a scream as she launched herself toward us.

"Nate," I started, looking away briefly, but no one was paying attention to me, still locked in their unmatched staring contest as the men were. A little louder—and with a rising note of panic—I repeated myself. "Nate!"

"What?" he bit out, his head swiveling to me—until he saw what was limping with surprising speed toward us. "Shit."

He still hesitated for a moment but then swung around, now training the rifle at the woman.

"What the—" the soldier I had been talking to asked, but was quickly cut off when the one who had been checking the corridor also saw her, and he and Nate started shooting in unison. Even with the ear plugs the rifles going off physically hurt, but my mind was too occupied with what they were shooting at to care much. Several bullets hit the woman and the wall beside her, making her body jerk—but not stop. If anything, the howl she let out was even louder, and it took a direct shot right between the eyes to make her go limp and drop to the floor, missing the entire back of her head.

For several seconds straight, all I could do was stare—and shake, as fear made muscles all over my body want to jump into action. My eyes were glued to the body on the floor, unable to take in anything else.

From up close, I could clearly see that it had been vomit, yes, and the darker stains on her legs and the lower part of her dress looked like… other bodily fluids. Even with the dust covering her entire body, it was evident that she had been sweating, and in the light streaming in from one of the labs, her skin looked pallid and sick.

Maybe it was simply because of the video that Nate had shown me, but there was one very distinct term that came to my mind, and it wasn't one that I'd ever thought to utter in earnest.

The sharp bark of male voices got me to tear my eyes away from her and focus on the now much more immediate threat of being shot—but while the two soldiers who hadn't fired a shot still had their rifles trained on us, the third had taken on a more relaxed, if still alert pose, and his eyes were firmly trained on Nate.

"What the hell are you doing here, Lieutenant?" he asked. His tone held a lot more bewilderment than surprise.

"Saving your ass, as usual, Martinez," Nate replied, offering him a toothy, if surprisingly real, smile before he focused on the other two soldiers, clearly dismissing any danger that might have come from his former… comrade? "Whatever you came here to do, forget about it. We need to get out of here."

The third soldier lowered his rifle ever so slightly, but the one in command didn't seem ready to let anyone boss him around who wasn't clearly above him in the chain of command—but the way his eyes kept flickering to the body on the floor spoke of a great deal less bravado than he showed otherwise.

"Just because you—"

"The building's gonna blow in less than seventeen minutes," Nate informed him succinctly, his gaze never straying from the soldier's face. "Even if you try to make it through the rubble that used to be the tunnel down to the BSL-4 lab, you'll never disarm all the charges we've set down there."

Part of me wanted to protest getting so openly included in the ongoings, but that number—seventeen—was much more alarming.

That neither of the three soldiers looked particularly disturbed just hammered down where the focus of their efforts lay—and it certainly wasn't in rescuing anyone.

Nate's radio went off again, giving a burst of static that made me jump before I could make out words in it.

"We have issues, boss," an undefined male voice reported between heavy pants, cutting off when several bursts of gunfire drowned it out. "Get that fucking thing off—argh!" More gunfire followed, interspersed with a disturbing amount of wet, crunching sounds, then steps echoing through a hallway as a different voice came on. "Several unidentified hostiles incoming! I repeat, hostiles incoming! The parking deck and loading bay are breached. We'll try to seal them off again but—"

The radio went silent, and I wasn't sure if that was a relief or not.

Martinez and the third soldier exchanged glances, then both stared at their comrade.

"Sixteen and counting," Nate informed them, his voice dry but with a hard note to it now. I could see the tension mounting in his shoulders from where I still stood slightly behind him.

"Screw it," the last soldier grumbled, turning around as he got back on his com. "Team eight is retreating. I repeat, team eight is retreating. They already set the charges. Sixteen minutes and counting."

Nate didn't hesitate to fall in behind the soldiers, and thankfully they set a pace that was almost too brisk to still call a walk. Over the drone their boots made, more gunfire and screaming sounded in the distance, but thankfully the corridors we crossed next were as deserted as when Nate and I had come up from the hot lab.

But what the ever-loving fuck was going on here?

We crossed two more intersections, then reached one of the connective hallways that went right by the seminar rooms below the cafeteria. Nate whistled loudly and held out his arm, making me stop and wait while he jerked his head to the side, indicating to the soldiers to take a right turn again. Now taking the lead, he veered back into the rabbit warren of the labs.

"Too much open space," he commented as I eyed him askance.

The fact that neither of the soldiers rebelled to him taking charge was telling.

The sound of scuffling feet—a lot, like ten or so, and the steps didn't sound like combat boots—picked up ahead of us, making Nate duck through a cell culture lab to traverse to yet another corridor. On the other side he stopped again and checked before we went on. I was glad that he knew where he was going, because I would have lost my orientation and likely run straight into the arms of, well, whatever else was out and about in the hallways.

Nate relaxed a little when we took another turn, and I realized that we'd made it into the wing that housed my workspace. The ground floor layout was different than the other levels, but still more familiar than any other part of the complex except for the hot lab.

"How much time do we still have?" I asked, trying not to sound too frantic, but failing.

Instead of replying, he got his radio out. "Status atrium."

It took endless ten seconds until static changed to a pressed, female voice. The Ice Queen, I assumed.

"We've a barricade by the hostages. All three staircases are blocked. Good luck getting out of there."

My stomach sank at the realization of what that meant, but Nate looked less grim than a second ago. Jerking his head to the side, he backtracked our steps for half a corridor, then went left and straight, wrenching open the door to one of the smaller stairwells.

"Didn't she just say that the staircases are blocked?" I asked.

"But this one's not connected to the atrium. Besides, how many staircases does the atrium have?"

He took the steps two at a time, forcing me to run after him if I wanted to keep up. I did a quick calculation in my head, not sure about the answer.

"Either six or eight."

"Six," he confirmed my guess. "Not three."

"She could have meant on one side?" I hedged, not sure why I was even contradicting him.

We reached the third floor—my floor—and Nate eased the door open slowly to look outside, then motioned me through.

"It was a message. All exits into the atrium are blocked except one, and that's our way out."

Slinking through the hallways I'd been walking through every day for the last fourteen months was eerie, but I tried not to let the familiarity lull me into complacency. Each step carried us closer to the atrium, and if I wasn't mistaken, we were angling for the side that was farthest away from the entrance. The intermingling sounds of voices and gunfire were more prevalent the closer we got, and it occurred to me that neither Nate nor the soldier had told their people to stand down. Our momentary truce seemed all the more temporary for that. Suddenly, having the soldiers at my back felt a lot less safe than seconds ago.

Then we finally reached the glass cathedral, and my pulse sped up with a twin feeling of hope and anxiety. I realized that we were standing roughly where I'd been peeking down into the atrium hours ago, not quite sneaky enough to avoid detection, which had ultimately lead to my capture.

A lot had happened since then, also to the structural integrity of the atrium.

Half of the opposite wall lay in ruins, partly caved in, glass shattered. At ground level I could make out what looked as if a giant had torn a hole through the wall, and a tank was stuck inside, flames and smoke billowing out of the hatch. The wall seemed to have collapsed around it, effectively closing off the breach it had presumably created, leaving barely enough room for a single person to squeeze through—if they didn't mind getting roasted or dying of smoke inhalation first.

Rubble, pieces of equipment, and at least fifteen dead or seriously wounded people in combat gear—and at least twice the number of other bodies—lay strewn across the floor, and an acrid smell made my nose itch and eyes tear up. Looking up and down the gallery we had stepped onto, I saw two more bodies on the floor to our left, with three of the not-quite-civilians standing over them.

Nate was shooting at them the moment I became aware of their presence, downing two. The soldiers took care of the last one. I shied back and tried to flatten myself against the wall, but Nate grabbed my arm and yanked me down into a crouching position instead. And not a moment too soon, as a barrage of fire opened from below, the bullets hitting the wall where my head had just been. The glass of the gallery balustrade cracked where a few of the less well-aimed shots struck, but it held, now looking like the safety glass car windshields are made of.

I was frantic with fear, the impulse to run contracting muscles all over my body, but the hand wrapped tightly around my forearm grounded me again. Nate didn't look at me, his eyes and the gun in his hand still trained on the heap of bodies a couple of yards down the walkway.

"Care to tell your guys to stand down?" Nate asked Martinez, but only got a shrug back from him when the soldier with the radio didn't react. Ignoring them for the moment, Nate turned back to me. "There are at least thirty of those fuckers down there, just waiting for us to be stupid enough to get up. Across the atrium, right opposite of us, there are four more. You need to listen carefully, and do exactly what I say, when I say it."

My ragged breaths were almost loud enough to drown out his low voice, but I felt myself nod as soon as he fell silent.

"Okay."

Just then, one of the doors of the seminar rooms burst open, spilling out an entire group of screaming, rabid figures onto the gallery, maybe ten feet from us. The soldiers on the other side of the gallery decided that they'd given us enough attention and seamlessly joined the full barrage of shots that went off from all around me. Clapping my hands over my ears, I shrieked, panic clawing at my throat. The bodies fell one by one, creating yet more obstacles, but as soon as the last one stopped jerking from the bullets that hit it, Nate grabbed my arm and started pulling me forward, using a half scuttle, half crouch as he led me around them. I tried not to look too closely, but even so it was impossible not to notice that at least half of them had blood smeared all over the lower halves of their faces—and a few were missing chunks from their necks and exposed arms with gaping, bloody wounds left behind.

Then Nate's phone made that annoying sound from before again, prompting him to utter a curse low under his breath.

"I hate to break it to you, but that was our ten-minute countdown. We have roughly three minutes to get down onto the ground floor, or this is going to end badly."

"Three minutes?" I shrieked, my voice breathless enough not to carry far, but I hated that squeak.

Something moved underneath the bodies, making me scramble after him as fast as I could, the soldiers hot on our heels.

Right before we reached the back corner of the gallery, shots were fired from the other side, whizzing past our unprotected backs. Nate cursed but kept his rifle pointed toward the floor as the soldiers from the other side of the gallery came toward us, moving as cautious as their comrades at our back—and a lot more intent on the dead than us. That he seemed to trust them all of a sudden made me incredibly wary, but then I remembered the police sniper on the roof. Just how many people did he know that some—like Martinez—felt confident to just fall in line with him if they got a good incentive for it?

Another of the doors behind the pile of bodies burst open, spilling an entire crowd out onto the gallery. The moment they saw us, they started surging forward, a mass of bodies so uncoordinated that they hindered each other immediately. Shots were fired, but

Nate kept pulling me forward, while the others kept up with us, providing cover fire.

That put us directly next to the bank of elevators, and I finally got what exit route he'd been talking about.

"Shit, no!" I murmured, my voice getting drowned out by the racket all around me.

"That should keep them busy," Nate grunted, then straightened and threw something at the mob. It dropped down right in front of them, then went up in smoke. "Incendiary grenade," he pointed out, tossing another one over the destroyed glass railings to the soldiers below. One of those with us was rattling off a frantic status report, the words "stand down, stand down!" less of a relief than I'd thought them to be.

Dropping his rifle so that it hung across his chest, Nate crossed the last feet to the elevators. Beyond him, fire and smoke continued to obscure the other side of the gallery, hiding what possibly lurked around there.

Shoving his fingers between the closed elevator doors, Nate started prying them open, one of the soldiers quickly stepping up to help. By the time I'd reached him, they'd come apart enough to let someone through sideways.

Into the empty elevator shaft, that was.

Just looking down gave me vertigo, and my fingers convulsed into a fist. I must have let out some sound of distress because Nate gazed up, a look of concern crossing his face before it turned to clear-cut determination. Looking deep into my eyes, he gripped the sides of my head with surprising gentleness.

"What you did down in the BSL-4 lab was crazy. Crazy, and crazy dangerous. This? This is just like climbing on the monkey bars at the playground. You've done great so far, and I know you will take this in stride just like everything else. Okay?"

My lip quivered with fright, but I forced myself to let his confidence wrap around the iron cage panic had locked around my heart, and ease its grip on me.

"Okay."

He held my gaze for another second, then dropped his hands, and after a last glance at the advancing mob eased himself through the doors.

For a moment it hit me as peculiar that, this once, he dropped his pseudo gentlemanly act, leaving me out here to the wolves, but when I followed him as quickly as my shaking limbs would let me, I saw that it was, in fact, the smart thing to do. Looking back, he made sure that I was watching him before he inched to the side of the shaft, gripped the rungs of the small ladder that was built right into the steel supports, and started climbing down.

He made it look so easy, and within seconds he was down an entire level. I knew I had to get going, but even when I didn't look beyond him further down the shaft, I felt like the entire world was spinning around me.

Then three shots hit the glass right where I was standing, startling me enough to almost let go of the strut I was clinging to and ending my sorry existence in the course of a seventy-foot fall. Screwing my eyes shut, I scrambled blindly for the next strut so I could move around the corner to the side, then forced them open as I started to lower myself.

Looking down between my body and the metal supports, I saw Nate hesitate below me, then send me an almost boyish grin.

"Just keep going. I'll catch you if you fall."

That was certainly impossible, but for some reason, his words made me laugh. It was a high-pitched, cut-off, hysterical laugh that reverberated through my entire body, but it was the thing that shoved me into motion again. As soon as I was out of the way, the first of the soldiers squeezed himself through the doors, followed by Martinez—effectively barring my way back. So forward it was.

The ladder was just wide enough to allow me to place one foot there per rung, forcing me to keep climbing down at an asymmetrical pattern as I could never keep both of my hands at the same height.

Quicker than I'd expected, I was down to level two, then one, and the tightness around my ribcage started to ease up.

Screams above me alarmed me to the fact that in my fright of falling down the shaft, I'd completely forgotten about the mob. How that was even possible, I didn't know, but that realization made me speed up.

Too late, I figured, when two bodies dropped down the shaft—one wearing combat armor, the other not—and the soldiers started shooting down the shaft, then four more bodies followed. Angry howls were suddenly loud below me, and something hot exploded across my left upper arm.

Shrieking, I let go before instinct could shut down the reaction. For only a moment I was airborne, then I crashed into something somewhat softer than the concrete floor and metal supports I'd expected to career into. Pain raced up from my ankle, but I managed to stagger to my feet just as Nate let go of me, pushing me into the corner that wasn't full of writhing, partly broken limbs. Not sparing a moment to check on me, he instead fired a couple of shots into the heap, his aim true.

I narrowly avoided being crushed by the next body falling down on us as I scrambled to the other side of the shaft, where strong hands grabbed my arms and pulled me up and out onto the main floor. Andrej gave me a quick grin before he pushed me forward, making way for Nate and the soldiers to follow me.

Panting heavily, I looked around. From here, the atrium looked even worse than three floors up. Except for the staircase the soldiers had apparently used to get up to the third floor gallery, all the exits were barricaded or otherwise blocked, a few of the doors so warped and twisted that they looked more like modern art than fire security doors. There were more dead bodies in the open spaces between the rubble than I'd thought, some of them burned. The front side of the glass cube had apparently been hit by something more powerful than guns, making it cave in, leaving shards of glass everywhere inside.

Around the elevator banks, extending almost to the wall on the side where the demolished tank had replaced the computer workstation, Nate's people had barricaded themselves behind desks and what was left of the computer equipment. I counted eight of the hostages, Gabriel Greene, his assistant, and Elena Glover among them. None of them had guns pointed at them, but they were still cowering on the floor behind the barricades.

At the front of the atrium I saw a few more overturned parts of what had been the barricade to the outside world, now held by the soldiers that had stormed the building—but something had clearly gone wrong along the way, and not just because of the heavy resistance they had met. As I'd guessed from up above, only the minority of the bodies on the floor wore combat gear, and the soldiers seemed much more occupied with keeping the barricades up toward the outside world than the people they had been sent to eliminate. There was a perpetual din of screams and the occasional gunshots, interspersed by shouts coming from both camps to each other.

"We're running out of time," the Ice Queen remarked dryly as she walked over to Nate, giving him a cursory glance. The soldiers now piling up behind him she completely ignored. "Seven minutes. Cutting it a little close, aren't you?"

"You know me. My life is so bland and boring, I always have to find ways to make it more interesting," Nate replied. "Who's in charge?"

"Old friend of yours," she said, just as a small group of soldiers—bristling with weapons—advanced on our position, all their rifles trained up at the upper floors. Glancing along their line of sight, I saw yet more movement above, making me guess that there were over a hundred people up there. Nate's guys finally managed to wrench the elevator doors down here shut, but that didn't seem to hinder the mindless jumpers that still thumped down into the elevator shaft with a sickening array of crunching and splatting noises.

"Ah," Nate murmured, turning toward the single man of the group not currently in a defensive position. "No surprise there."

"Miller," the man grunted out as he gave Nate a hostile look.

"Bucky," Nate acknowledged, relaxing as if we had all the time in the world at our leisure. Turning to me, he explained, "That would be Captain John Hamilton, but you know how the guys are. Some need the nickname for the ego."

In fact, I didn't know, but thankfully no one expected me to join the conversation. Nate barely paused before he turned back to the soldier.

"What do you want? Twenty words or less, we're kind of on a schedule here."

Bucky gnashed his teeth, but sounded surprisingly jovial as he replied.

"The vaccine."

Did everyone know about this damn virus but me?!

"There is no vaccine," Nate replied, his tone more neutral than I expected, considering his personal involvement in the entire affair.

"I know that they were working on it. It has to be…"

"There is no vaccine," Nate repeated. "They never managed to develop a working version of it. Before you ask, we have video footage of the lead scientist of the project getting infected after being dosed with their most promising candidate. Curious detail on the side, the one who infected him killed herself earlier last night. Besides, what stocks there were kept in the viral vault were manually destroyed."

Bucky took that in with a stony look on his face, before his eyes zeroed in on me.

"Her?"

"Just my technical advisor," Nate divulged, glancing at his watch again. "We're out of time. The first charges will blow in just under a minute, and then we have exactly enough time to get out of the blast radius if we run like hell."

I would have loved to know what the soldiers were doing here, and why anyone would send them for a vaccine that whoever had funded the project must have known wasn't working—the part about Thecla not only infecting Raleigh but also dosing him with the supposed antidote was new to me, but Nate had clearly known about that from the start—was beyond me, but absolutely not my most pressing concern.

Bucky kept glaring at us, but after a moment he gave a brief jerk with his chin that might have been a nod.

"What a shame." To his soldiers he asked, "Anyone still deeper in the building?"

Martinez shook his head. "We lost contact with two other teams. And considering what came after us—" He let that hang between them, but the howls and shouts coming from the gallery were answer enough.

Bucky gave another nod, then hollered back to his men. "Everyone, get ready. We're moving out." He spent another second glaring at Nate, but turned away without saying another word. The soldiers flocked to him, only Martinez hesitating for a moment.

"How is your arm?" Nate asked me, his focus on switching magazines for his rifle, letting the empty one drop to the floor. Yet he picked it up and lobbed it at one of his people in full gear.

At first, I didn't understand what he meant, until I realized that he was referring to my left arm where the bullet had grazed me in the elevator shaft. As if my body had been waiting for that moment, the dull ache flared to life, but it was just one more distraction compared to how battered I felt overall. Clenching my fingers, I made a fist, figuring that if the muscles and tendons still worked, it couldn't be that bad.

"I'll live."

"That you will," he said, a ghost of a smile crossing his face. "We'll patch you up once we're outside." He turned to the Ice Queen next. "Casualties?"

"Fifteen at last count. Three more down with heavy injuries." She glanced at the huddle of hostages to her right. "Three of them started coughing blood so we put them out of their misery. It's not looking good."

She and Nate shared a look that I really didn't like—particularly the hint of fear crossing her features before she reined them in, becoming the cold killer again—and he gave a nod that wasn't unlike Bucky's. I was really burning to know what history those two had—but not as much as I wanted to get out of here.

"Okay, people, listen up—" Nate started, but never got further than that, as his last word got drowned out by the boom of a series of explosions.

Chapter 24

For a moment, I thought that the countdown on my life had already reached zero before I realized that the detonations had happened outside of the building, not inside.

Peeking over the barricade, I could make out a few soldiers by the exit before a cloud of dust blew over them. As it settled, I could see torn-up earth and debris where the thick wall that had surrounded the entire complex had been. In a series of smaller explosions, what I presumed were buried mines went off, either activated by the shock wave or remotely detonated like the charges that had brought down the wall. They tore through the few somewhat disoriented, filthy figures that had started wobbling around the grass. I quickly looked away, my heart thudding in my throat.

Nate's nudge against my knee brought my attention back to him. "Whatever happens, you stay with me." He didn't wait for me to acknowledge his order before he shouted, "Everyone, go!" He reared up, his gun ready. All around us, the others followed, the roar of so many feet hitting the floor even drowning out the racket from above.

Then we were moving, like everyone around us. Barricades were pulled away, and suddenly the outside world lay just in front of us, only barred by the glass walls of the foyer that quickly shattered under the impact of bullets. Glass crunched under my plastic lab clogs, not built for this kind of abuse—and then we were out in the open, running for our lives.

Air burned in my lungs, and I stumbled when the muscles in my legs wanted to give out. I forced myself to keep going, knowing that we weren't out of the danger zone yet. Nate let go of me after pulling me to the right, and I ran after him, my eyes glued to his back.

The architecture of the atrium had worked like a funnel for the stream of people trying to leave the building like rats a sinking ship, and now they fanned out. To my left I saw Elena Glover stumble down the main path, going for the easiest way. That was, until a few steps later two figures materialized out of the smoke, taking her down as teeth and claws bit into her. Her scream cut off in a wet gurgle as one of them went for her throat.

Greene had been right behind her, but he managed to stagger to the side, looking around frantically. For a moment our gazes crossed, and suddenly I regretted that I'd declined Nate's offer of a gun. Then he looked away, quickly surveying the situation, and went after a couple of soldiers who were running across the lawn but angling away from us.

I staggered and almost pitched forward when my toes snagged on something uneven in the grass, but I caught myself in the next two steps. My clumsiness put Nate ahead of me, but as if he'd felt my absence, he turned around, gesturing at me to hurry up. I did, ignoring everything else but him, and just ran.

We'd barely made it across half of the distance to the remnants of the wall when the real explosions went off.

I more felt than heard them at first, the ground underneath my feet shaking. A deep rumbling followed, until off to my far right grass and earth heaved up and fell away as the hot lab buried underneath blew up. Nate shouted something at me that I didn't understand before he grabbed my hand and physically pulled me forward.

More detonations followed high up behind us. Over my shoulder I saw parts of the upper three floors of the building blow apart, then disappear in a cloud of debris. A shock wave hit me, hard enough to stagger me, but not enough to make me fall. His fingers tightened around mine and he kept pulling me forward, ever forward.

Another figure in a billowing white lab coat appeared in front of us, and I had only a moment to recognize one of my former fellow hostages before he stepped on a mine, the bottom half of his body disappearing while the rest fell to the ground. I was close enough to feel the much smaller shock wave hit me and instinctively tried to shy away, but Nate pulled me right into the just spawned crater.

I hit the ground with the full length of my body, unable to cushion the fall when my limbs wouldn't respond fast enough. My face was only inches away from the gory remains of what had seconds ago been another human being. I tried to scramble up, but then Nate's entire weight landed on me, pressing me even more firmly into the disgusting ground. I struggled, but he somehow managed to get one arm underneath me, pulling himself flush with my body, while the fingers of his other hand entwined with mine.

Something was beeping loudly right next to my face, and I had just a second to realize that it was the alarm of his watch that had gone off before the sky came raining down on us.

Day Zero

Awareness returned slowly, one agonizing body part at a time.

It took me a while to remember what had happened.

There'd been an explosion, then many, many more, joining in one continuous boom. A sense of vertigo as the immense pressure of the blast had picked my body up and thrown it around like a rag doll. Pain, panic, then nothing.

Until now.

I opened my eyes, or tried to. Something was keeping them shut. I tried to raise my left arm to my face, but couldn't. I tried my right, then realized I couldn't move it because it was trapped under my own body. Shifting, I managed to free it. Something sharp scraped across the back of my hand, re-igniting the sting of the burn mark the coffee had left.

Coffee. Water. My throat was parched, my tongue so dry that it felt like a swollen, foreign something in my mouth.

Finally, skin. There was grit everywhere, covering my face, gluing my lashes shut. I wiped at it until I could pry my eyes open.

Everything around me was dark. Not pitch black—there was some light filtering in from somewhere up ahead—but not enough to see colors, only vague shapes.

Concrete, steel, and clumps of earth everywhere.

Inhaling sharply, I got dust into my lungs, which brought on a painful coughing fit. Muscles tensed, relaxed, and suddenly my other arm was free. My upper arm hurt like hell, and something was wrong with the last two fingers of my hand, but I managed to raise both hands to my face and scrub it until all the dust was gone.

Awareness slowly gave way to actual consciousness, if not rational thought. Clearly, we hadn't made it out of the blast radius, but the fact that I was still alive meant that we hadn't gotten caught in the primary explosion.

Checking my limbs next, I realized that I could feel every hurting inch of my body, but my right foot was trapped. I tried kicking at the massive chunk of concrete that pinned my leg down from the middle of my shin to my toes, but it wouldn't budge.

Shit.

But I was alive. Alive. ALIVE!

A single tear of joy made it out of the corner of my eye, leaving a track down the side of my face.

I was alive. I'd beaten the odds, I'd cheated death. And it hadn't been entirely my doing.

Nate had kept his promise. He'd gotten me out of there alive. He'd protected me with his body, likely saving me from the worst of the blast, even if I felt as if I'd been picked up by a giant and smashed repeatedly into a wall. I dimly remembered lying on the ground, horrified, afraid, the scent of blood and earth filling my nostrils, his weight heavy on me. Now I was lying on my back, facing up. Where was he?

"Hey," a gravely voice said out of the darkness to my left, an answer to my silent question.

Looking around, it took me a few moments to make out a head, shoulder, arm, and torso amidst the concrete blocks.

"Hey," I replied, stretching as much as my trapped leg would allow to reach his hand. His fingers were as warm as I remembered, the calluses of them rough even on my dirt-caked skin.

"Are you okay?" Something in his voice nagged at the back of my mind, but it was hard enough to keep my thoughts straight with pain still radiating through my body whenever I moved, or took a breath.

"My leg is trapped, but I think I'm mostly unharmed."

"Told you I'd get you out of there," he whispered, then coughed. It was not a dry cough like mine had been, but an awful, wet sound. It reminded me of blood-soaked bandages and hands.

"You?" I asked, rising dread starting to tighten my throat.

"Me? Not so much," he admitted, followed by another cough.

Moving forward as far as I could, I managed to look around a small boulder that lay between us. There was no color, but against the light fabric of his shirt, if terribly stained now, the spreading, dark patch looked exactly like what it was. Blood. He'd been speared by a rebar sticking out of the concrete slab he lay buried under.

"It's okay," he murmured when I could think of nothing to say. "I've always known I'd die somewhere in horrible pain, alone." He tried to laugh, but it turned into another horrible cough. How he could find humor for the remark was beyond me.

"You're not alone!" I retorted, my voice thick with tears that wouldn't quite come. I clenched his hand harder, and he gifted me with a sad smile.

"No, I'm not."

His lids fluttered, then drifted closed, and my heart gave a painful pang much worse than any physical discomfort I felt until I saw his chest rise again. He kept his eyes shut for a while, as if it cost him what was left of his strength just to stay conscious.

The sound of voices coming from the direction of the dim light made me perk up, then shout when I thought I recognized Andrej's. Within a few minutes, dust started raining down on me as rubble was moved, followed by blinding sunlight when the last piece finally fell away. I'd never been this happy to see familiar faces as when Andrej and Martinez pulled me out. But my elation was short-lived as I gestured at the hole in the cement blocks they had freed me from. "Nate's still down there. But it's not looking good."

Andrej and Martinez traded looks, then Martinez crawled into the artificial cavern. I could hear his and Nate's voice but not what was said, and a few moments later Martinez was back, looking concerned.

"Not good, but could be worse," he offered, glancing around. "I need someone who's a little stronger than me."

One of Nate's people who had been standing close was quickly recruited, and the two men disappeared one after the other again. Looking around, I only noticed now that the sun was still shining on my face, the likely reason for why my eyes were watering.

"Don't worry, he'll make it," Andrej told me with a lot more confidence than the situation warranted.

"He was speared. Like, literally pierced by a rebar!" I ground out, disbelief heavy in my voice.

"Will leave nice scars," came a dry remark from behind me. Whipping around, I saw Pia stagger toward us from where she moved away from the line of soldiers who had started to set up... a perimeter defense? At least that was what it looked like, with several of them crouching on the ground, guns and rifles out, propped up on makeshift barricades. All around us, people were dragged from the debris, looking as dirty and disheveled as I felt.

"Scars," I deadpanned, unable to comprehend why they both sounded so calm. She gave me a toothy grin before she joined Martinez and the other guy below.

Looking at the settling dust around us, I got my first good view of the site, trying to find something to distract myself with before I got the news I really didn't want to hear.

The Green Fields Biotech building was gone, plain and simple. Where the concrete-and-glass behemoth had towered over an entire city block, only a giant field of broken rubble remained. The detonations had broken the windows of close buildings, but all in all, the destruction was less catastrophic than I had expected.

It certainly didn't account for the sirens wailing in the distance from all over town that I now noticed as the ringing sound in my ears lessened. Pulling out the earplugs, the sounds were amplified immediately, making the fine hairs on my forearms stand on end. Glass crashed somewhere in the distance, and a few shots rang out, followed by a scream that cut off suddenly.

Before I could look around and find the source of the noise, my attention was drawn back to the hole in the ground when the would-be rescuers emerged—dragging Nate along on unsteady feet, the foot of rebar still sticking out of his side. Everything inside of me screamed to run to him, to make sure that he was okay, but Andrej held me back before I could do more than tense.

Nate managed to remain upright as Martinez helped him onto a block of concrete before he focused on the rebar again. Nate's jacket was gone, as was most of his shirt, cut away to inspect the wound.

"Just pull it out and glue me up," Nate ground out, his eyes scanning the surroundings rather than focusing on what was about to happen to him. How this was even possible, I had no idea, but he actually did look better than he had sounded below.

"The wound will get infected," Martinez objected but was already rummaging around in his pack for something.

"I'll have to live another day or two to even get an infection, and that won't happen if I have a fucking iron bar driven right through my abdomen," Nate replied, just condescending enough to make the Ice Queen snort.

"True," Martinez offered, making me twice as uncomfortable as moments before. "Then let's hope that no major organs are ruptured, right?"

He didn't wait for Nate's reply—or even give him time to steel himself—but simply grabbed his shoulders, while Pia went for the rebar. One hard jerk and she staggered back, the bloody, rusty bar in her hand. Nate gave a low sound that held a lot more pain than any human was supposed to be able to tough out, but he remained upright even when Martinez let go of him to quickly grab a syringe that he'd readied before. It looked almost like a miniature glue gun, and seemed to work like that, too, as he inserted the nozzle-like tip and squeezed something into the wound on Nate's front, and the rest at the back. Some kind of patches followed, and lots more bandages and gauze, yet they remained white except for the blood that had fountained out of the wound and now stuck all over Nate's lower torso that Martinez hadn't completely cleaned away.

Considering what else I'd seen today, I didn't even protest the plausibility of this.

But there was still the bloody rebar and the heap of bloody, torn shirt, making me sick if I just looked at them. Turning around, I took a few steps away, out of the worst of the rubble and toward what had been the street in front of the building. The rescue effort seemed to be winding down now, most either accounted for or dead, and still no ambulances in sight. Also no onlookers drawn to the site by the incredible noise that a building coming down must have made.

The only one I saw besides the soldiers was a young girl coming out of one of the houses down the street. She looked around, as disoriented as I felt, her eyes passing over the rubble and soldiers without snagging on anything. Her gaze moved on, skipping over me, slow enough to make me realize that her eyes were completely empty.

The cold fist of fear around my heart that had been my companion for the last hour inside the building returned, squeezing, whispering at me to run. Instead, I took a step toward her, then another, morbid curiosity warring with fright.

"Sweetie, are you okay?"

At the sound of my voice, her head jerked in my direction, sightless eyes remaining unfocused. She opened her mouth and closed it without making a sound, then again. She took a hesitant step toward me, mimicking me, then another, a little faster now.

"Bree?" I heard Nate call out behind me, but I ignored him. She was much closer now, stepping out into the sunshine, giving me a much better look at her. Too good a look, I realized, as what my eyes took in made my brain fire straight into the "flight" part of the fight or flight reaction.

Her eyes were glazed over, filmy, and looked so strange because the sockets around them were dark with subcutaneous bruising. In the shadows, her dark skin had hidden the blood caking her neck from where it had dripped from her ears, eyes, and nose. The underlying color of her skin was wrong, with an unhealthy tint that made it look like wax. But the worst were her fingers—bloody and broken from where she'd apparently clawed her way out, with no apparent regard for her health.

"What happened to you?" I asked under my breath, more to myself than her, but at the repeat sound of my voice, she gave a jerk.

And then she was coming at me in a surprising burst of speed that belied the former shuffling motion of her feet, her face turned into a feral grimace.

"Bree! Get down!"

I instantly dropped to the ground on Nate's command, and not a second too early as a series of shots rang out from behind me, hitting the girl in the legs and chest. She went down without making a sound, but instead of bleeding out on the ground, her head snapped back up, her eyes still focused on me, and she started dragging herself forward, her legs useless from a bullet that must have ripped through her spinal cord. Scrambling back, I tried to put distance between us, but she only stopped when a last shot turned the right side of her face into so much bloody gore.

Panting heavily, I looked up at where Nate was standing above me, a shotgun braced against his torso, his fingers white around the black metal and plastic of the weapon. Behind him, Andrej and the Ice Queen lowered their rifles, while Martinez put his pistol away.

At the shots, several of the soldiers had come running, Bucky among them. If he'd looked grim in the atrium before, his face had turned to stone now, and he glared at the body of the girl for a moment before he glanced at our huddle of people.

"Everything in the green over here?"

Nate nodded. I thought he was trying to relax, but his fingers were shaking even now that he'd let go of the gun and let it dangle from its shoulder strap. Sweat stood heavy on his brow, but his eyes were clear, belying the pain he must have been in.

"A-okay," he ground out.

"Get ready. We're moving out in five," Bucky told him, about to turn away, but stopped when I called after him.

"Care to tell us what the fuck is going on?" He shot me a long look, then glanced at Nate, what little emotion there still was on his face closing down. "Don't bother with any bullshit! Where are the first responders? Why aren't there even any people? And what the fuck is going on with these maniacs?" I didn't need to point at the corpse close to us to indicate what I meant.

Bucky gave me a humorless grin that made me even more uneasy.

"Just how long have you been holed up inside that lab?"

I shrugged, not sure what that had to do with anything. "Since yesterday morning when I went to work. Why?"

His snort was dismissive in a way that made my hackles rise, but I could keep my tongue if it meant finally getting some answers.

"So you missed the whole fun of when the shit hit the fan?" Bucky jeered and laughed, a hard, short bark. "You're a smarty-pants scientist, right? Just what does this look like to you?"

He walked over to the corpse and lifted it by the back of the nightshirt the girl had been wearing, thrusting the ghastly thing in my face. I jerked away, trying to put as much distance between me and that as I could. Death really didn't become her. And from up close, it was impossible to ignore the blood stains on her teeth and lips that were way too massive to just come from bleeding gums.

"Exactly what does this look like to you?" Bucky repeated, and when I still didn't reply, he was only too happy to fill in the blanks for me. "Like a fucking zombie." Taking a step back, he dropped the thing in front of me and spread his arms wide.

"Welcome to the fucking zombie apocalypse."

The story continues in

Green Fields #2

Acknowledgement

Like so many other things, writing a book takes a village. Or at least a bunch of very patient souls, some of them needing relentless badgering to dip their toes into the zombie / post-apocalyptic horror genre (or simply a gentle nudge because they are awesome like that.) Foremost, I'll be forever grateful to my guy for keeping me hooked on an infinite caffeine drip, and listening to me rave and rant about the idiosyncrasies of made-up characters.

Shayla and Jaana, you're the best beta readers anyone can wish for. A round of applause goes to all the people who slogged through this manuscript one time or another in any of the stages. Thank you!

About the Author

Adrienne Lecter has a background in Biochemistry and Molecular Biology, loves ranting at inaccuracies in movies, and spends increasingly more time on the shooting range. She lives with the man and two cats of her life in Vienna, and is working on the next post-apocalyptic books.

You can sign up for Adrienne's newsletter to never miss a release and be the first to know what other shenanigans she gets up to:

http://www.adriennelecter.com

Thank you

Hey, you! Yes, you, who just spent a helluva lot of time reading this book! You just made my day! Thanks!

Want to be notified of new releases, giveaways and updates? Sign up for my newsletter:
www.adriennelecter.com

If you enjoyed reading the book and have a moment to spare, I would really appreciate a short, honest review on the site you purchased it from and on goodreads. Reviews make a huge difference in helping new readers find the series.

Or if you'd like to drop me a note, or chat a but, feel free to email me or hit me up on social media. I'll try to respond as quickly as possible! If you'd like to report an error or wrong detail, I've set up a separate space on my website for that, too.

Email: adrienne@adriennelecter.com.com
Website: adriennelecter.com
Twitter: @adriennelecter
Facebook: facebook.com/adriennelecter

Books published

Green Fields
#1: Incubation
#2: Outbreak
#3: Escalation
#4: Extinction
#5: Resurgence
#6: Unity
#7: Affliction
#8: Catharsis
#9: Exodus
#10: Uprising
#11: Retribution
#12: Annihilation

Beyond Green Fields
short story collections
Omnibus #1
Ombinus #2

World of Anthrax
new series coming 2022

Made in the USA
Middletown, DE
21 May 2025

75875263R00187